JILTED

When Eustacia Hope is jilted at the altar, her parents send her to stay with her godmother Lady Agatha Rayner, a clergyman's widow. Her mother warns her to shun Lady Agatha's brother, the notorious Lord Ashbourne and his son Lord Ilam. And she soon discovers that her godmother isn't all she seems either. Then Eustacia meets Lord Ilam and the two are attracted to one another. But it is only after the arrival of Eustacia's estranged fiancé and the unexpected appearance of Lord Ashbourne that matters can be resolved in a way that is satisfactory to all parties.

ANN BARKER

---◆---

JILTED

Complete and Unabridged

ULVERSCROFT
Leicester

First published in Great Britain in 2008 by
Robert Hale Limited
London

First Large Print Edition
published 2009
by arrangement with
Robert Hale Limited
London

The moral right of the author has been asserted

British Library CIP Data

Barker, Ann.
  Jilted
  1. Young women- -Family relationships- -Fiction.
  2. Sponsors- -Fiction. 3. Love stories.
  4. Large type books.
  I. Title
  823.9′2–dc22

  ISBN 978–1–84782–816–3

For my in-laws, with love and gratitude

Acknowledgements

I would like to thank Sir Richard Fitzherbert for his careful stewardship of Tissington Hall and village, both of which inspired me for the setting for this book.

I would also like to thank the kind ladies at the Tourist Information Office in Ashbourne who dealt with my questions so tolerantly; and, as always, my grateful thanks to all at Robert Hale, and especially to Gill Jackson my editor, who does her best to keep me in order.

1

'This,' declared her ladyship, 'is the most humiliating moment of my life.' After a surreptitious glance behind her, in order to establish that her husband was within easy reach, Lady Hope sank back gracefully, her eyelids fluttering closed.

Sir Wilfred Hope, who had made it his study to please his wife from the very first moment that they had met, did not fail her now. Leaping forward with an athleticism surprising for one of his years, he caught her neatly in his arms before she came anywhere near making painful contact with the stone flags on the floor of their local church.

He glanced up anxiously at his daughter, who was looking nonplussed to say the least. 'Eustacia! Do not stand there staring like a looby! Put those flowers down and go and fetch your mother some water! Hurry, now!'

Eustacia Hope put her wedding bouquet down on the nearest pew, and looked up at the vicar for guidance.

'Water? Oh, oh yes, Miss Hope. There is a flask in my vestry,' uttered the Reverend Timothy Stroud in rather abstracted tones.

More than half of his attention was directed towards the unconscious Lady Hope.

This was not at all surprising, Eustacia reflected, as she walked through the chancel of St Peter's Church, turning left just before the altar, and going into the vestry. For as long as she could remember, her beautiful, statuesque mother had always managed to make herself the centre of attention. Eustacia was so used to this, that she had long since ceased to resent it in the general way of things. Today, however, when she had just been left standing at the altar by the gentleman to whom she should by now have been united in marriage, it did seem a little hard that her feelings should not come first.

She had been engaged to Morrison Morrison for two years. The engagement had never been intended to last for so long, but a bereavement that Mr Morrison's family had suffered had put the wedding off. Eustacia had always been strongly attracted to her handsome fiancé. She had known him ever since his family had come to live in the area when she was eight years old. They had not got to know each other well at that stage, for he was soon away at Eton, and she had her school in Harrogate to attend. When at the age of sixteen she met him once more at a picnic, his lean figure, dark eyes and floppy,

2

silky brown hair had make her heart beat a little faster, and she had confided to friends that she might like to marry him one day. Morrison, taking in the agreeable sight of Eustacia's plentiful dark curls, laughing eyes, and generous but neat figure, had given the impression of being similarly impressed. The marriage was desired by their families, both fathers being pleased to avoid all the expense that a season in London would entail.

Eustacia had another reason for eagerly desiring the match. The truth was that above all things she wanted to have her own establishment. It was not that she did not care for her mother and father; on the contrary, she loved them both very dearly. She had always been aware, however, that as far as her father was concerned, she came very much second to her mother, whose wants always had to be considered first, and whose able handling of household affairs left her daughter with very little to do. Lady Hope cast a long shadow from which Eustacia had expected to emerge. This now seemed to be unlikely for the foreseeable future.

She was roused from her moment of reverie by the sound of someone else entering the vestry. Turning, she saw the vicar standing on the threshold. 'Have you found it?' he asked her. His eyes met hers briefly, then darted away in search of the flask. It occurred to her that he was embarrassed by her situation. She wondered whether that would be her fate: to be a source of embarrassment as The Jilted Miss Hope from now on. 'Ah, there it is,' he exclaimed at last in relieved tones, spotting the flask where it stood half concealed behind a pile of musty-looking books. With hands that shook a little, he poured some water into the glass that acted as a lid for the flask. Eustacia wondered whether in thirty years of ministry such a thing had ever happened to him before.

When they had set off from Woodfield Park that morning, nothing had occurred that might have acted as a warning that Mr Morrison would let her down. Sir Wilfred, looking pleased and proud and still upright and well proportioned at the age of fifty, with a dash of distinguishing white at his temples, had handed his daughter into the barouche. Eustacia, in a gown of cream silk embroidered with golden roses, had looked charming and bridal.

Her gown had, of course, been chosen by her mother. Lady Hope, 5'8" in her stockinged feet, and built on generous lines, had never tried to make her daughter into a copy of herself. Eustacia, at just 5' and petite, with a neat shapely figure and her father's lustrous dark-brown hair and hazel eyes, would have looked absurd trying to wear the kind of styles that her mama carried off so well. Lady Hope had gone to the church earlier, looking ravishing in a delectable pink gown that complemented her blonde beauty to admiration. No doubt on arrival at St Peter's she had made a stunning entrance as always, filling the church with clouds of perfume and overwhelming all those present with the force of her personality.

Before her marriage, Lady Hope had been an actress. Unlike many of her profession, however, she had employed a strict chaperon and had never permitted any admirers to take the slightest liberty. Her acting career had ended where it had begun, in Bath. After a brief, meteoric rise in her career, at the zenith of which seats at the Theatre Royal were almost impossible to procure, (and some of which had even been occupied by royalty), she had abandoned the stage in order to marry Sir Wilfred Hope after a brief courtship.

Sir Wilfred was not the most handsome of her suitors, although he did cut a very fine figure in riding dress. Nor was he the richest or the most dashing of the supplicants for her favours. Her striking beauty had attracted the attention of a number of rich and titled gentlemen, one of whom had been the notorious libertine, Lord Ilam. Sir Wilfred did, however, have two distinct advantages over his rivals. The first was that his estates were situated in Yorkshire, well away from Bath and London, so that it was unlikely that Claire Delahay, as she was then, would find her past coming back to haunt her. He was, furthermore, one of the few who offered marriage, and Miss Delahay wanted to be respectable above all else.

Needless to say, there were cynics who predicted that the former actress would soon take steps to relieve the tedium of her country existence by taking lovers, or even by deserting her husband for long periods in search of the thrills that only a big city could provide. They were to be disappointed. Once settled on their country estate, Sir Wilfred and his lady seemed content to remain there. They made occasional visits to York and Harrogate for shopping and for the assemblies and concerts. Sir Wilfred travelled to London on business from time to time, but always unaccompanied, and Lady Hope concerned herself with the needs of their tenants and the running of the house. With all this evidence to hand, onlookers were forced to conclude that along with the obvious reasons that the lady had had for accepting the modestly circumstanced baronet, she might well have a very genuine regard for him.

Since Sir Wilfred's affection for his wife was legendary, it was quite useless to try to imagine a situation in which Lady Hope, unlike her daughter, would ever have been left standing stupidly at the altar, wondering what had happened to her prospective bridegroom.

Eustacia was, and always had been, their only child, and she never doubted that she was loved by both her parents. Sometimes, nevertheless, she felt that she was a bit of a disappointment. This was partly because the estate was entailed upon a distant cousin, so that Sir Wilfred always had at the back of his mind the notion that should anything happen to him he would need to find some way of caring for his womenfolk. It was a question that preyed upon her ladyship's mind as well. When she was at a very low ebb, she would sometimes talk sentimentally about Charlie. Charlie was the name that she would have given her son, had she been fortunate enough to have had one. He would have been tall, as fair as she was herself, with her sapphire-blue eyes, and he would have towered over her and teased and protected her. At such times, Lady Hope would look at her daughter and sigh, and Eustacia would think to herself, if only I could have been tall and blonde! At least that would have been *something*.

Their arrival at the church, perhaps not surprisingly, had caused something of a stir. The entrance of a bride ought, in all ordinary circumstances to cause a degree of excitement. But the mood of those present seemed to be more one of consternation mixed with prurience.

As Eustacia had entered on her father's arm, she could see Mr Morrison's groomsman, Mr Bartrum, but of the groom himself there was no sign.

'Did you not come together?' Sir Wilfred had asked Bartrum in a low-voiced conversation, conducted in front of the altar and a very puzzled-looking clergyman.

'We were about to set off, when he suddenly muttered about having left something behind; something for the bride, he said. So I came on ahead and he said that he would join us.'

'Then he should soon be here,' Sir Wilfred had replied, looking indignant. 'By heaven, I shall have stern words to say to him about this. A bridegroom late! I never heard of such discourtesy!'

It was at this moment, whilst they were all still gathered about the altar with the congregation talking uncomfortably amongst themselves in low tones, that a small boy, plainly but respectably dressed, had hurried into the porch, slithered to a halt on the tiles, then walked up the aisle with a clattering sound, all the more noticeable on account of the silence which had swiftly fallen once more upon the congregation.

As he had reached the group of persons gathered at the top of the nave, he had cleared his throat then said in a piping voice that could be heard all over the church, 'Please, which one's the bride?'

It was such a ludicrous question that Eustacia had felt a spasm of hysterical mirth bubbling up into her throat. She was glad that her father had said, 'Don't be a fool, boy. This lady is the bride. Why do you ask?' She was afraid that if she had opened her mouth to say anything, completely inappropriate laughter would have burst from her lips and shocked everybody.

'Got this for her,' the lad had answered, handing Eustacia a folded piece of paper. The message inside was brief and if not tactfully phrased, at least had the merit of being clear and unequivocal.

Can't go through with it. Gone to join the army. Sorry.

Morrison.

'Give that to me,' Sir Wilfred had said, snatching the note from Eustacia's hand. She was still having some difficulty in taking it in. No sooner had Sir Wilfred glanced through the note than Lady Hope, with all the grace that she had ever had, had glided over to them, taken the note and read it in her turn. It was at this point that her ladyship, with her fine instinct for drama and her almost inborn ability to seize the moment, had keeled over, whilst excited chattering had broken out amongst the congregation, who had gathered to witness a wedding and were actually seeing something much more exciting unfold.

Eustacia had stood holding her wedding bouquet, feeling slightly sick and wondering what to do next, whilst the small boy, alone unmoved among the whole throng, had piped up with 'Can I have sixpence now? The man what handed me the note said someone'd give me sixpence.'

It was almost a relief to Eustacia that her father had sent her to find water at this point. She badly needed someone to tell her what to do.

The vicar went back into the church with

the water and for a moment, Eustacia stood looking at the door through which he had gone. Then she remembered that there was another door in the vestry, the one that led out into the churchyard.

Glancing around, she saw an old cloak of the vicar's hanging on a peg. Quickly, she took off her wedding bonnet and, leaving it on the table next to the musty books, she picked up the cloak and wrapped it around her. Fortunately, although it was May, the day was not particularly warm. With her wedding finery concealed from all but the keenest observer, she would, she hoped, be able to walk the short distance home unobserved.

Carefully taking a quiet path rather than the road which everyone used, she walked slowly along beside the brook, thinking about Mr Morrison's courtship. Like her, he was his parents' only child and as such was destined to inherit all of his father's property. Although Sir Wilfred's estate was entailed, there was provision for a handsome jointure for Lady Hope and a similarly generous dowry for Eustacia, so the match had been considered suitable by all concerned. Yet after the engagement had been announced, politely attentive though Morrison had been, Eustacia had often had the impression that when he was in her company, he would much rather have been elsewhere, doing something else.

Looking back with the benefit of hindsight, there had been moments when she now wondered whether he had been on the point of confiding in her. There had been an occasion when they had gone to Derby and had seen the militia marching through. They had been a fine sight, the sun glinting on the brightly polished metal on buckles and buttons, and on the gold facings of the officers' uniforms.

'God, I wish — ' Mr Morrison had begun, before breaking off abruptly.

'You wish what?' Eustacia had prompted him curiously.

He had collected himself and had responded in his usual light, cheerful tone, 'I wish we could get something to drink, that's all. I'm devilish thirsty.'

By a strange irony, had they been closer, had there been more between them than a rather lukewarm affection, at least on his part, he might have brought himself to confide in her concerning his military ambitions. He was young — only three years older than herself. No doubt he had become fearful at the idea of tying himself down for life when he still wanted to do many other things. Obviously she came a very distant second to his own ambitions. She could only wish that he had been more honest with her, and thus saved her that humiliating scene in the church. He was surely old enough to have been able to envisage how dreadful that would be. For the first time since it had happened, she started to feel angry.

At that point, she came in sight of Woodfield Park and saw the carriages waiting outside. One was the barouche in which she and her father had travelled to the church. With a sinking feeling, she recognized the other as being an equipage belonging to Mr and Mrs Morrison, her errant bridegroom's parents. Clearly everyone was intending to chew the whole matter over and start trying to apportion blame. She had never felt so humiliated in all her life before, and she did not know how she was going to begin to face anybody. The only thing that she wanted to do was to creep up to her room and lick her wounds in secret.

She entered the house with that very intention, and handed her borrowed cloak to the butler, who simply said, 'I'm very sorry, miss.' This brief expression of regret from a man she had known all her life threatened to reduce her to tears when she had remained dry-eyed throughout the scene in the church and since then until now.

'Thank you, Cumber,' she said, and headed

for the stairs. She even had her foot on the bottom step when she heard the sound of raised voices proceeding from the drawing-room. No doubt Mr and Mrs Morrison would take great delight in blaming her for Morrison's defection. She was sure that her mother and father would defend her admirably. Then a voice deep inside her seemed to say, why should they? Pride came to her aid as she stiffened her spine and walked to the drawing-room door, dismissing Cumber, who had been about to open it for her. It would do those Morrisons no harm to see her in her wedding dress. On hearing her mother's voice, she paused briefly outside the door. Lady Hope had raised that powerful instrument to the volume which Eustacia had always privately called 'rear stalls level'.

'I repeat, where is the wretched boy?' her ladyship demanded, rolling her r's on the word 'wretched' and thus giving it added emphasis. 'He belongs to you, does he not? Surely you must have some idea where he is?'

'The same might be said of your daughter, ma'am,' retorted a voice that Eustacia recognized as belonging to Mr Morrison senior.

'My daughter's whereabouts are irrelevant, sirrah,' said Lady Hope haughtily. 'She, after all, has not just left someone standing at the altar.'

'But she must take her share of the blame,' replied Mrs Morrison.

Judging that to remain outside the room any longer could be construed as eavesdropping, Eustacia pushed the door further open and walked in.

'She drove him to it,' quavered Mrs Morrison, pointing at Eustacia with a short, plump, trembling finger.

Eustacia had intended to be quietly respectful and sympathetic to Mr and Mrs Morrison who, after all, had suffered as severe a shock as had she. Instead, she found herself saying tartly, 'No doubt I planned to get myself jilted from the very beginning.'

This response had the effect of making Mrs Morrison dissolve into tears, whilst Lady Hope raised a hand to her brow and stalked across to the window, where she stood gazing out across the meadow towards the church from which they had come so recently.

Sir Wilfred, who until now had kept silent, left his position at the fireplace with his foot on the fender, encouraged his daughter to take a seat with a sympathetic smile and a warm grip on her shoulder, and approached Mr Morrison, holding out his snuff box. 'Whatever may be our own feelings on the matter, there is no sense in coming to cuffs about it,' he said pleasantly, waiting for the other man to take some before doing so himself. 'Today's events were not of my contrivance, nor were they of yours.'

'No indeed,' agreed the other man, hesitating briefly before taking a pinch. He looked at Eustacia in rather an embarrassed way. 'They were not of yours either, my dear. I'm very sorry for what I said just now. I spoke in haste. I'm also very sorry for what has happened today, and my wife will be too. Just now she is overwrought.'

Eustacia nodded her thanks. As before, this expression of kindness almost overset her, and she could not trust herself to speak.

Sir Wilfred nodded. 'It might be better to postpone further discussion until we are all cooler,' he said. 'Of one thing I am certain, however: I have no desire to give the neighbourhood any kind of entertainment by being at odds with you.'

Mr Morrison being in agreement, soon bore his stricken wife away with him.

'I think I will go to my room,' Eustacia said, after the couple had gone.

Neither her mother nor her father sought to detain her. 'Now what?' asked Lady Hope after a short silence.

'There's a lot of food to eat,' her husband remarked.

'Heavens,' declared his wife turning towards

him and throwing her hands in the air. 'It will all be wasted.'

'Not quite all of it,' her husband replied mildly. 'We have to eat, after all, and so do the servants.'

'Poor Eustacia,' said Lady Hope. 'Do you think that I should go to her? It is at times like this, my dear, that we need our loved ones to cherish us.'

'Very true,' agreed Sir Wilfred. 'But I have a feeling that Eustacia might like to be left alone, at least for a time.'

Upstairs, Eustacia allowed her maid to help her off with her wedding gown. It was very strange, but although she did not seem to have done a great deal, the emotional turmoil of what had taken place had left her feeling very tired.

Like the butler, her maid Trixie looked very sympathetic and, as she helped her mistress into bed and laid a light cover over her, she said quietly, 'He wasn't good enough for you, miss, and that's a fact.'

2

Eustacia did not join the family downstairs again that day. To her surprise, for she had thought that she would choke on just one mouthful, she managed to eat a small portion of the chicken that Trixie brought to her room, accompanied by a large glass of wine, with Sir Wilfred's orders that she was to drink it all.

That night, she found herself quite unable to sleep. Eventually, in the early hours of the morning, after she had gone through the entire scene in the church several times and come to the reluctant conclusion that however she might have behaved, she would still have ended up looking ridiculous and pathetic, she decided to go to the library and find something to read. She would normally have had several books in her room, for she was a voracious reader, but all her things had been packed away ready to be taken on her honeymoon.

On reaching the library, she went at first to the shelf on which the novels could be found. After a moment's hesitation, however, she decided that the antics of fictitious persons held no interest for her at present. She could, she thought, tell a tale far more compelling than any of theirs.

In the end, she picked up a copy of Mary Wollstonecraft's *A Vindication of the Rights of Woman*. Its title seemed to promise the kind of book that would be in keeping with her present mood.

Her mother had purchased it whilst she and Sir Wilfred were in the throes of one of their rare disagreements. Her ladyship had swept off to York, with an air of affronted dignity, taking Eustacia with her. After a very tiresome shopping outing during which Lady Hope had not been pleased by anything, she had eventually spotted the book through a shop window and had pounced upon it eagerly. 'I will show this to him, Eustacia,' she had declared, brandishing it before her daughter in the carriage as they returned home. 'Then he will see that I am not a woman to be trifled with.'

Eustacia had accepted what her mother had said in silence. Indeed, she could not imagine anyone ever supposing for a moment that Lady Hope was to be trifled with.

On their arrival home, Sir Wilfred had been waiting on the steps with a huge bouquet of his wife's favourite blooms. 'Forgive me, my dear,' he had said, his hand on his heart, thus proving that his wife was not the only one of the family with an instinct for drama.

'Wilfred, my darling, of course I will,' Lady Hope had replied, giving him her hand. Eustacia had brought the forgotten book in from the carriage, and put it in the library. Now, she took it upstairs with her. Once back in bed, she began to turn the pages. Written and published just two years before in 1792, the book seemed to be saying things that were personally directed to her.

> *Destructive, however, as riches and inherited honours are to the human character, women are more debased and cramped, if possible, by them, than men, because men may still, in some degree, unfold their faculties by becoming soldiers and statesmen.*

'Oh yes indeed,' she said out loud in bitter tones. 'I wonder what he would have said if *I'd* sent a note to *him*, saying that I was joining the army!' She read on.

> *But the days of true heroism are over . . . Our British heroes are oftener sent from the gaming table than from the plow; and their passions have been rather inflamed by hanging with dumb*

suspense on the turn of a die, than
sublimated by panting after the adven-
turous march of virtue in the historic
page.

'If I ever find that he was not joining the army but just looking for an excuse, I'll kill him with my bare hands!' She declared savagely.

★ ★ ★

The following morning, she woke up with a start, having eventually fallen asleep after having heard the clock in the hall chime four. It took her a moment or two to recall the events of the previous day. Then the humiliation of what had happened swept over her once again. How could he have done it, and in such a way? Even a letter sent to the house to arrive before they had started for the church would have been better than that. Before she could start brooding in good and earnest, she rang her bell and asked Trixie to bring her hot chocolate, and some water for washing.

What a very peculiar day, she thought to herself as she dressed. It was a day that should not have happened — at least, not in this form. She should have begun this day as Mrs Morrison Morrison. Yet here she was, still Miss Hope. What should she do now? A week ago, her days had been packed with fittings, last minute visits, sending and receiving letters and opening gifts. Now, she supposed that she would have to undertake all the various tasks involved in informing people that the wedding had not taken place. Then she would settle down again to being Miss Hope, 22, unwed, unsought, and now tainted with scandal.

As she had expected, she breakfasted alone. Her mother never ate breakfast and seldom appeared before eleven o'clock. Her father would have eaten long since and gone for his morning ride. The last time that she had accompanied him had been three days ago. She sighed. Although she had slept poorly, she could almost wish that she had gone with him. It would at least have given the day some semblance of normality.

Very conscious of the sympathetic gaze of the servant who waited upon her, Eustacia ate her breakfast of toast and marmalade, drank some coffee, and forced herself to read the paper which her father had left behind him. In it, she read about the latest excesses taking place in France as the revolution there proceeded on its bloody path. If she did not follow the stories therein with quite her usual attention, the exercise did at least have the effect of reminding her that there were other things going on in the world apart from her own woes.

Arming herself with these thoughts, she determined to begin packing any gifts that she had received so that they could be returned to the donors. She had also intended to write a short letter to go with each gift, but this small task proved to be far more time-consuming than she had expected. She simply could not think what to put. 'My fiancé has thought better of it', seemed to be the most honest thing to say, but she could not bring herself to write it. It made her sound so second rate. In the end, she contented herself with a brief note in the third person stating that the marriage between Miss Hope and Mr Morrison would not now take place for private reasons, and thanking the donor for his or her kindness in remembering them.

She was saved from further reverie by the entrance of her mother. Lady Hope was clad in peach and cream and looking as delectable as always. If Eustacia closed her eyes, she could picture the fatuous expression that had adorned Morrison's features as he had looked at her elegant mother. Every man of their acquaintance, apart from Sir Wilfred, seemed to lose half his wits when her mother was about.

Before she had become engaged to Morrison, she had gone with her parents to visit Harrogate. There, they had attended a number of assemblies, where a handsome gentleman had seemed to be very smitten with her. It was only after she had admitted to herself that she was beginning to like him very much, that she had discovered he had only pursued her so that he could get close to her mother. Remembering that humiliation, and adding it to the total sum of her experience of men, she resolved never to marry unless she could find a man who could face the full barrage of her mother's beauty, charm and authority unmoved.

'How are you today, my love?' Lady Hope asked her daughter, bending to bestow upon her a scented kiss.

'Keeping myself busy, as you see,' Eustacia replied, gesturing towards the neatly wrapped parcels. She had been feeling quite composed until that moment; but it was as if bringing her voice into use required more effort than she was capable of. To her surprise, she found tears pricking at the back of her eyes.

'Oh, my dear child!' exclaimed Lady Hope. 'Come to Mama!'

'Your gown,' murmured Eustacia, hesitating.

'A fig for my gown,' declared her ladyship with a dramatic snap of her fingers before taking her tearful daughter in an extravagant embrace. Those who did not know her well, suspected that her theatrical manner was a symptom of insincerity. They were completely wrong. There was, and no doubt always would be, something of the actress about the former Miss Delahay; but her affections were sincere, and her loyalty fierce. Eustacia never doubted either for a moment.

'That Morrison!' Lady Hope declared, when her daughter's tears had subsided. Her consonants were becoming more pronounced. 'I could wring his neck with my bare hands! Oh, what a crowning pity that Charlie is not here to take matters in hand!'

Eustacia, knowing how deeply moved her mother was by this reference to the son that she had never had, said reassuringly, 'Not even Charlie could have stopped Morrison from deserting me.' She took a deep breath. 'To be perfectly candid, Mama, I have no wish to be married to a man who would much rather be doing something else.'

Although her mother agreed, Eustacia had the distinct feeling that she did not quite understand. Probably no gentleman had ever been in company with Lady Hope while at the same time wishing that he was doing something else.

'Shall we take a turn about the garden?' her

ladyship suggested. 'You and I can have a cosy chat while Papa is out of the way.'

'Yes of course, Mama,' Eustacia replied, although to be truthful she could not imagine a conversation with her overpowering mother ever being cosy.

Lady Hope tucked her hand into her daughter's arm, and drew her out of the French doors and into the garden. It was a glorious day, the weather refusing to be affected by the dismal nature of the previous day's unfortunate events.

'We must also decide what you ought to do now,' her ladyship went on.

'Do?' Eustacia murmured. Her mind had not taken her beyond returning the wedding presents.

'Certainly,' her mother answered. 'I am sure that you would like to get away from this neighbourhood where every eye must be upon you, for instance.' Eustacia looked at her mother in surprise. Lady Hope laughed. 'You think that I cannot possibly understand after my experience of being on stage; but I do, I promise you. The feeling of being observed when one is unprepared, for example, is excessively unnerving.'

Eustacia eyed her mother keenly. 'You fainted on purpose, didn't you — so that everyone would stop looking at me?'

26

Her ladyship gave a little laugh. 'My faints used to be legendary,' she mused. 'I was quite noted for them. I flatter myself that no one in the church, except perhaps for your father, realized that I was acting. As for your present situation, I have been giving it quite a lot of thought, and I have come to the conclusion that you should go to Agatha.'

'To my godmother? But did she not send apologies for my wedding?'

'Indeed she did, and very properly, for she is still in mourning,' Lady Hope replied in tones of approval. 'I do not see why you should not pay her a visit, however. It will help to lift her spirits. You will go at the end of the week.'

'So soon?'

'It cannot be soon enough for your reputation, I think.' Eustacia knew from the way in which her mother had referred to her life in the theatre that she must think that the case was desperate. She never alluded to her former career except in situations of dire emergency.

'Had you not better write to her first?' suggested Eustacia tentatively.

'I should not dream of sending you without that courtesy,' her mother replied, in her most magisterial of tones. 'There is no need to wait for a reply from her, however. If she is well, she will be delighted to welcome you.'

27

'And if she is ill?' ventured Eustacia.

'If she is ill, then you may make yourself useful. If she is dead — '

'Mama!' exclaimed Eustacia, shocked.

'Well these things happen; you cannot deny it. If she is dead, then, grievous though such a situation would be, it would at least mean that you would be on hand to help to arrange the funeral. No, on second thoughts, if she is dead, you must come home immediately. Ashbourne, reprobate though he is, would never sink so low as to miss his own sister's funeral. Upon no account must you meet Ashbourne.'

'Very well, Mama,' answered Eustacia. She knew better than to ask why. It had always been drummed into her that the Earl of Ashbourne, Lady Agatha's younger brother, was a rake and not to be trusted. He had been one of the court that had flocked around Claire Delahay in her acting days. At that time he had not yet inherited the earldom, and had the courtesy title of Viscount Ilam. Unlike Sir Wilfred, he had made a dishonourable proposal, and had been firmly repulsed.

'If Agatha is there and still alive, he will not come anywhere near the place, so you will be quite safe,' her ladyship went on in satisfied tones.

'Why not?' asked Eustacia curiously.

'Because they are not upon good terms,' her mother explained. 'You may be obliged to see Ilam, I fear. He is Ashbourne's son, and his residence is in the village where Agatha lives. I have no idea as to his character, but as he is Ashbourne's son I suspect the worst, so you must be on your guard. I cannot say too strongly, Eustacia, that given your present unfortunate situation, you must above all avoid the company of rakes. Believe me, I have had experience of them and I know how cunning they can be!'

'Yes, Mama,' replied Eustacia, but she could not help thinking of Morrison Morrison and reflecting that he had managed to do her plenty of harm, despite his blameless reputation.

3

'You are determined upon Eustacia's going, then,' the baronet observed when he went to his wife's bedchamber later on in order to bid her good night. 'By the way, that's a very fetching night-cap, my dear.'

'Do you think so, indeed?' replied her ladyship coyly. 'I had it from Radcliffe's in Harrogate. Yes, I am *quite* determined. I think it will be a very good thing for Eustacia to get away from here after what has happened.'

Her husband nodded. 'We live in such a small society here,' he agreed. 'Everywhere she goes, she will meet people who know about her humiliation. In Derbyshire, she will be able to make a new start.'

'That Morrison Morrison!' exclaimed her ladyship after a short silence. 'I would like to tear him limb from limb!'

'I think that that is probably my duty,' answered Sir Wilfred, his mouth going into a thin line.

'Do you intend to seek him out?' asked Lady Hope, the emotion in her voice increasing subtly. 'Wilfred, my darling, if you were to fight a duel with him, I do not think that I could bear it.'

He smiled whimsically. 'Nonsense, my dear. You would adore it!'

'Well, perhaps,' she admitted, smiling reluctantly. 'But only if it was over me, and if you won.'

'I shan't duel with him,' replied Sir Wilfred. 'But if I find him, I shall make it plain to him where his duty lies.'

Her ladyship sat up very straight in her bed. 'Wilfred, I am not at all sure that I want Eustacia married to such an irresponsible person,' she declared.

'I quite agree. But he must be made to say publicly that he has treated Eustacia abominably, and that it was not her fault in any way. Also, he must write her a very handsome apology. If he is not prepared to do these things, well, I have a friend or two in high places, and in military circles as well, come to that. I could make life quite uncomfortable for him if I chose.'

Lady Hope shuddered artistically. 'Wilfred, my love, I do so adore it when you become determined and masterful,' she declared.

'I know,' he answered, leaning forward to kiss her.

★   ★   ★

Once the decision had been made that Eustacia should go away to her godmother, the whole business took very little time to arrange. Eustacia's trunks were already packed in preparation for her wedding tour and although it seemed a little strange in some ways to be setting off as a single woman with the things that she had expected to use and wear as a married lady, clothes were clothes, and her new things were much too good to waste.

Unlike his wife, Sir Wilfred had never bemoaned his lack of a son, or called upon the spirit of the mythical 'Charlie'. He thought the world of his daughter, and had always given her as much time as he could spare, teaching her to ride and to shoot, and taking her about the estate with him. He had declared himself very willing to accompany her to lllingham but she had refused his offer. 'Mama needs you,' she told him. 'Besides, it is only a short distance, not even a day's journey.'

'The house will seem strangely quiet without you, my dear,' he told her. He had summoned her to his study after breakfast on the day of her departure. Now, he handed over what seemed to her to be an obscenely large sum of money for a stay with a widowed lady in a country vicarage.

'Quiet? With Mama still in residence?'

questioned Eustacia with a chuckle in her voice.

'Well, you know,' her father responded ruefully. 'Are you sure you do not want me to come with you? It is not too late to change your mind.'

'I will have Peter Coachman and Roger the groom to look after me, and with Trixie accompanying me in the chaise I shall come to no harm.'

'You mean that with *you* in the chaise, *Trixie* will come to no harm,' Sir Wilfred answered bluntly. 'She is the flightiest piece this house has ever seen, and why your Mama puts up with her — '

'You know why Mama puts up with her,' Eustacia replied.

When Lady Hope had retired from the theatre, she had brought Honor, her dresser with her. Honor had soon married the head footman and Trixie was the only offspring of that union. Honor's death fifteen years ago had so distressed her husband that he had run away to sea, leaving his infant daughter in his sister's care.

For the child's mother's sake, Lady Hope had always taken an interest in Trixie and, when she was of a suitable age, had decided to train the girl to be Eustacia's abigail. There was something quite fitting, she decided, in her own dresser's daughter growing up to perform a similar function for her child.

Needless to say, it was not Lady Hope herself who did the training. The abigail whom she had taken on after Honor's death, had been given that task. Florrie Niblett was very unlike Honor, being of strict Methodist stock, and she would rather have died than have endured any besmirching connection with the theatre. Nevertheless, she knew her work; and she had the advantage that her disapproval of her employer's acting career meant that she was quite willing to participate in her ladyship's determination never to mention her previous occupation, except in an emergency.

Unfortunately, Trixie was not prepared to further this deception, at least as far as her mother was concerned. She was proud of Honor's work in the theatre and, Eustacia suspected, from the gleam in Trixie's eye, took no small degree of pleasure in mentioning it in Miss Niblett's hearing. Had she ever mentioned Lady Hope's previous career, then her presence would not have been tolerated; she never did so. Nor did she ever attempt to flirt with Sir Wilfred, which would have obtained her instant dismissal.

She might still have been dismissed despite her heritage, for in addition to her insolence towards Miss Niblett, she had an irrepressible tendency to flirt with all the male servants. Her saving grace was that she had inherited her mother's clever fingers and eye for colour. Be Eustacia's curls never so recalcitrant — and sometimes they were very recalcitrant indeed — Trixie could always coax them into order. An odd piece of ribbon which did not match anything else, in Trixie's hands became a cleverly contrasting piece of trim that gave a cachet to a whole new outfit. A gown that had been spoilt by the flat iron could be altered and pleated so that the finished result looked better than the garment had done when it was new.

Decidedly, then, Trixie must go with her mistress, although she could not be depended upon as a chaperon. Her escort could only be considered sufficient because the journey could be accomplished in one day, with no overnight stops.

'Give Agatha my fondest love,' Lady Hope said, as she and Sir Wilfred stood outside the house ready to wave off their daughter and her companion.

'Of course, Mama,' Eustacia replied.

'Trixie, see that you behave yourself,' Lady Hope added in minatory tones.

'Oh yes, my lady,' answered Trixie respectfully. Like the rest of the household, she looked up to her ladyship as to a being on a higher plane.

'And should Ashbourne appear, keep out of his way, both of you. Remember, once a rake, always a rake.'

'Yes, Mama,' replied Eustacia, her heart sinking into her shoes, for she knew what the reaction from Trixie would be as soon as they were out of earshot.

'A rake?' exclaimed the maid, her eyes gleaming for all the world as if she had been promised an outing to Astley's Amphitheatre.

'Yes, but he is *years* older than we are and no doubt has lost all his looks with over-indulgence,' said Eustacia firmly. 'He probably will not come anywhere near where we are staying. What's more, if he does and if you misbehave in any way, I will box your ears and tell Mama, *and* you will not have that pink gown from my trousseau which I did not like from the very first but which you adored.'

Trixie had indeed had her heart set on the pink gown and Eustacia had caught her holding it in front of herself and admiring its effects with her blonde prettiness in the mirror on more than one occasion. 'Oh, all right, Miss Stacia,' replied the girl sulkily. 'You're mean, you are. I only wanted a little sport.'

The trouble was, what seemed like sport to such as Trixie could mean heartache to others. It had not been very long since a new groom had come to work in the stables at Woodfield Park. For a week after his arrival, Trixie had been in bed with a nasty chill. During that week, one of the housemaids had become enamoured of the lad and had been trying, in a modest way, to attract his attention. Once Trixie was on her feet, however, she had flirted outrageously with the young man, and little Miriam had not had a chance. Eustacia had noticed the girl's downcast looks. She hoped that now that Trixie was away, the housemaid might be able to reanimate Trevor's affections.

Contemplation of Trixie's previous triumphs brought a very unwelcome notion into Eustacia's mind. 'Did you ever flirt with Morrison?' she asked suspiciously.

'Not I,' replied the girl virtuously. 'Her ladyship'd've had a stick across my back if I had. Besides,' she went on, spoiling the effect, 'I tried, but he wasn't interested.'

'You tried?' demanded Eustacia indignantly.

'He wasn't interested,' Trixie repeated in a tone that was so close to insolence that Eustacia would not have tolerated it, had they not been almost the same age, and known one another all their lives.

'No, he obviously wasn't very interested in me, either,' replied Eustacia in a deflated tone, after a brief pause.

Trixie leaned across and grasped her mistress's hand. 'I told you he wasn't good enough for you,' she said. 'You'd do better to have a look at that rake that her ladyship was talking about.'

'I don't think so,' said Eustacia, chuckling despite herself. 'If Morrison wasn't good enough for me, then I'm sure that Lord Ashbourne would be much too bad, as well as being far too old. *And* he probably has gout.'

'How old is he then, Miss Stacia?' asked Trixie, sitting back comfortably in her seat.

'I think he is a little younger than Mama,' replied Eustacia. 'I know that my godmother is two years older than Mama, and that she is Lord Ashbourne's older sister by a few years.'

'Too old to be a match for you, then,' Trixie observed. 'Maybe not too old for a little flirtation, though.'

'Trixie,' said Eustacia in warning tones. But Trixie was already leaning back with her eyes closed, and a faint smile upon her lips.

As the girl dozed off, to dream, no doubt, of being chased by rakes, Eustacia sat and thought about her godmother. She knew that Lady Hope and Lady Agatha had met in Bath when Lady Hope, then Claire Delahay was the toast of the town. Miss Delahay had appeared at one or two select evening parties, always accompanied by her chaperon, giving poetry recitations and then remaining as a guest. A drunken gentleman — possibly Lord Ilam, although Eustacia had never found out for certain — had made a nuisance of himself and Lady Agatha had intervened, rescuing the actress from serious assault. The two had been firm friends ever since, the earl's daughter blithely disregarding those of the polite world who said that befriending a woman from the theatre would prove to be her social ruin.

Had Lady Agatha ever been obliged to pay for that unwise friendship, Eustacia wondered. Was that why she had married a country clergyman, albeit of a good family, instead of enjoying the glittering career that should surely have been the lot of a wealthy earl's daughter? What attitude had her mother and father taken?

Her mind turned to her own home and parents, and a tear slid down her cheek. She could not remember the last time she had gone away without Mama and Papa. She had looked forward to the idea of her own establishment; she had not anticipated leaving them like this!

After a moment or two, she brushed her tears away determinedly and opened the book that she had brought with her to while away the journey. It was the volume by Mary Wollstonecraft that she had taken to her room after she had been jilted. She read for a little while before coming upon a sentence which seemed appropriate to her own situation.

My own sex, I hope, will excuse me, if I treat them like rational creatures instead of flattering their fascinating graces, and viewing them as if they were in a state of perpetual childhood, unable to stand alone . . . I wish to persuade women to endeavour to acquire strength, both of mind and body . . .

The author was right, she decided. She must not be so childish. She had become so used to thinking about her future as being entwined with that of Morrison that she had lost sight of her own strengths and abilities. It was time for her to stand on her own feet. Perhaps this time spent with her godmother would help her to do so. At length, like Trixie, Eustacia, too, closed her eyes, and soon she was asleep.

★   ★   ★

It was only mid-afternoon when they arrived at the village of Illingham, set in the heart of the Derbyshire peaks. It was not a large village, comprising little more than a single street, a few houses around a village green, together with a pretty inn — the Olde Oak — a fine Norman church, a small shop and a manor house. On entering the village, they immediately began to descend a gentle slope, soon passing the manor house on their right-hand side, and what looked like a well on the left.

The manor house was a handsome building, constructed in the Elizabethan style, and was only a matter of steps away from the village street. Eustacia was impressed to see what was clearly a gentleman's residence right at the heart of a village, as opposed to being hidden at the end of a very long drive. She was still wondering whether this might be the residence of Lord Ilam when the carriage made a left turn through a pair of open gates and up a short drive that led to a squarely built house that appeared to be about thirty years old. It was the kind of house that would certainly merit further examination at a later date. For now, their view of it was somewhat obscured by a small equipage that was standing near the front door. As their own driver hesitated, deciding how to deposit his passengers most comfortably, Eustacia and Trixie were treated to an astonishing sight.

A black-clad, long-legged figure, possibly a clergyman, came scuttling out of the house, his hurried movements and skinny limbs causing him to bear more than a passing resemblance to a spider fleeing from a broom. The reason for his haste became apparent when a diminutive dark-haired lady came bustling after him, a closed umbrella raised threateningly above her head.

'But my lord bishop,' bleated the clergyman, half raising his hands in order to protect his head, as he turned to address his pursuer.

'A fig for the bishop, sirrah,' exclaimed the lady in authoritative tones. Her manner, if not the activity in which she was engaged, reminded Eustacia very much of her mother in full flight. 'How dare he send his minions to hound a defenceless widow in her own home?'

'But madam, the church owns — '

''My lady' to you, insect,' she of the umbrella interrupted. 'The church does not own the right to put me out into the street.' She indicated the carriage in which Eustacia and Trixie were sitting. 'See, now, here is the carriage of my kinsman, Sir Wilfred Hope. Heaven only knows what he will say to this intrusion.'

At once, Eustacia sat back in her seat, not wanting to be seen, then briefly leaned forward to push Trixie back in hers. Unsurprisingly, Trixie showed a distressing tendency to gape out of the window at the unfolding scene.

By dint of rather an impressive degree of athleticism, the clergyman managed to scramble into his carriage without sustaining more than a glancing blow or two. 'The bishop will hear of this outrage,' he declared, rendered braver once the carriage was in motion.

'And God will hear of my complaints in my prayers,' retorted his opponent in a very unprayerful manner, before turning to greet the new arrivals.

The departure of the clergyman had vacated the space by the front door. As Eustacia was assisted down, the lady of the house, who had taken a few threatening steps in pursuit of the unwelcome visitor, turned back with her free hand extended. 'Eustacia, my dear, this is delightful! It must be at least two years since I saw you last. I had not expected you so soon, but now you can join my campaign.'

'Your campaign, Godmama?' ventured Eustacia.

'My campaign to defeat the Church of

England, of course,' answered the other lady. 'It promises to be great sport. Come inside and let me show you to your room. There will be time enough for all of that when you are rested.'

Wondering how much time it would take for her to be rested sufficiently to build up enough strength in order to bring down the Anglican Communion, Eustacia obediently followed her godmother into the house.

4

The entrance hall was bright and airy. From it, a fine marble staircase led up to the next landing, then divided in two, going left and right in front of a large rectangular window. Above the foot of the stairs, a modest dome set into the ceiling let in more light.

'This is charming, Godmama,' said Eustacia spontaneously as she looked around.

'It is indeed,' agreed her godmother with a decisive nod. 'Perhaps you now begin to understand my determination to remain here; apart, of course, from the fact that justice is on my side,' she added hastily.

'Of course,' Eustacia agreed. 'This is Trixie, my maid, by the way.'

'Hm,' said Lady Agatha, eyeing Trixie in a way that was strangely reminiscent of Lady Hope. Then she looked at her goddaughter again, paying special attention to Eustacia's hair, becomingly arranged beneath her head-gear, and the choice and arrangement of her apparel and accessories. Eustacia was wearing a blue carriage dress trimmed with dull gold, and her bonnet, with blue ribbons and gold flowers, conformed to the same theme. 'The young woman seems to know her business, at all events. Go with Grimes to the kitchen,' she said to Trixie, indicating the elderly butler who was standing close by, looking as if the recent contretemps with the departed clergyman had taken its toll. 'My housekeeper will meet you there and acquaint you with the house and the other servants. Grimes is my right-hand man, Eustacia. Grimes, Miss Hope is my goddaughter and is to stay with us for the time being.'

Grimes bowed in a stately manner. 'I trust your stay will be a pleasant one, miss,' he said, before indicating to Trixie that she should go with him. Trixie threw her mistress a surreptitious wink before disappearing in the direction of the kitchens.

'Come along,' said Lady Agatha to Eustacia. 'I've had the most delightful room prepared for you. I know you will love it.'

Lady Agatha walked ahead of her, her black silk skirts rustling as she mounted the stairs. She was clad from head to toe in black, even to the lace cap that she was sporting atop her hair, which was still black, with just a few strands of grey. In stature, she was a little taller than Eustacia with a neat figure. At the age of 48, her ladyship was still a handsome woman, with just a suggestion of tiny lines at the corners of her mouth and eyes. She also had a very determined chin.

The room to which Lady Agatha took her goddaughter was indeed delightful. Decorated in shades of green with a thick carpet on the floor, it was set into the corner of the house and had two windows, one with a view facing onto the drive and the other looking across a lawn towards a scattering of beech trees which marked the boundary between the garden and the fields beyond.

'This is lovely,' declared Eustacia. 'I shall be very comfortable here, I'm sure.'

'I'm glad,' replied Lady Agatha, taking her hands and giving them a squeeze. 'I will leave you to refresh yourself from your journey. Have a little rest if you like, but come down when you are ready. We'll have some tea and you can tell me all about your dear mama.'

The subject of Eustacia's broken engagement hovered in the air between them. No doubt it would have to be discussed at some point, but if Lady Agatha was tactful enough to leave the timing of that discussion to her goddaughter, then Eustacia was very thankful for it.

She took off her bonnet, smoothed down her hair and stood looking out of the window for a few minutes. Just a few days ago, she should have been united in marriage to Morrison Morrison. Where would she have been now, if her wedding had taken place? Might she have been standing looking out of some other window, and might she then have felt the clasp of Morrison's hands on her shoulders? She glanced round quickly, almost surprised to find that she was alone. She looked down at her gown, and recalled that blue was Morrison's favourite colour. Suddenly conscious of a prickling behind her eyes, she fumbled in her reticule and pulled out her handkerchief. She had shed a few tears over Morrison's defection, but never in public. Even with her mother, she had only dabbed at moist eyes for a moment or two. Any extravagant displays of temperament in the Hope household were the province of her ladyship. Eustacia always felt that her part was to be more restrained in her behaviour.

Now, however, there was no audience and no likelihood of interruption. Trixie, she knew, would be enquiring into the appearance of any male servants on the premises. Lady Agatha had withdrawn, telling her not to come downstairs until she was ready. So she sat down on the edge of the comfortable four-poster bed with its green coverlet, patterned with pink flowers, and sobbed into her handkerchief.

It was not a very cheering thing to be rejected in favour of a career in the military, she decided. No doubt had she been tall and blonde and classically beautiful like her mother, Morrison would have turned up at the church with his tongue hanging out!

After her tears were done, she spent a little time splashing her face, then waited to recover her complexion before going downstairs. On her arrival back in the hall, she found Grimes, who conducted her to the drawing-room. This room, she decided, must be almost exactly beneath her bedroom, for the aspect was just about the same. Unlike her chamber upstairs, however, this room was decorated in apricot. Lady Agatha was seated writing at a little table in front of one of the windows, but at Eustacia's entrance, she got up and asked Grimes to bring tea.

'I have just been writing to the bishop,' she explained. 'I think that he should apologize for the mannerless intervention of that insect who came today. Not that he will, of course. My opinion of the bishop is not very high! Enough of him for now. Come and sit down. It is a shameful thing, but I have barely seen you recently. Tell me all about your mama and papa.'

'And about Morrison Morrison?' Eustacia asked, proud of her tranquil tone. The subject could not be avoided indefinitely, so the sooner that it was raised and then dropped for good, the better she would like it.

'If the fellow does not think my god-daughter good enough for him, then the less said about him the better, in my opinion,' replied her ladyship decisively.

Eustacia was conscious of an instinct to leap to his defence, which she instantly repressed. 'I only thought that you might want to hear what happened.'

At this point, Grimes came in with the tea tray, but after he had gone, Lady Agatha said 'My advice to you, my dear, would be to put the whole matter behind you. I had a friend who was left at the altar and she told the story at great length to every acquaintance. It became very tedious. Not only that, but it drove new suitors away as well. She became known as 'The Jilted Miss Maybury.' You would not want to become known as 'The Jilted Miss Hope,' would you?' Eustacia shook her head, remembering how she had imagined herself being given that very title. 'The best plan would be to put Morrison Morrison out of your thoughts. I have to say that his parents must have very commonplace minds if they could not think of a Christian name that differed from his surname. Imagine if your parents had called you Hope Hope?'

Eustacia had to laugh at that. 'I should

then have been doubly annoyed with Morrison for not giving me the chance of changing my name,' she agreed. 'I have to admit, too, that I sometimes wondered whether speaking to him as a married woman, I would have been assumed to have been fashionable and dashing, or rather vulgarly familiar.'

'Your dilemma is solved, then,' declared Lady Agatha, pouring the tea and passing Eustacia a cup. 'Now let us not say another word about him. He has occupied far more of our time than he deserves already. Indeed, I urge you not to mention the matter to anyone. It could damage your chances of achieving a good match in the future, you know. I have put it about that you have come to stay with me for your health.'

'My health?' echoed Eustacia.

'Certainly. You are inclined to be delicate, my dear Eustacia. I have always suspected it.'

'But Godmama, I am in the very best of health,' Eustacia protested. 'I am like Mama — never ill. I ride every day — '

'Hush, my dear,' replied her ladyship reprovingly. 'It is not at all the thing for a young woman to boast about her robust health. As soon go round with your face covered with freckles! Now let us put your troubles aside and instead, let us think about my own personal difficulty, which concerns how to put the bishop in his place.'

'Why should the bishop need putting in his place?' ventured Eustacia.

'Because he is out of it, of course,' retorted Lady Agatha. 'A bishop should be in his palace, or in his cathedral communing with his God, not throwing poor defenceless widows out of their homes.'

Eustacia stole a look at her godmother over the top of her tea cup. The older lady was straight-backed in her handsome silk gown. Her eyes sparkled with a militant light, and her chin was raised. Anyone less like a defenceless widow Eustacia had never seen. 'Is that what the bishop has been trying to do?'

Her ladyship gave a decisive nod. 'Hardly a Christian attitude for a clergyman to take,' she said scornfully. 'Is that tea to your liking, my dear?'

'Yes, it's very good,' Eustacia replied. 'That gentleman who was here today — '

'That clergyman,' Lady Agatha corrected. 'Not a gentleman, but a clergyman. There is a difference.'

'That clergyman, then. Was he here at the bishop's instigation?'

'He certainly was.' Her ladyship sniffed. 'As if I would be intimidated by such a skinny, lanky creature as that.'

Eustacia sat in silence for some moments before venturing to say, 'This house, God-mama: to whom does it belong?'

There was a pause. 'Do you mean technically or morally?' her ladyship asked with a touch of hauteur.

Realizing that she had made a *faux pas*, Eustacia hastened to recover herself. 'Techni-cally, of course,' she replied, then added craftily, 'I can see that morally there is no question as to who is the rightful owner.'

Lady Agatha's expression relaxed visibly. 'You are right in asking the question. It will enable you to follow my reasoning as I describe my campaign.' She paused briefly. 'You will be aware that I was married to the vicar of this parish, the Reverend Colin Rayner.'

'Yes, I was aware of that.'

'My husband, Eustacia, died in the performance of his duties. Had he not been vicar here, then his death would never have occurred in the manner in which it did, and we would probably have enjoyed a ripe of old age together.'

Eustacia had never discovered how the Rev'd Colin Rayner had died. It had not been discussed in front of her at home, even when the death had occurred six months before.

She had heard part of a conversation that had taken place in the kitchen between the man who had brought the news and one or two of the upper servants. She had been able to make out very little beyond something which sounded like 'falling into a pit of his own making'. This phrase had been followed by stifled laughter, and Eustacia had left hurriedly, rather shocked by the callous attitude displayed by those she had overheard.

Sir Wilfred had not referred to the matter at all, nor had her mother made any comment, beyond telling her to send a letter of condolence to her godmother. When Eustacia had asked about the circumstances so that she might make her letter more sensitive, her mother had replied that these need not concern her and that she was by far too young to understand such matters.

Looking back, it seemed to her that she must have been very incurious. At the time, however, she had been far too preoccupied by the immediate prospect of a visit from some of Morrison's relations to worry about the death of a gentleman whom she had never met.

'About what duties was he engaged, ma'am?' Eustacia asked, feeling that it would be impolite not to say anything at all.

'He died within sight of his church, whilst clad in his vestments,' her godmother replied with dignity.

'That must have been of some comfort to you,' Eustacia murmured.

'Indeed it was, child, and the fact also provides me with a powerful argument. If he died in such circumstances, it could be maintained that he never actually ceased being the vicar here. If that were the case, how could they appoint another man? Despite this argument — which I have put most forcefully — the church still wants to throw me out of this house — the house to which I came as a bride thirty years ago. Indeed, it was only just finished when I moved in, so it has never been occupied by anyone else. I have lived in this house for longer than I have lived anywhere else. I have made it my own. I have stamped my taste upon it. It some senses, it might even be said that I created it. Who has a better right to live in it? Doubtless the bishop would enjoy throwing me out whilst Ashbourne looked on, rubbing his hands.'

Eustacia could not think of anything to say that would be pleasing to her godmother. Had they been having this conversation six or even three months previously, she could have agreed with Lady Agatha without so much as a qualm. After the vicar had been dead for half a year, however, it did not seem to her to be unreasonable for the bishop to want to install another clergyman in his place. This kind of response would clearly not be acceptable. Instead of commenting directly upon the situation, therefore, Eustacia asked, 'How does Lord Ashbourne come into this?'

Her ladyship's back straightened and her expression became even more outraged than before. 'Ashbourne! Pah! In a civilized society, I, as the elder, would be the one with the title and lands, and he would be the one begging for a foothold in a miserable vicarage.'

Eustacia found herself very much in sympathy with some of this speech. She recalled some words of Mary Wollstonecraft that she had read during the night after she had been jilted. *The society is not properly organized which does not compel men and women to discharge their respective duties*, that lady had written. No doubt her godmother would agree with this sentiment, taking the argument further by saying that as Ashbourne obviously was not discharging his duties, his sister ought to be allowed to assume them, along with his title.

It did, however, seem odd to her that Lady Agatha was so eager to remain in a place that she described as miserable. Resisting the temptation to remark upon this curious anomaly, Eustacia said merely 'Is Lord Ashbourne siding with the bishop?'

Lady Agatha gave a snort of laughter. 'Side with the bishop? He would as soon take orders himself! The truth of the matter is that the property is very stupidly divided, which in this instance works to my advantage, because it means that I can play one party off against the other. The vicarage and the land upon which it stands belongs partly to the church and partly to the Ashbourne estate. At one time, the church had the chief responsibility concerning the appointment of the vicar, although the earl was consulted as a matter of courtesy.

'Then, some years ago, in the reign of Charles II I think, the bishop and the earl were fierce rivals over some wench that each of them wanted to make his mistress. They played cards for her, the game got very heated, and the earl came away from the table with not only the wench, but also a large amount of property, including this village and part of the land on which the church and the vicarage stand. The consequence is that the bishop and the earl of the day are obliged to agree upon the choice of incumbent for the parish. If they disagree, then the earl has a second vote, and his decision stands.'

'I see,' remarked Eustacia in enlightened

tones. 'So you can appeal to your brother.'

Lady Agatha could not have looked more outraged had Eustacia suggested appealing to the Devil himself. 'Appeal to Ashbourne?' she exclaimed. 'I would rather have my head shaved. No, my best course must be to make sure that my brother knows nothing about this. He is in Italy gambling and whoring himself silly, and the longer he remains there, the better.'

'Surely, the church will consult him, if they have not already done so,' Eustacia objected, colouring a little at her godmother's broad speech.

'Not if I can help it. He was in Greece for goodness knows how long, and that is the last that the church knows of his whereabouts. Now his travels have taken him to Rome. The church has no idea where he is and I have not told them.'

'How do you know where he is?'

'I have my sources,' said Lady Agatha mysteriously. 'They will not disclose their information to the enemy.'

Wondering what her mother would think to this description of the Established Church, Eustacia said, 'What have you told the church authorities in the meantime?'

'I have told them that my brother will naturally be taking my side in the matter.'

'It is what any brother would do, I

suppose,' murmured Eustacia.

'Poppycock! The only course that my brother would take in such circumstances would be to do the opposite of what he thought I wanted. More tea, dear?'

Eustacia accepted and sat drinking it while Lady Agatha had a conversation with Grimes who had come in to raise some household matter with her.

When her ladyship came to sit down again, Eustacia said cautiously, 'Forgive me, God-mama, but for how long do you intend to . . . to . . . '

'To hold the church to ransom?' suggested her godmother, her eyes twinkling. 'For as long as I possibly can,' she replied frankly. 'Oh, I know I shall be obliged to leave here eventually. The bishop will find his way around my schemes, and no doubt Ilam will disoblige me by colluding with him, but this battle is so entertaining. Packed away in the dower house at Ashbourne, I should be bored to death.'

Eustacia would have liked to ask why the daughter of a wealthy earl could not live as high as a coach horse, but she knew that that would be unpardonably intrusive. Instead, she asked her hostess to tell her something about the history of the village and so changed the subject.

5

It was while they were drinking tea, and while Eustacia was still taking in the fact that her godmother was deliberately deceiving the church in order to remain in a house to which she was clearly not entitled, that the door opened and a lady wearing a neat but unremarkable bonnet and a modestly cut smoky-grey gown came into the room.

'Oh, I beg your pardon,' she said in a soft musical tone.

'Come in, Jessie,' said Lady Agatha. 'Allow me to introduce Eustacia Hope, my god-daughter. You will remember that I told you that she was to come and stay with us for a while. Eustacia, this is Jessie Warburton, who resides with me as my companion.'

Eustacia got up to exchange polite greetings with the newcomer. Miss Warburton was taller than Eustacia by a good three or four inches, and she looked to be in her thirties. Her hair, neat and smooth beneath her plain straw bonnet was of an ordinary shade of light brown. Her eyes were also brown, and her features held nothing to displease, but nothing to catch the eye either.

Altogether she was the kind of woman that one might easily pass in the street and instantly forget. This was Eustacia's opinion, until the other woman smiled, whereupon her face was lit up with an expression of such sweetness that her appearance was instantly transformed to something that was very like beauty.

'I'm sorry that I was not here to greet you, Miss Hope,' said Miss Warburton. 'I was doing a little visiting on Lady Agatha's behalf.'

'Visiting?' echoed Eustacia.

'I like to keep an eye on the parishioners,' said her ladyship. '*Someone* has to do so, if there is no priest here.' Then, before anyone could comment upon the connection between the lack of an incumbent and her refusal to quit the house, she said, 'Take off your bonnet, Jessie, and ring for more tea. This is cold.'

'I have already had tea with Mrs Swanage,' Jessie replied, doing as she was bid. As she removed her head covering and walked to the bell, her movements were as smooth and gentle as the tone of her voice.

'Tea with Mrs Swanage!' exclaimed Lady Agatha in disgusted tones. 'Cat's wee with a wet hen!'

Eustacia coloured again at her godmother's

forceful language, for Lady Hope, despite her former connections with the stage, never expressed herself in unladylike terms. Jessie, who was obviously more used to it, simply smiled and enquired about the visitor's journey.

'It went very smoothly, thank you,' Eustacia replied.

'Until the last few minutes,' her ladyship put in. 'That insect Henry Lusty came again and I had to eject him.'

'You do Mr Lusty a disservice,' said Jessie calmly. 'He is only doing what he believes to be right.'

'Ha!' ejaculated her ladyship. 'He would not come here nearly so often if *you* were not here. Still, you're better off entertaining his suit than sighing over Ashbourne, I suppose.'

Jessie coloured faintly, but made no response to this, simply enquiring for how long Eustacia was intending to stay. 'I am not sure as yet,' Eustacia told her, as Grimes came in with more tea. 'For how long have you resided with my godmother, Miss Warburton?'

'For the last eight years,' Jessie answered. Eustacia was surprised. She had expected to hear that Lady Agatha's companion had come to live at the vicarage on the death of the vicar.

'Never mind that. It's all past history,' said Lady Agatha dismissively. 'The main thing is that we now have reinforcements.'

'Reinforcements?' repeated Jessie and Eustacia, almost at the same time.

'Yes indeed,' responded Lady Agnes, smiling like a cat that had not only got the cream, but also knew from where to procure the next bowlful. 'A young girl, all alone, jilted, penniless, and in delicate health: how could the church be so heartless as to throw her out?'

'But I'm not alone and penniless, and I've already told you that my health is excellent,' Eustacia protested, mystified.

'Yes, but they don't know that, do they?' answered her godmother, still beaming.

★   ★   ★

Over the next few days, Eustacia frequently found herself wondering what her mother would have made of the situation in which her daughter found herself. Her intention in sending Eustacia to her godmother had been that she should be cared for at some distance away from the scene of her jilting, with all the scandal that that entailed. No doubt Lady Hope had anticipated that her daughter would benefit from the wise counsel of her old friend, the vicar's widow. What Eustacia's mother could never have expected was that the same vicar's widow would seek to embroil her young guest in an intrigue which involved falsifying the opinions of a peer, deceiving ecclesiastical authorities as to the nature of her, Eustacia's, circumstances, defrauding the church of its rightful property and denying the village the priest that it was entitled to have.

She recalled how Lady Agatha had visited them once when she, Eustacia, was only seventeen. She had taken her goddaughter to York and they had gone to an inn and, as there was no parlour, they had sat in the taproom. She remembered another occasion when Lady Agatha had taken her driving in the country. When they had found a secluded spot, her ladyship had taken out brandy and cigars. Eustacia had tried both and been vilely ill. In many ways, it was not surprising that a lady with such a capacity for plots and plans should still be plotting now.

It was odd, though, that at one moment, her ladyship seemed to be saying that they should keep quiet about Eustacia's Unfortunate Experience, and at another that she should be advocating using this sad circumstance as a weapon in her fight against the bishop. Part of her rejoiced at this piece of intrigue. At Woodfield Park they had always led a very quiet life. Most of the time, Eustacia did not mind. Sometimes, though, she thought of her mother's exciting and slightly scandalous past, and wanted to have adventures of her own. This scheme of her godmother's, surely harmless in its way, promised a little intrigue and excitement, if only for the short term.

How strangely things fell out, she thought. Her mother, the former actress, would always be tainted with immorality in many people's eyes. Yet her mother was a pillar of the local community, a vigorous supporter of the church, and a fierce opponent of falsehood. Lady Agatha's approach seemed rather entertaining in comparison.

There had been no further visits from the church authorities, and no correspondence from them either. On the other hand, a letter had arrived from another source that very morning which had brought to her ladyship's face that self-satisfied smile with which Eustacia was beginning to be very familiar. 'Ashbourne is still hell-raising in Italy,' she had declared. 'He will have no interest in my concerns.'

'What if the bishop writes to him?' Eustacia had ventured.

'Ha! If anything arrives for him with the

frank paid for by the bishop, he'll throw it in the fire,' her godmother had stated positively. 'We'll not see him here.'

Throughout this discourse, Miss Warburton had sat quietly in her place, buttering her toast with careful precision and cutting it into small, neat squares.

Now, although she had not finished, she stood up. 'If you will excuse me, I think I will go to my room,' she said in even tones.

'Shall we go for a walk in a little while?' Eustacia asked her. The two younger ladies had quickly formed the habit of walking together each day.

'I shall be ready,' Jessie replied, before leaving the room.

'Poor Jessie,' said Lady Agatha shaking her head. 'I fear she has always had a weakness for my brother, but it would never do. A rake like Ashbourne would never look her way. She's not the kind of pretty slut that appeals to him at all. In reality, she wouldn't like it above half if he did pay her any attention, although she'd never believe it if I told her so. Unfortunately, the alternative is no better in my opinion.'

'What is the alternative?' asked Eustacia curiously.

'Henry Lusty, of course,' her godmother replied scornfully. 'You don't think this business with the bishop is the only reason he calls, do you? If I thought he was really interested in her, I would encourage him tomorrow. Unfortunately, I suspect that he believes that by courting her, he will get a foot into this place. If you've finished your breakfast, you might as well go and find her. She seems to have taken to you.'

To Eustacia aged 22, Miss Warburton at 30 seemed venerable. The notion that this lady could at one and the same time be smitten by a rake and pursued by a curate was novel indeed. They had talked about all kinds of things as they had strolled about the village together, but their conversations had not encompassed either of these two gentlemen. The truth was that in Miss Warburton, Eustacia had discovered the kind confidante that she had not found in her godmother. Jessie's gentle sympathy had drawn out the whole sorry story of Morrison's desertion, and it had been about him and about Eustacia's own life that they had talked.

Now, Eustacia felt guilty. She had poured all her troubles out to Jessie without ever wondering whether Jessie might have things that *she* wanted to talk about. Eustacia resolved that she would remedy the situation that very day. The essential thing would be to show herself ready to listen to Jessie's problems without looking as if she was being vulgarly intrusive.

In the event, it was Jessie herself who raised the matter. 'I suppose you must be wondering why I fled the breakfast-table this morning,' she said.

'It seemed to me that you left just after my godmother spoke about Lord Ashbourne,' Eustacia replied. They were walking down the drive, making the most of the sunny day. Eustacia, dressed as usual by Trixie, was in a dark pink gown, set off handsomely by dove grey gloves and kid boots, and a charming bonnet with pink flowers and pink and grey striped ribbons. Jessie, in a mustard-coloured gown with a plain bonnet, managed to look several years older than she really was.

'You must think me such a fool,' Jessie said, after they had walked along in silence for a short time.

'Of course I don't,' replied Eustacia without hesitation. The other woman's gentle kindness had won her heart almost from the very first. It made a welcome change to Lady Hope's imperious conviction that she must know best for everyone, and Lady Agatha's inclination to make use of other people quite shamelessly in order to further her schemes, and to discount any concerns that did not affect herself.

'Well I do,' Jessie replied frankly. 'I have told myself time out of mind what a fool I am, but it does not seem to make any difference, I'm afraid.'

'Have you known the family for long?' Eustacia asked her.

Jessie nodded. 'Mama and Lady Agatha were friends for years. My father was a squire with a small income, but he wasn't very wise with his money, I fear. After he died, Mama and I were left without a home, so Lady Agatha persuaded Lord Ashbourne — the present Lord Ashbourne's father — to provide us with a cottage on his estate and somehow we managed. Mama was ill for some years before she died, and I looked after her. Then after her death eight years ago, Lady Agatha invited me to come and live with her.'

'Is Lord Ashbourne like his sister?' Eustacia asked.

'A little,' replied Jessie.

'Is he handsome?'

'Yes, he's very handsome,' answered Jessie wearily. 'Handsome and wicked and careless, and he's never cast so much as a glance my way. Perhaps if I met him every day, I would get used to him. If I never saw him at all, that would be even better; but I see him just enough to keep him in my mind.'

'Forgive me for asking,' said Eustacia tentatively, 'but surely Lord Ashbourne must be a married man.'

'He is a widower,' answered Jessie. 'His wife died giving birth to his only son. Ilam was brought up chiefly by a local farmer's family. Ashbourne has been kicking over the traces ever since. Mercifully his fortune is immense, or he would have run through it years ago.'

'Have you never thought of anyone else?' Eustacia asked curiously.

'Not really,' replied Jessie simply. 'However, it may be that that situation could be on the point of changing.'

Eustacia remembered her godmother speaking about the curate, Henry Lusty. Could it be that Jessie was considering encouraging his suit?

By now, they were walking along the main street. Eustacia and Trixie had travelled the other way down it when they had first arrived in the village. Now, the two ladies strolled up the gentle incline. As they reached the gates of Illingham Hall, Jessie said impulsively, 'Would you like to see Ashbourne's portrait? There is one inside.'

'Would it be allowed?' Eustacia asked.

'The housekeeper likes showing people around,' Jessie told her.

'What about Lord Ilam?'

'He would not mind. In any case, he is from home.'

'Is he gambling in Italy with his father?' Eustacia asked, remembering her mother saying that he might be a rake as well.

'Oh no,' replied Jessie positively. 'He and his father are not upon good terms. Shall we go in?'

Eustacia allowed herself to be persuaded. In truth, she was feeling rather curious about Lord Ashbourne. Her mother had warned her about this notorious rake before she had ever come here. Now, she had the chance to see him for herself.

The housekeeper, a thin, wiry-looking woman with iron-grey hair, obviously knew Miss Warburton very well, seemed to be gratified to meet Lady Agatha's goddaughter, and was quite happy to permit the two ladies to make a tour of the house without her.

'I won't take you all the way round,' said Jessie confidingly as they made their way up the stairs that led up from the hall. 'I expect Lady Agatha will want to do that. I would be grateful, however, if you will perhaps not mention today's visit.'

'Of course,' Eustacia replied, as they climbed the stairs. Like the majority of the house, it was Elizabethan, and richly carved with vines and grapes, in the style of Grinling

Gibbons. There was a sharp turn to the right at the top of the stairs, and Eustacia gasped with admiration, for she found herself standing at the end of a long gallery, with huge windows on one side, and bookcases which extended from floor to exquisitely painted ceiling on the other. The windows looked out onto a well kept old-fashioned parterre.

'This place seems well managed,' remarked Eustacia looking round her with the eye of one accustomed to a father's diligence and a mother's good housekeeping. The house was obviously cared for, with highly polished wood and sparkling windows, and the fabric of the place looked to be in good order. How much was Ilam responsible for this good care, she wondered? She bent to examine an exquisitely decorated table, and slipped her reticule off her wrist when it got in the way.

'The gardens are beautiful, aren't they?' said Jessie. Eustacia looked up and wandered over to join her at the window. Beyond the parterre was a terrace with a summerhouse, and a variety of trees behind. 'They were tended especially by Ilam's grandmother. Ilam was born here, as his grandfather was alive at the time, and Ilam's father was the viscount. He and the previous Lord Ashbourne hated each other. It runs in the family, I'm afraid — fathers and sons hating one another.

Do you want to see the portrait now?'

They went into an anteroom set in a corner of the house, with latticed windows in two of the four walls. With two doors diagonally opposite each other, there was little space for furniture or wall decoration. There was one large picture in the room, hung to face the window to the left of the door through which they had just come. The gentleman in the picture was dressed according to the fashion of about twenty years ago. He was leaning negligently against a heavy wooden desk, his arms folded, one leg crossed over the other. It was an unusual pose.

There was only one portrait of Eustacia's father at her home. In that picture, he was depicted as being outside in the grounds, the house appearing in the background. Beside him was seated Lady Hope with a diminutive Eustacia upon her knee. There was also a sketch of her father, again outside with the house in the distance. In this drawing, he was shown with his gun, and his dog lying obediently at his feet. On visits to other stately homes, Eustacia had seen similarly stylized depictions of the owner in a family group, or in a pose which sought to convey his sporting prowess. Often, too, there were portraits of peers in the ermine robes of their rank.

The stance of the sitter in this picture, however, seemed to suggest an attitude which might best be described as 'If you want to paint me, you'll do it here, damn your eyes.' His expression was not a pleasant one; yet it was a handsome face as Jessie had said, if rather a lean one, with high cheekbones, soaring brows, a well-shaped but thin-lipped mouth and dark, rather hard eyes with a hint of a cynical smile behind them.

'Was the painting done here, or at Ashbourne?' Eustacia asked, wondering why it remained here when the man who had sat for it was resident elsewhere.

'It was done here, when he was Lord Ilam,' Jessie replied. 'His father only died ten years ago.' She paused for a short while, then said, 'Shall we go now? I really ought to stop myself from looking at this picture. It does me no good at all.'

Eustacia readily agreed. As for the picture doing Jessie no good, doubtless she was right. After all, the picture was only a depiction of a man who, according to his reputation, had never done any woman any good either.

6

It was not until they were just a few steps away from the village shop, from which Lady Agatha had asked Jessie to procure some black thread, that Eustacia realized she had not got her reticule.

'Are you sure you had it when we set out?' Jessie asked, with half an eye on the shop. She wanted to get there before it closed for the customary two hours during the middle of the day.

'Yes I did,' said Eustacia after a moment's thought. 'I took my handkerchief out to use it just as we arrived at Illingham Hall, if you remember. I think I took it off my wrist in the long gallery when we bent over to examine the marquetry on that table in the window. I'll go and get it while you buy the thread. Then I'll meet you here.'

'I could come with you after I've bought the thread if you like.'

'No need for you to suffer for my mistake,' said Eustacia cheerfully. 'I'll be back in no time.' It would be as well for Jessie not to have another opportunity to gaze at Lord Ashbourne's portrait, she told herself as she hurried back to Illingham Hall.

She was almost there when she saw some very pretty wild flowers that she did not recognize, growing by the side of the road. She bent to pick a few, meaning to ask Jessie if she knew what they were called. Moments later, she berated herself for her foolishness. She could have taken Jessie to the spot and shown them to her just as easily. Now they would wilt long before she got them home. Telling herself that what was done was done, she walked on to Illingham Hall with the flowers still in her hand.

The housekeeper was nowhere to be seen, but the servant who came to the door was very happy to allow her to return to the gallery once she had explained what had happened. Her reticule was on a chair near to the far window in the gallery. She picked it up, thankful that no servant had discovered it and taken it away for safe keeping. Then, after a moment's hesitation, she put it down again and walked into the little anteroom that housed Lord Ashbourne's portrait.

There was a signature at the bottom of the portrait, and she leaned forward to see if she could make it out, setting her flowers down on the little table that stood in front of the picture. She could not decipher the writing, so instead she stood back, wondering how old

Ashbourne had been when this likeness was taken. She knew that he was a little younger than her mother and the father of an adult son, so he would probably now be in his mid forties. Judging by his clothes, she would surmise that he must have been in his twenties when this was painted. What had happened to him by this time to make him look so hard? Was it because of the death of his wife?

It was while she was still looking at the picture that she became aware that she was no longer alone. Turning, she saw the figure of a tall, broad-shouldered man standing in the doorway and she gasped in surprise. Some magic must surely be at work, for there before her in the flesh, not roistering in Italy as she and everyone else had supposed, was Lord Ashbourne!

Suddenly remembering his reputation, and that she was all alone, she stepped back, her hand to her throat. Then he took a step or two into the room and as the light from the window fell upon his face, she realized that she must have been mistaken. This could not be Lord Ashbourne, for he was only the same age as the man in the portrait, and probably only a few years older than herself. Furthermore, although there was a likeness between them. the man who had just entered was built more heavily. His brows were a trifle thicker and without the pronounced arch which gave Ashbourne a look that was almost satanic. His hair, rather than straight and black, was wavy and very dark brown, and caught behind his head with a ribbon, whereas the sitter's hair draped his shoulders; his eyes though were the same shade of grey.

'Forgive me for startling you, ma'am,' he said. His voice was deep, and his tone, though courteous, was a little on the blunt side. 'Were you looking for anything — or anyone, perhaps?'

Eustacia blushed, glanced involuntarily up at the portrait and back at the newcomer again. 'I just came . . . that is — '

'It's all right,' he interrupted, his voice becoming a little world-weary. 'You need not bother trying to explain yourself. I'm well used to the spell that my father seems to cast over half the female population. I'm sorry to have to disappoint you, if you were in search of him, but he isn't here.'

'I am well aware of Lord Ashbourne's whereabouts, Lord Ilam,' Eustacia replied, guessing the identity of the gentleman. She had merely intended to sound haughty. To her chagrin, the gentleman raised his brows ironically. In so doing, he gained more of a look of his father.

'Are you indeed?' he replied. 'Then what brings you here? Are you spying out the territory? I regret to have to inform you that this is not my father's home but mine.'

'I was doing no such thing,' Eustacia protested, now red as much from anger as from embarrassment. 'I was here earlier with a friend — as no doubt Mrs Davies will testify — and I left my reticule behind in . . . ' Her voice petered out.

'In?' he prompted her.

'In the house,' she replied, her chin high, determined not to be bested.

'Indeed?' he responded, looking and sounding unconvinced.

'Certainly,' she answered swiftly. 'You can see it in there.'

He glanced round. 'Ah. In the gallery. So you came to find your reticule, and decided that you would take another delicious look at his lordship.'

'No,' she protested, then realized that what he had said was true, at least in part. 'I mean yes, but not for the reasons that you are implying. And I do not think that Lord Ashbourne is . . . is . . . '

'You'll forgive me if I keep to my own view on that,' he replied. 'And now, having looked your fill at his dark beauty, perhaps you would like to leave? I am more than happy for people to look round my house, but I'm damned if I'll tolerate his female courtiers sighing over him and offering their homage.' He picked up the flowers that she had laid down. 'Take your tribute. It's quite wasted on him, believe me.'

With an infuriated squeak, she snatched the flowers out of his outstretched hand, threw them in his face, then hurried out through the gallery almost at a run, snatching up her reticule as she went.

7

By the time she reached the village shop where Jessie was waiting, Eustacia had regained her composure. She did not say anything about her encounter to her companion as they resumed their walk. Had she done so, she might not have been able to avoid confessing that she had gone back to have another look at Lord Ashbourne's picture. She did not want Jessie to think that Ashbourne had cast his spell over her as well.

For a moment or two, she toyed with the idea of casually telling Jessie that she had bumped into Ilam, but it did not take her long to decide against this. Jessie knew the family well, and she might therefore feel bound to go back and greet him after his absence. In those circumstances, Eustacia would have to accompany her, and then Jessie would learn how she had thrown the flowers at him. What was worse, Ilam would think that she had gone back for yet another look at his wretched father.

If only the truth were told, she was rapidly becoming sick of hearing about the man. As for yearning after him, she had experienced quite enough heartache and humiliation at the hands of Morrison. She had no desire to pursue a rake who was noted for dealing out that kind of treatment. She would do well to put Ilam out of her mind as well. He was probably no better than his father, as her mother had suggested.

★ ★ ★

News of the viscount's arrival did not reach the vicarage until the following day. 'Ilam's back,' Lady Agatha announced at the breakfast table. 'He returned yesterday.'

'That's funny. We didn't see him, did we, Jessie?' said Eustacia quickly.

'Been to the hall, have you?' said her ladyship, her eyes narrowing. 'You shouldn't keep mooning over that portrait you know. It'll do you no good at all.'

Eustacia realized that in her haste to establish the fact that she had not seen Ilam, she had put Jessie in an awkward position. She glanced at Jessie and saw that she was looking at her reproachfully. 'Jessie did not go to moon over the picture, I promise you, Godmama,' she said, anxious to make amends. 'I asked her if you and your brother were alike and she offered to take me so that I could see. That was all.'

'Hmph,' replied Lady Agatha, only half convinced. 'You know of Jessie's hankering after my brother. I would have thought that you would have refrained from mentioning him at all.'

'I'm sorry, Godmama,' said Eustacia contritely. 'I'm sorry, Jessie.'

'It wasn't your fault, Eustacia,' replied Jessie readily. 'I should never have mentioned the picture.'

'Have done with this mutual exonerating exercise at once,' Lady Agatha commanded. 'It is very tiresome. No doubt Ilam will be round this morning in order to pay his respects. I would like you both to be present, if you please.'

Eustacia hurried upstairs to prepare for the visit. Much to her irritation, she was conscious of a feeling of nervousness at the thought of encountering Lord Ilam again. For some reason, this seemed to necessitate her looking her very best. So Ilam had mistaken her for one of his father's fancy pieces, had he? He would soon discover his error. She rang for Trixie, and when the maid arrived it was to discover her mistress looking through her wardrobe. The maid looked a little put out and Eustacia wondered whether she had interrupted the girl in the middle of a promising flirtation.

'Change your gown, miss?' Trixie asked, bewildered. 'But I dressed you not above an hour ago.'

'Yes, but I think I may have spilled some fat on it at breakfast,' Eustacia replied mendaciously.

'Fat!' exclaimed Trixie in horror-stricken tones. 'We'll be lucky if I ever get that out! Where is the mark, then?'

'Oh . . . er . . . was it just here?' murmured Eustacia, catching hold of a fold of her skirt. 'No, it was there, I think. Oh well, never mind. You'll just have to look for it later. Help me out of this gown, and into something else — something demure.'

Trixie looked at her suspiciously, but said nothing, simply taking out a charming gown of white muslin with a modest neckline, trimmed with tiny rosebuds. 'I suppose you want your hair to look demure as well,' she said, as soon as she had fastened her mistress's gown.

'Yes please,' answered Eustacia, watching as her maid worked busily amongst her dark curls with clever fingers. 'That ought to do it,' she said in satisfied tones when Trixie had finished, and she was standing looking at herself in the full-length mirror. She looked the image of a virtuous debutante from the highest rank of society. She also looked her very best. That, of course, was entirely beside the point.

'Do what, miss?' asked Trixie as she picked up the discarded gown for cleaning.

'Never mind,' replied Eustacia, turning to look at herself from another angle. 'I just want to look my best for my godmother's visitor, that's all.'

'Is it the rake, miss?' said Trixie avidly.

'I don't know whether he is a rake,' replied Eustacia. Then she bit her lip because she hadn't meant to tell Trixie anything. Deciding that to say no more now would be worse than to explain, she said 'It's Lord Ilam, Lady Agatha's nephew.'

'I'll come and have a look at him,' said Trixie slyly. 'I can tell a rake when I see one.' This time, Eustacia was reminded not so much of someone hoping to take in Astley's Amphitheatre as a would-be visitor to the menagerie in the Tower of London.

'If I catch you so much as peeping at him from round the corner, I'll box your ears,' Eustacia threatened.

'Oh, all right then,' answered Trixie sulkily. 'I'll go and see to this gown, but if you ask me, the mark on it is a bit like some other things that are going on here — not quite what it seems.'

As soon as Trixie had gone, Eustacia

hurried downstairs to find her godmother. She now felt very foolish for not mentioning that she had seen Ilam. She would be obliged to make more of the matter, which was the last thing that she had intended. It was either that, or run the risk of Ilam revealing that they had met, thus making her guilty of being seen to have told falsehoods for no good reason.

She ran her godmother to earth in the library, bent, as usual, over some ecclesiastical documents, and told her that she had seen Ilam at Illingham Hall when she had gone back alone to look for her reticule. 'In that case, why on earth did you not say that you had done so?' Lady Agatha asked her, her fine brows drawn together.

'I hadn't said anything about him to Jessie before this morning, and I thought that it would sound rather silly if I suddenly admitted that we had met.'

'I suppose that's understandable, given that you said nothing in the first place. What I still do not understand is why you said nothing to me privately about Ilam's presence at the Hall.'

'Because he was very rude,' Eustacia replied forthrightly. 'He made some unpardonable assumptions about my purpose for being there, and he very nearly threw me out on my ear.'

Lady Agatha laughed briefly. 'That doesn't surprise me,' she said. 'He has none of his father's polish. Sometimes I think that he cultivates a boorish demeanour just to be as different from his father as possible. Raff says that he has the shoulders of a coal-heaver and the manners to match.'

'Raff?'

'My brother is Raphael, Lord Ashbourne. I always called him Raff when we were children.'

'Is Lord Ilam not a rake like his father, then?'

Lady Agatha gave a bark of laughter. 'Never let him hear you say so,' she said. 'Ilam's a very principled young man.'

'Yet there is a physical likeness between father and son,' observed Eustacia. 'In fact, when he appeared in the doorway, I thought that it was Lord Ashbourne at first.'

'If he knew that that was what you thought, then no wonder he nearly threw you out,' retorted Lady Agatha. 'There is a likeness between them as you say, but they would both die rather than admit it.'

'It was partly because of the likeness that I didn't tell Jessie,' Eustacia said. 'Then I thought that perhaps she would want to go back and greet him, and she would have to see the picture again.'

'That picture is very bad for her,' agreed Lady Agatha. 'In fact, I've been wondering whether to send her away for a short holiday. She gets away from here very seldom, and a change of scene would do her good. The only question is where.'

'Does she have any relations?' Eustacia asked.

'None. I shall have to give the matter some thought. For now, we'd better repair to the drawing-room in order to receive Ilam. I don't want him to see all these papers. Please do not mention this tiresome dispute of mine. Gentlemen, in my experience, are very bored by ecclesiastical matters, unless they are clergymen themselves.'

They arrived at the drawing-room door at the same time as Jessie came down the stairs. She was dressed in a neat, plain grey gown which complimented neither her colouring nor her figure.

'Jessie, I did see Ilam yesterday,' said Eustacia quickly. 'I didn't tell you because I didn't want to upset you.'

'Upset me?' Jessie echoed.

'Because he's like Ashbourne, I expect,' put in Lady Agatha as the doorbell rang. 'Sit down, both of you. Not there, Eustacia; over by the window.'

Eustacia immediately recognized the gentleman who entered, admitted by Grimes. He was dressed very much as on the previous day, as far as she could remember. On this occasion, his coat was dark green, and he wore it with a buff waistcoat, buckskin breeches and shiny but serviceable top boots. All his clothes were of a good cut, but the fit was comfortable rather than skin tight. Altogether, he looked like a well-dressed country gentleman rather than the fashionable man-about-town which Eustacia suspected his father must be.

'Good day to you, Ilam,' said Lady Agatha in response to his polite greeting, which had included Jessie Warburton as well as his aunt. 'I'm glad to see you looking well.'

'I'm in good health thank you, ma'am, and trust that you are the same,' replied Ilam in the same deep, rather harsh voice that Eustacia remembered from the previous day.

'I'm pleased to hear it,' said Lady Agatha. 'No doubt you are feeling strong enough to make your apologies to my goddaughter for your rudeness yesterday.'

Eustacia now saw the reasoning behind Lady Agatha's decision to send her into the window seat. It meant that Ilam had been unaware of her presence until the moment when her godmother chose to disclose it.

Ilam turned his head in the direction which Lady Agatha indicated. Whereas the previous day, he had had the advantage of surprise on his side, today that advantage belonged to Eustacia. Furthermore, because she had her back to the light, it was not possible for him to read her expression. She got to her feet. From where she was standing, she could see the look of dawning recognition on his face, followed by a dull flush. 'Your goddaughter, ma'am?'

'My goddaughter, Eustacia. You may call her Miss Hope.' She gestured to Eustacia to come to her side.

He bowed. It was a gesture which conveyed power and energy rather than elegance. 'Your servant, Miss Hope.'

'Good day, my lord,' replied Eustacia, her curtsy as demure as her gown. She was beginning to enjoy herself.

'Your apology, Ilam,' prompted Lady Agatha.

'My apology?' he echoed, drawing those uncompromising brows together.

'For your rudeness to Eustacia yesterday.'

He turned to Eustacia. She noted that his grey eyes were uncomfortably penetrating. 'Forgive me for having startled you, ma'am,' he said, his tone not perceptibly contrite. 'Had you made yourself known to me at the time, I would have been less . . . ' He paused.

'Rude?' suggested Eustacia sweetly.

'I was going to say 'direct',' he replied.

'You would say that you were direct rather than rude, then,' put in Lady Agatha.

'Yes, I would say so,' he responded. 'Unlike your goddaughter's aim.'

'Her aim?' Lady Agatha's brows soared. It was Eustacia's turn to blush as her godmother looked at her in enquiry. 'What have you been throwing at Ilam?'

'She threw a bunch of flowers at me,' said the viscount. 'I thought it rather an extravagant gesture at the time, especially when we had only just met.' There was no change in his expression, but there was a softening in his tone that although not a chuckle, had the potential of developing into one.

Eustacia eyed him with some annoyance. 'Had you not been unpardonably offensive, then I would not have needed to throw them,' she retorted.

'That settles it then, ma'am,' said Ilam, turning to Lady Agatha after a brief silence during which he directed a penetrating gaze at Eustacia. 'I will certainly *not* beg Miss Hope's pardon.'

'Your reasons, Ilam?' her ladyship demanded haughtily.

'She has declared my behaviour to be unpardonable,' he responded. 'That being the case, begging her pardon would surely be a fruitless exercise.'

Lady Agatha gave a bark of laughter. 'You have your father's quickness, I'll say that for you,' she declared.

'I'll not pretend to be flattered by the comparison,' Ilam responded. 'I'm prepared to cry quits with Miss Hope if she will do the same. To be at odds over such a trivial incident seems a trifle unnecessary to me.'

Eustacia could either agree or appear ungracious in the extreme. 'Very well, my lord,' she said, in as pleasant a tone as she could muster. 'Let us consider the matter closed.' Inwardly, she was seething. He had leapt to quite unwarrantable conclusions about her presence in his house. Perhaps she should not have thrown the flowers at him, but he had been the first one to be rude. She had only been retaliating. He had offended her, both by what he had said and by his manner of saying it. Now, he had as good as implied that she was making something out of nothing. Well, she would not give him the satisfaction of making a fuss like a silly schoolgirl. Let him be on his guard, though. She would find a way to turn the tables on him one way or another.

The viscount only stayed for half an hour, as was proper, but he left having accepted an invitation to dine with them later in the week. 'It will just be ourselves, so we shall be a very quiet party,' said Lady Agatha.

'If you say so, ma'am,' answered Ilam politely, with a swift glance at Eustacia.

'I hope you do not mean to imply that I intend to start a brawl,' she said archly.

'I will do my best not to provoke you, Miss Hope,' was his reply.

★　★　★

The following morning, Eustacia received a letter from her mother. In it, she informed her daughter that both she and Papa were missing her very much, but glad that she was in safe hands. No more had been heard or seen of that wretch Morrison Morrison. Eustacia smiled. She could almost hear her mother rolling her r's as she said it. The Morrisons had gone away for their health. Another family had come to live in the district. They were renting a house that had belonged to the late Lord Coulter. They seemed quite genteel. Eustacia smiled again. Nobody could be quite so high in the instep as her mama when she chose to be.

'And how is your dear mother?' Lady Agatha asked. She had been perusing her own correspondence. Since she had not begun spitting feathers, Eustacia assumed that none of it was from the Church of England.

'She is well, as is my father,' Eustacia replied. 'She says that she misses me. Oh, and she sends her love.'

Lady Agatha frowned. 'Misses you, eh? I wonder whether she might like to have a visit from Jessie? You remember we were talking about sending Jessie on holiday only the other day.' The two of them were alone in the breakfast parlour, Miss Warburton not yet having come downstairs.

'Can you spare her?' asked Eustacia

'I can spare her very well,' answered her godmother. 'Now that I have you, it's the perfect opportunity, and she won't even suspect. The beauty of the scheme is that Ashbourne will never be mentioned there, because Claire can't abide him. It will also test Lusty's interest in Jessie. If it's genuine, he'll go after her. If his only interest is in this vicarage, then he'll keep away, and he'll certainly have fewer reasons for coming here, which is all to the good. Who knows, she might even meet someone else while she's there. What do you say?'

'Mama would be more than happy to have her, I'm sure,' agreed Eustacia.

'Then it's settled,' declared her ladyship. 'I'll have a word with Jessie.'

'Shall I write to Mama?'

'No, I will do so myself. I have been meaning to send her a few lines.'

8

On the evening Ilam came to dine, Eustacia dressed with particular care. She was determined that he would have no cause to say that she looked like someone who might start a brawl. Trixie assisted her to dress with her usual skill, and was soon fastening her mistress into a sky-blue gown trimmed with beads that caught the light.

'I suppose his lordship'll be walking here this evening,' said Trixie in resigned tones. She had been rather disappointed to discover that there were no male servants worth looking at in Lady Agatha's household. The arrival of the viscount meant that he might bring more men in his train, but because Illingham Hall was so close to the vicarage, Lord Ilam never used his horses to visit his aunt.

'I expect so,' replied Eustacia.

'He's very handsome, isn't he, miss? Not a rake like his father, though, according to the staff here.' She sounded regretful.

'Be thankful for it,' Eustacia replied. 'If you got yourself entangled with a rake, I'd send you home straight away. In fact, for two pins,

I could have sent you with Miss Warburton this morning.'

Jessie had left quite unsuspiciously earlier in the day. She had seemed to accept Lady Agatha's reasoning, namely, that since she now had a companion in the person of Eustacia, she, Jessie, was free to go on holiday. Lady Hope was missing her daughter and was probably feeling a little lonely. Eustacia wondered whether Jessie herself might be glad to be free of a place where so many things, even her own employer's face, reminded her of a man she could never have.

Eustacia had made sure that she had a private word with Jessie before she left, as she had something very important to say to her. 'Whatever you do, don't mention Lady Agatha's conflict with the bishop,' she had said. 'Mama is a pillar of the church and she would send for me at once if she thought that my godmother was doing anything to undermine it.'

'I won't breathe a word,' Jessie had promised. 'I'm very grateful to Lady Agatha, but there are times when I get a little tired of her scheming.'

'I'm rather enjoying it,' Eustacia had admitted.

'Was you wishful to wear your gold pendant tonight, or your pearls?' Trixie asked, choosing to ignore her mistress's last remark.

'The pearls, I think.' While Trixie was fastening these, Lady Agatha scratched on the door and came in.

She eyed her goddaughter's appearance critically, then said to Trixie, 'You might be a flighty piece, but you know your work, I'll say that for you. Shall we go down, Eustacia?'

They could not have been downstairs for much more than five minutes when the doorbell rang, and moments later, Grimes admitted Lord Ilam to the drawing-room. He was attired correctly, if rather severely, in a black evening coat and knee breeches and a pearl-grey figured satin waistcoat. Presumably because he never expected to do anything more energetic than dine or dance in them, these garments were cut more closely to his shape than those which he had worn during the day, and Eustacia felt bound to acknowledge that it was a very good shape indeed with broad shoulders, powerful chest and muscular thighs and calves well in proportion.

'Aunt Agatha, Miss Hope,' he said, as he stepped forward to take his aunt's hand.

'Welcome, Gabriel,' she said. Eustacia started a little to discover that he had such an exalted Christian name.

Ilam grinned. Eustacia realized that it was

the first time that she had seen him smile. It lightened the severity of his features and revealed that he was in fact a handsome man. 'Now I know I'm no longer in disgrace,' he said. He turned to Eustacia. 'My aunt always calls me Ilam when she's vexed with me,' he told her. 'As soon as she reverts to Gabriel, I know I'm forgiven.'

'My mother does something similar,' replied Eustacia, unbending a little. 'If I have offended her then she calls me Eustacia Mary Louisa.'

'I shall try to remember that,' said her godmother. 'Shall we go into dinner? Gabriel, you may give us each an arm.'

'Does Miss Warburton not join us this evening?' he asked, doing as he was bid.

'She has gone to stay with Eustacia's mother for a holiday,' replied her ladyship.

Lady Agatha took the head of the table, with Gabriel on her right and Eustacia on her left. Dinner was a well-cooked but simple meal, the fare being ample but not extravagant, and Eustacia noticed that Lord Ilam had a good appetite. No doubt he needed plenty of fuel for that large frame.

'Well, Gabriel, you have been away for some weeks this time,' her ladyship said when they were all enjoying the beef, rabbit pie and stewed vegetables which constituted the chief dishes of the first remove.

'Yes, I have been finding out about some new farming methods,' he told her. 'I am convinced that the land could be more productive, and I want to put some of these methods into practice.' He briefly explained some of the innovations that he was planning and Eustacia listened with interest, for she had heard her father speak about such matters.

'A pity Ashbourne cannot show a similar interest,' Lady Agatha said to him. 'He does not care what happens to his land from one year's end to the next. I do not suppose you have any idea when he is likely to return and take some responsibility?'

Eustacia raised her glass to her lips in order to hide a smile. She now had a reasonable idea of how her godmother's mind was working. She was convinced that that lady was far more concerned that her brother should not return to interfere with her dispute with the church than that he should come back to till his acres!

The viscount glanced briefly at Eustacia before shaking his head. 'I am not in my father's confidence, I fear.'

Looking at her godmother seated at the head of the table with very much the air of the *grande dame*, Eustacia wondered, not for the first time, why a lady with her position and opportunities should have married a country vicar. Had some scandal damaged her ladyship's reputation, and made her glad to receive an offer from any quarter? An idea stirred at the back of her mind which she could not quite grasp.

She was roused from her reverie by the sound of her own name being spoken. 'Certainly I would be very grateful if you would take Eustacia,' her godmother was saying. 'I know that she would feel the same, would you not, my dear? As long as you are careful not to tire her, Ilam. She is rather delicate.'

'Yes indeed,' Eustacia replied, not having any idea to what she might be agreeing.

Ilam looked at her, his brows raised. They did not and never could have the pronounced arch to be found in those elegant features which adorned the faces of his father and his aunt, but at that moment he had very much a look of both of his older relatives. 'The thought of crawling through the final cavern with the water lapping halfway up your person does not alarm you then?' he said blandly. 'Very well then, Miss Hope, we'll go tomorrow.'

'I beg your pardon?' exclaimed Eustacia involuntarily, her face a picture of consternation.

Ilam burst out laughing, a full rich sound. 'Confess it, Miss Hope. You were miles away.'

Eustacia was glad that because she was blushing due to her inattention, she did not have to worry about anyone suspecting the impertinent nature of her thoughts concerning her godmother's past. 'I am obliged to own to it, my lord,' she replied. 'I was wondering whether my parents might be dining with Miss Warburton at this very moment. Please tell me that you are not really intending to make me crawl through a foot of water.'

'No indeed,' he replied. 'Though if ever you do wish to visit the caves at Castleton, I would be more than happy to oblige.'

'Gabriel was offering to lend you one of his mounts,' said Lady Agatha, taking pity on her. 'I keep no horses as you know, but I am aware that you are accustomed to riding with your father in order to build up your strength.'

'I am indeed,' agreed Eustacia, fighting down a feeling of irritation because yet again he had managed to make her feel foolish. 'Thank you, Lord Ilam.' She was about to add that although she had enjoyed some invigorating walks in the area, she had missed her daily ride when her godmother kicked her sharply under the table and she fell silent, remembering that she was supposed to be delicate.

He inclined his head politely. 'It is I who am indebted to you,' he answered. 'The horse I have in mind is not up to my weight, and would otherwise lack exercise. Shall we say, tomorrow morning at ten o'clock?'

'Thank you,' she said again.

Lord Ilam did not linger in the dining-room at the end of the meal. 'He never does so,' said her ladyship, when they had sat down together in the drawing-room and taken up their sewing. 'If it were Ashbourne, now, I dare say we should not see him again, and he would be put to bed by his valet.'

'How old is Lord Ilam, ma'am?' Eustacia asked, after they had each set a stitch or two in silence.

'He is just twenty-five.'

'I am surprised. I took him to be older.'

'He takes his responsibilities seriously, and that has aged him a little, I think. That blunt manner of his doesn't help, either. I sometimes feel as though I am the younger relative whom he is trying to control.'

Eustacia smiled. 'He looks younger when he laughs,' she said.

'Yes, he does, doesn't he?' Lady Agatha agreed, looking at her sideways. 'You look thoughtful, my dear.'

'I was just wondering about their names,' replied Eustacia. 'Raphael, Gabriel: they are not exactly the kind of names that one comes upon every day.'

'The men in my family are always named after angels,' Lady Agatha told her. 'It's rather ironic, really. Raff is no more of a rake than was our father, so angelic names were not really appropriate for either of them.'

'There can't be many names to choose from,' Eustacia reflected.

'Only three sensible ones,' her ladyship agreed. 'Gabriel, Raphael and Michael. The latter was my father's name. If you think that Gabriel is unusual, then reflect how it would have sounded had he been called Barachiel or Zachariel.'

'So if there are more than three boys born in the family, then I suppose that some of them are saddled with very peculiar names.'

'It's only happened once as far as I know. On that occasion, they named the fourth one Angel. He was part of the court of Charles II and was the worst rake of the lot.'

'They could have called him Lucifer,' Eustacia pointed out. 'After the fallen angel, you know.'

'Doubtless they thought that it would be tempting fate,' replied Lady Agatha, causing both of them to laugh.

Her ladyship was proved to be correct in her prediction, when Ilam entered the room a bare quarter of an hour after they had left him, very properly, to his port.

'Ah, Gabriel,' she said. 'As you are on your feet, will you please ring for the tea tray?'

He did as she asked, but when he sat down, there was a serious expression on his face, and his aunt remarked upon it. 'There is a matter that is troubling me greatly,' he admitted. 'I have been away for some weeks, as you have rightly said. Now that I have returned, I find that the church has not yet seen fit to send a new incumbent. Are you still having to make shift with a visiting curate from the next village?'

Eustacia was glad that his direct gaze was not turned upon her. She was not at all sure whether she would have been able to withstand its power. She could not help feeling a tiny dart of pleasure. Here, perhaps, was her opportunity to turn the tables on him for his rudeness and mockery, by aiding Lady Agatha as she pulled the wool over his eyes.

That lady did not seem to be similarly constrained and she met her nephew's eyes blandly. 'I fear so,' she replied. 'I am in regular contact with the bishop, but without success.'

He raised his brows. 'Perhaps I should pay

him a visit myself. My weight added to yours should make a difference.'

'It is very kind of you to suggest it,' replied Lady Agatha, with what Eustacia considered to be breathtaking audacity. 'However, I understand that the bishop has become incensed at Ashbourne's profligate behaviour.'

'As have we all,' agreed Ilam as the tea tray was brought in. 'I fail to see what that has to do with the matter.' There was a brief pause in the conversation as the table was arranged, and Grimes withdrew.

'Possibly. There is an additional problem, though. You must forgive me, Gabriel, I have no desire to distress you.' The viscount made no comment, but continued to look at her with that uncompromising gaze. Eventually, with a show of reluctance, Lady Agatha said, 'It gives me no pleasure to say this.'

'Go on, ma'am, go on,' said Ilam, his brows snapping together.

'There is a rumour going round that it is a case of like father, like son.'

'Damnation,' he exclaimed, springing up out of his seat. 'Then I must most certainly see the bishop and disabuse him of that idea.'

'Calm yourself, dear boy,' said Lady Agatha soothingly. 'You would do much better to leave the whole matter in my hands. If you go to see him in that glowering sort of way, he will think that he is being bullied and dig his heels in. Believe me; I will make sure that your sentiments are made known to the bishop. If I feel the need to call upon your powers of persuasion, rest assured that I shall inform you of it.'

* * *

'I thought that passed off quite well,' said Lady Agatha calmly after Ilam had gone. She had walked out into the hall with him, while Eustacia had stayed in the drawing-room.

'Quite well?' echoed Eustacia. 'He was furious, Godmama.'

'Yes, I suppose he was quite annoyed,' her ladyship agreed. 'I was quite pleased with the bit about the church thinking that he was like Ashbourne. The last thing we want is for Gabriel to have any conversations with the bishop or any of his minions. Moreover, he does have other properties to see to, so I don't suppose he will stay here for long.'

'In the meantime, though, he is here. What is more, I am to go riding with him tomorrow. What am I to do if he asks me any questions about my health or about the church?' She thought about saying that she was sure that she would not be able to lie with her godmother's effrontery, but she decided that that would be uncivil.

'He will not do so,' Lady Agatha replied tranquilly. 'That is what I was ensuring when I went with him to the door.'

'Godmama, what have you told him?' Eustacia asked with a feeling of deep foreboding.

'I warned him not to talk about the church for fear of upsetting you. I said that you had been jilted by a clergyman.'

'Jilted by a clergyman and delicate!' exclaimed Eustacia. 'Whatever next?'

'Probably the one caused the other,' her ladyship replied blandly.

'But you told me that you did not want my circumstances to be bruited about,' Eustacia protested.

'Oh, Ilam won't tell tales. In any case, that was purely a matter of decorum. This is to do with my strategy, and therefore far more important.'

Eustacia could only stare at her, completely lost for words.

★ ★ ★

That night, as Trixie was preparing her for bed, Eustacia remembered the thoughts that had gone through her head as she had been eating her dinner. 'Trixie,' she began.

108

'Yes, miss?'

For a moment, Eustacia paused in indecision. Then she recalled that Trixie, for all her apparent empty-headedness was in fact exceedingly shrewd, and utterly loyal to her mistress's interests. 'Trixie, have you heard talk of any scandal in my godmother's past?'

'What, recently, miss?'

'No, before she was married. It's just that I would have expected someone in her position to have looked much higher for a husband. I'm wondering whether something happened to prevent that.'

'Perhaps she fell in love, miss,' Trixie suggested.

'Perhaps.'

After a brief pause, Trixie came to sit down next to her on the bed. 'You mustn't worry about what happened to you, miss,' she said reassuringly. 'We're living in more modern times, now. After all those nasty goings on in France, people know that there's worse things to worry about than that.'

'Yes, of course,' Eustacia replied. She hadn't been thinking of her own situation at all; but now she realized that all the time, it had been there at the back of her mind.

'As for that other business, I'll see what I can find out, miss. At least it'll take your mind off your own troubles.'

9

Lord Ilam arrived promptly at the vicarage at ten o'clock the following day. He raised his brows at the sight of Eustacia coming down the stairs, becomingly attired in a mulberry-coloured riding habit topped by a pert little hat of the same shade.

'Is anything amiss?' she asked him calmly, drawing on her gloves. She knew that her appearance was faultless. Trixie was never satisfied with anything else.

'By no means, ma'am,' he assured her bowing. 'I am merely surprised by your punctuality.'

'My father dislikes keeping his horses waiting as much as any man,' Eustacia told him. 'Shall we go?'

He inclined his head, and gestured for her to go before him. She gave silent approval to his own dress. As on two other occasions when she had seen him during the day, he was dressed neatly and with style, but with a practical concern for ease of movement. Yet again, he was in buckskin breeches and comfortable-looking boots and his blue coat seemed to impart something of that shade to his grey eyes.

When she stepped outside into the bright July morning, an involuntary cry of delight broke from her lips.

'Is she to your liking?' asked Ilam as they both looked at the dainty mare being held by the viscount's groom. 'She's still quite fresh and lively. I hope that she won't prove to be too much for you.'

'I hope so indeed. She's beautiful,' said Eustacia as she approached the mare. 'I shall very much enjoy riding her.' She went to the mare's head and crooned to her.

'Her name is Butternut,' said the viscount. 'She was bred at Ashbourne. Her father was a winner at Newmarket. I was thinking of selling her quite soon, but I shall retain her for your use while you are here. Shall I put you up into the saddle, ma'am?'

Eustacia thanked him, and in no time, she was perched on Butternut's back, effortlessly controlling her fidgets.

'You've the mastery of her and no mistake, ma'am,' said the groom, releasing the mare as soon as he was sure that Eustacia could manage her.

'I was just thinking the same, Briggs,' remarked his lordship as he mounted his own horse, a fine long-tailed grey.

Soon Ilam and Eustacia were setting off on their ride, followed by his lordship's groom.

'We'll have to walk them through the village, but then we'll have a clear run to shake the fidgets out of them,' said Gabriel.

It did not take them long to negotiate the quiet main street of the village, and, as Ilam had promised, they were soon enjoying a refreshing canter across the fields, Briggs riding at a respectful distance.

'That was wonderful!' Eustacia exclaimed, as they drew to a halt next to a clump of trees.

'Wasn't it just?' agreed Ilam, turning to look at her. 'I hope that it was not too much for you. I fear that I have been rather thoughtless.'

'Not at all,' she answered, amused and a little irritated at the same time by her godmother's fiction. 'I am feeling stronger every day.'

She smiled at him. His hair was a little dishevelled, as was her own, no doubt. His face was flushed and animated, his generous mouth curved up as he returned her smile, and something about his appearance made her catch her breath. For a long moment they looked at one another.

He seemed on the point of speaking, paused, and eventually said, 'What do you usually ride when you are at home, Miss Hope?'

'I ride a grey mare a little bigger than Butternut, and very like yours in colouring,' she replied.

'And who will be riding her while you are away? Your mother?'

'Oh no, Mama never rides,' replied Eustacia, barely repressing a chuckle at the thought of her stately mother on horseback. 'I expect one of the grooms will take her out. Papa may ride her occasionally, although he has his own favourite mount. He is not so . . . ' She paused, colouring. 'He is not so big a man as you.'

He laughed. 'If I tried to ride Butternut, she would have permanently bowed legs, I fear. Harry does me very well.' He patted his own mount.

'Was he bred on your estate as Butternut was, my lord?' Eustacia asked him.

'My father's estate,' he corrected her, his expression losing some of its humour. 'There is a difference. No, Harry was bought from a friend who wanted to reduce his stables. What of your mare? Does she come from your own stock?'

Eustacia shook her head. 'We are not horse-breeders,' she replied. 'Papa bought her from a local breeder. The same man provided me with my very first pony.'

'How old were you then?' Ilam asked her.

After giving their horses a few minutes to catch their breath, they were now walking on slowly, leaving the clump of trees and beginning to skirt the edge of a meadow, in which grew a profusion of wild flowers.

'I was six,' said Eustacia. 'My parents pretended that Papa had forgotten my birthday, and Mama brought me down to the stables to show him my first riding habit as a reminder. He was there with a broad grin on his face, holding Maisie by her bridle. I was so excited, I begged him to teach me to ride that very day. Did *your* father teach *you* to ride?'

He had been smiling at her description of her birthday surprise. Now, his smile disappeared. 'No, he did not,' he answered. 'To be blunt, Miss Hope, my father did not give a damn about me, save that he had an heir.'

'But surely you must be mistaken in him,' she put in. 'Any father must be proud of his son. My mother . . . ' She was about to tell him about Charlie but when she saw the expression of contempt and disbelief on his face, the words froze on her lips.

'But you see, I have no mother, Miss Hope,' he replied.

'No, but — '

'Have done, ma'am. I accept that as far as

your parents are concerned, you are perfection itself. Allow me to know my own father. Believe me, he still finds me quite beneath his notice, and that suits me very well. Another day, if you will permit it, I will take you to meet the man who put me on my first pony. We have come in quite the wrong direction to do so today. Shall we canter again?'

Eustacia nodded in assent, and for a short time further conversation was impossible, and she was glad of it. When they spoke again, their conversation touched such undisturbing topics as the nature of the terrain, and the seasonal changes to the countryside.

On her return to the house, she invited Ilam to come inside, but he declined. 'I must refuse your invitation on this occasion,' he told her. 'I have business to transact. Pray send my duty to my aunt.'

She would have liked to apologize for over-stepping, but the groom was there, and there was no chance for private words with him.

She went inside thoughtfully. Jessie Warburton had said that Ilam and his father did not get on. If anything, she had understated the case. The viscount clearly detested his father, and believed that the sentiment was mutual. She would have liked to discuss the matter with someone, but Jessie had gone, and talk that involved Lord Ashbourne obviously did her no good anyway.

Lady Agatha appeared from the direction of the library as soon as she entered the hall. 'Did you have an agreeable ride?' she asked.

'Yes, it was very invigorating,' Eustacia replied.

'You are looking exceedingly well,' replied the other, making her remark sound like a criticism. 'Change your habit and come downstairs, and we will have a cup of coffee together. I am very ready to put down my work for a short time.'

Trixie was summoned, and although she tut-tutted over the state of her mistress's habit — a smear of mud having got onto the skirt — Eustacia had no doubt that the girl would soon have it looking as good as new again.

'I've got some news about what you asked me the other day,' said Trixie as she was fastening her mistress into a charming gown of white muslin sprigged with tiny purple flowers.

'Really?' Eustacia was more than half regretting asking Trixie to find out some gossip for her. However, she consoled herself with the thought that she would certainly not repeat the gossip to anyone else. Furthermore, Lady Agatha, a mistress of intrigue herself, could surely not object to her god-daughter doing a little intriguing of her own.

'It seems that Lady Agatha's chances were very good, as you said. She ruined them herself, by making friends with an actress. The vicar she married was the youngest son of an earl and the best she could get.'

'She must have a had a dowry from her father,' Eustacia observed.

Trixie shook her head. 'When she befriended the actress, her father refused to give her most of the money that was her due. She had *some* money, but the vicar was a gambler and lost it all.'

'Trixie, I don't think you should be saying that about a man of the cloth,' said Eustacia reprovingly.

'It's no secret, miss,' Trixie assured her. 'He even borrowed Cumber's savings and lost them all. Part of the reason why her ladyship is so short of money now is because she's been paying back everything that he owed.'

'I see.'

'Oh, miss, do you think your mama was the actress she befriended?'

'I don't know,' replied Eustacia. 'Thank you, Trixie. Don't repeat any of this, will you?'

'As God is my witness,' said the abigail solemnly.

It was while Trixie was brushing her hair that they heard the sound of a carriage arriving. 'Perhaps it's the rake, miss,' suggested Trixie, her eyes sparkling.

'I doubt it,' Eustacia replied. 'Trixie, come away from the window,' she added hastily, for the girl had gone tripping over to look out.

'It's only a clergyman,' said Trixie in disappointed tones. 'Well there's an end to excitement for the day.'

'I suppose Godmama will want me to go downstairs,' reflected Eustacia.

'Well I can't do your hair quicker than I can do it,' replied Trixie, almost giving the lie to her own words by the speed and skill of her fingers. 'There. Now it's done.'

Eustacia walked slowly down the stairs, thinking about what she had learned from Trixie. Of course, mixing with an actress would have damaged Lady Agatha's reputation. But witness how carefully Lady Hope had gathered those around her who were prepared to forget that association. Despite the dangers, however, Lady Agatha had not hesitated to offer her friendship, and in doing so she had ruined her chances of a good marriage. Perhaps Rayner had been prevailed upon to marry her, with the living as his reward. That must be the explanation. Obviously the present Lord Ashbourne had not seen fit to pay his sister what their father had kept from her. Perhaps that was why they were not upon good terms.

If indeed this was the true version of events, then Claire Delahay's daughter owed Lady Agatha a good deal, and no effort expended on her ladyship's behalf could be too much to ask. It did seem strangely ironic that of the two ladies, it was the actress who had made the good marriage, whereas the peer's daughter had not achieved what might have been expected of her.

Her ladyship was waiting in the drawing-room, looking imposing in her usual black silk. At the sight of Eustacia, however, an expression of consternation crept over her features.

'Oh heavens, child, you have been far too quick,' she declared. 'You must not be in here when Lusty comes in. I have planned what to say to him and your presence will spoil it entirely.'

'I'll go back up to my room then,' replied Eustacia, making as if to leave the room by the way she had come.

'No, no, not that way. He will see you,' answered Lady Agatha in agitated tones. 'Go into the parlour and wait there.'

Eustacia slipped quickly into the little room where they always had breakfast. She did not close the door. If she were to be shoved out of the room so ignominiously, she would have no compunction whatsoever in listening to what was said.

No sooner had she pulled the door to, than she heard the sound of another person entering the room that she had just left. 'Lady Agatha,' said the voice of the newcomer. Its sound was faintly familiar.

'Mr Lusty,' replied Lady Agatha. 'I presume you have a very good reason for intruding upon me at such a time as this.'

'Forgive me, my lady, but I have always understood that this is a perfectly reasonable hour for visiting,' Lusty replied.

'I am referring to my mourning state,' Lady Agatha declared with dignity.

The clergyman flushed. 'I am aware that you are in mourning, ma'am,' he said. His voice was a pleasant one, and Eustacia now remembered that she had heard him speaking briefly, just as she was arriving at the vicarage at the beginning of her visit.

'I should think you might well be aware of it,' Lady Agatha replied, 'since my late husband was a clergyman. He must indeed be turning in his grave at the abuse visited upon me by his brethren in holy orders.'

Eustacia had to smile. Although, unlike Lady Hope, she had never trod the boards,

Lady Agatha was clearly an actress of no mean order.

'You have my sympathies, my lady, but — '

'Yes, so you have said,' Lady Agatha interrupted wearily. 'Your sympathy appears to be a house of straw, sir. It makes not a whit of difference to my situation as far as I can see. However, that is not the matter that I wished to draw to your attention at this time. What is of far more concern to me is the health of one who is near and dear to me.'

'Miss Warburton!' exclaimed the clergyman in anxious tones. 'Do not say that she is ill?'

'Jessie? No, she is not ill. She is presently on a visit to my dear friend Lady Hope.'

'She is from home?' The clergyman still sounded anxious.

'Yes, she is from home,' said Lady Agatha at her most haughty. 'What is that to you?'

'Why . . . why . . . '

While Mr Lusty was struggling for words, Lady Agatha spoke again. 'While you are making sentimental enquiries about a lady who is far above you, sir, my goddaughter lies upstairs upon a bed of pain.'

Eustacia almost choked. She clapped her hands over her mouth. She was at a loss to understand what her godmother might be about.

'A bed of pain?' echoed Lusty. 'But she

seemed in perfectly good health when I last saw her.'

'Through a carriage window whilst you were leaving in haste — rather too hastily for politeness, in fact,' said Lady Agatha, seemingly oblivious to the fact that his haste had been due to the fact that she had been at his back with an umbrella in her hand. Eustacia bit back a giggle at the memory.

'But what ails her?' asked the clergyman, a question which Eustacia very much wanted to echo.

'If the doctors could say what it might be, then they could no doubt effect a cure,' replied her ladyship scornfully. 'Her mother has sent her to me in the hope that the milder climes here in this sheltered spot may be helpful to her. Imagine the scandal should she be thrown out of this refuge, only to perish on the street! What the newspapers would make of it, I dread to think.'

'Surely it cannot be so serious?'

'Are you calling my goddaughter's mother a liar, sirrah?' her ladyship demanded.

'No, no, of course not,' responded Mr Lusty hastily. 'I am just . . . surely . . . if the illness does not even have a name . . . ' His voice tailed away.

'Every illness has to acquire a name at some point,' said her ladyship haughtily.

'Then, of course, there is my brother, Ashbourne, to be considered.' She sighed heavily.

'What of Lord Ashbourne?' asked the clergyman.

'Ashbourne is very attached to my goddaughter,' replied her ladyship, surprising the young lady in question very much. 'It was by his expressed wish that she should be placed in my care. I dread to think what he might say should he find that she had been ejected by the church, in her delicate state of health.'

'I see,' responded Mr Lusty. 'Do you think . . . ? Should I go and offer her some spiritual solace, perhaps?'

Eustacia took a deep breath, wondering whether she ought to run up the stairs and fling herself upon her bed. Her godmother's next words reassured her.

'Perhaps on another occasion. I have not had time to prepare her mind today. However, I am sure, Mr Lusty, that a man like you with such a deep sense of the needs of the sick will appreciate that my goddaughter cannot possibly be moved now, or indeed for some considerable time.'

'Well, yes, indeed, my lady. However, you must understand that — '

'*Must* understand, young man?' echoed her

ladyship at her most magisterial. 'And what, pray, is it that I *must* understand?'

'I . . . I was just going to say that I must take advice from the bishop,' he murmured.

'Very wise,' agreed her ladyship condescendingly. 'I am sure he will advise against murdering a sick girl and alienating a powerful landowner. For now, I must not delay you. No doubt you have other families to evict before dinner.'

'My lady, I — '

'I would be obliged if you would not bruit the news of my goddaughter's delicate health throughout the neighbourhood. The shock of having herself the subject of gossip could easily prove to be the end of her. Good day to you, Mr Lusty.'

Evidently the clergyman could not summon up his courage to think of a riposte to this, for there was simply the sound of mumbling, followed by the closing of a door. Eustacia waited until she was quite sure that the visitor had gone before slipping out of her hiding place.

'Hah!' exclaimed Lady Agatha, in a satisfied tone. 'That's dealt with him very nicely for the present.'

Eustacia could not help laughing, but eventually she asked with a hint of reproach, 'Godmama, how could you?'

'What do you mean, how could I?' responded her ladyship, honestly puzzled.

'I have already told you that I am not ill. In fact, I enjoy remarkably good health, and seldom have even so much as cold. Now, thanks to you I have to play the role of a person with some nameless illness whenever anyone from the church comes near.'

'None of them will,' replied the other. 'Now that they know you are sick, they will stay away out of respect.'

'Perhaps for a time, but not for ever. Mr Lusty is sure to come back, *then* what do I do? I might not be out of sight next time. I might be out riding or going for a walk. As far as Lord Ilam is concerned, I am getting better, but Mr Lusty now thinks that I am getting worse by the day. If I am to play a part, I would at least like it to be a consistent one. And another thing: Lord Ashbourne is supposed to be concerned with my welfare, but I have never even met the man! What if *he* turns up?'

'He will not do so,' declared her ladyship confidently. 'As for Lusty, I have told him that you are here for your health, remember? You would need to take part in all these activities in order to build you up. Besides, there are some illnesses in which the sufferer gives the illusion of perfect health, especially just before the end. Ring for wine, would you, my dear? I am so glad that you have come to stay with me. You are going to be such a help to me, I can see. Oh, how entertaining this all is! I am having such fun!'

Eustacia stared at her godmother in amazement. She had always known that the older lady was something of a rogue, yet it was Lord Ashbourne's wickedness that everyone spoke about. To Eustacia, it seemed that it was rather his sister who had absolutely no scruples whatsoever.

10

To Eustacia's great relief, the question of sustaining the role of a seriously ill person did not demand much of her over the next few days. Lord Ilam came to take her riding again, but the subject was not broached. She concluded that Mr Lusty must have kept the information to himself, as Lady Agatha had requested.

With this in mind, she was able to face a visit to church with equanimity. Mr Lusty took the service, and afterwards, he shook her hand in the church doorway with a look of deep sympathy on his face. 'And how are you feeling today, Miss Hope?' he asked solicitously, holding her hand as if it might break.

'Quite well,' she murmured. 'My godmother takes very good care of me.'

'That's enough of that, Lusty,' said Lord Ilam's rather harsh voice from behind. 'No need to monopolize Miss Hope.'

'Oh, indeed, my lord, um . . . ' Lusty's voice faded away.

Eustacia turned to look at Lord Ilam, and in doing so caught a fleeting glimpse of her godmother's face, which bore a most uncharacteristic expression of anxiety. No doubt a conversation between the curate and her nephew was the last thing that she wanted. For her own part, she, too, would be glad of as few words as possible between the two men. She was not at all sure which role she ought to be playing and for whose benefit.

There did not appear to be any need for either of them to be concerned today, for Ilam seemed intent upon drawing Eustacia away from the clergyman. For church attendance, the viscount was dressed in a well-cut blue coat with a discreetly striped waistcoat, buff breeches and shiny top boots. He did not look the dandy — he was too muscular for that — but he could have made an appearance in Bond Street without having to blush for his attire. She was glad that she had taken the trouble to dress in one of her new gowns, one of amber trimmed with blond lace, which showed off her excellent figure to great advantage.

Eustacia looked up at his lordship again. The day was cloudy, but at that moment the sun appeared and a ray of light, falling upon his hair, brought out a glimmer of chestnut. In his grey eyes there was a hint of concern. 'That Lusty fellow wasn't bothering you, was he?' he asked her.

She stared at him blankly for a moment or

two. Then she recalled that she was supposed to have been jilted by a clergyman and blushed. The other possible meaning of what he had said struck them simultaneously a few moments later and they both laughed. Following the laughter — during which each had been thinking how engaging the other looked when amused — Eustacia asked, 'Why would you suppose that he was bothering me?'

Ilam seemed a little uncomfortable. 'He just looked to me as if he was being a bit pressing, that's all. May I introduce you to my family?'

'Your family?' she looked around, but amongst the crowd at church that day could only see Lady Agatha whom she knew to be related to Ilam.

'I should say my foster family,' he replied, holding out his arm to escort her towards a small group of people. 'I was taken to live with a local family from an early age, as I'm sure you know already. They farm some of the land on the other side of my estate. Would you like to meet them?'

'I should be pleased to do so,' replied Eustacia warmly.

The small group to which Ilam led her comprised a sturdy-looking man in his late forties or early fifties, a comely woman of about the same age with curly brown hair, a young man of about Lord Ilam's age, a girl who appeared to be about seventeen, and a boy who was probably about twelve or so. They looked pleased at the advent of his lordship, and all smiled expectantly at Eustacia, apart from the young girl, who seemed rather serious.

'Miss Hope, may I introduce to you Mr and Mrs Crossley, their daughter Anna, and their sons David and Elijah? Aunt Bertha, Uncle Tobias, this is Miss Hope, my aunt's goddaughter.'

As Eustacia responded to the formal greeting, she noticed that all the family were dressed well in clothing which, if not expensive, was undoubtedly of very good quality. Anna's gown, of white muslin, was certainly not of the kind usually worn by a farmer's daughter who only had one or two to her name. She guessed that they were one of the more prosperous and successful tenant families. No doubt their prosperity had been increased by the service that they had done for Lord Ashbourne by caring for his son in infancy.

'It is a pleasure to meet you, Miss Hope,' said Mrs Crossley, speaking with a pleasant light country burr. 'Are you staying with Lady Agatha for long?'

'It is not yet decided,' Eustacia replied.

'Miss Warburton has gone to visit my mama, so I would guess I shall stay until the two ladies grow tired of the exchange.'

'Are you liking the countryside around here?' the farmer's wife asked her. 'Many people come here for holidays, I do know.'

'It is very agreeable. Lord Ilam has taken me riding and there have been some lovely bursts of scenery.'

'Do you hunt, ma'am?' asked Mr Crossley.

'I have never cared for the sport,' replied Eustacia. 'I am too soft-hearted, I fear.' Glancing at Anna, she saw a scornful expression on her face.

'Have you brought the new horses today?' Ilam asked.

'I have indeed, my lord,' replied Crossley. 'Would you like to inspect them?' He turned to Eustacia. 'By your leave, ma'am.' Ilam bowed and turned to accompany his foster father, and David and Elijah did the same.

'Anna!' said Mrs Crossley firmly when her daughter made as if to follow them. 'You'll stay with me if you please.'

'But I haven't seen Gabriel for ages,' Anna protested pleadingly.

' 'His lordship' to you, miss,' said her mother tartly. 'Miss Hope, you must come and visit us at the farm. You will be very welcome.'

131

'Thank you,' replied Eustacia, smiling. 'I will ask Lord Ilam to bring me next time we go riding together.' She turned to look at Anna Crossley and found that the younger girl was regarding her with a decidedly stony face. Could the girl be a little possessive with regard to her adopted brother?

After a few more exchanged comments, Mrs Crossley took her leave and, escorting Anna, walked over to the family trap where the men were still inspecting the horses. Ilam stayed to help the farmer's wife and daughter into the trap. Eustacia, watching, saw the look on Anna's face as Ilam walked away after making his farewells, and made a startling observation. The girl fancies herself in love with him, she thought to herself. I wonder if he knows.

By the time Ilam had returned to the church, Lady Agatha had joined Eustacia on the path.

'I have been wondering whether you would both care to dine with me?' Ilam asked. 'It is time I returned your hospitality. There are others whom I ought to invite, but they will not be arriving until just before the garden party. With any luck, that will put off the need to invite any of them to dinner, at least for a while.'

'Very gallant,' remarked his aunt as she took his arm and they began to walk,

Eustacia following behind as they negotiated the path towards the ancient lych gate. 'I cannot imagine Ashbourne issuing an invitation in such a way.'

'Believe me, ma'am, nothing you could have said could possibly have pleased me more,' he answered, a little tight-lipped.

'I dare say,' her ladyship answered serenely. 'Are any other persons the lucky recipients of your gracious invitation?'

He grinned at that. 'I was thinking of inviting Dr Littlejohn. It's time I paid him that courtesy.' He turned to Eustacia. 'Doctor Littlejohn was my tutor before I went to Harrow. He lives in a cottage on the Ashbourne estate.'

Lady Agatha nodded approvingly. 'He is a sensible man. It will be a pleasure to meet him again. Tell me how your plans for the garden are progressing.'

As they left the church grounds, Eustacia fell into step beside them, and Lord Ilam started to tell them about the changes that he was proposing to make to the ancient parterre behind Illingham Hall. 'It's not a fashionable design,' he admitted, 'but I like it. It suits the house. Besides, it mirrors the pattern of the ceiling in the great hall. Any changes I make will be ones which will not affect the geometric pattern.'

'I have a fancy that your grandmother made some alterations in the choice of plants, and the ones she chose have not prospered as well as they might.'

Ilam nodded. 'The originals were the best,' he agreed. 'There are records of the first planting which I intend to examine.'

'That must be fascinating,' said Eustacia. 'My father's house is of a much later date than yours, my lord, but there was another house on the site, and the plans of the parterre are kept in the steward's room, even though the parterre has long since gone. Was it very common for landowners to use the same design for their garden as for aspects of their houses?'

'I have no idea,' replied Ilam. 'I shouldn't be surprised. You must examine the plans when you come to the Hall, Miss Hope.'

'I should be delighted,' replied Eustacia truthfully.

⋆   ⋆   ⋆

The following day was wet and miserable, with no chance of a ride, so Eustacia and her godmother stayed indoors sewing, writing letters and reading.

Part way through the morning, they both grew tired of their occupations and Lady

Agatha sent for coffee while they laid their work aside. It was then that Eustacia ventured to ask a question that had been occupying her mind for some little time.

'Why does Ilam so resent his father?' she asked. 'I know that he feels himself to have been rejected as a child, but could that still make him angry now?'

Lady Agatha sighed. 'You are right of course,' she agreed. 'He does believe that Ashbourne rejected him when he was a baby. I think that Gabriel would understand better if he had ever really known my father. He was an implacable man, and the pressure that he could put upon one was quite unbelievable. In addition to that, Ilam has always believed himself to be second best.'

'Second best? To whom?' asked Eustacia.

After a short pause, Lady Agatha said, 'Raff fathered another child before Ilam was born. It was that child's mother that Raff wanted to marry. It wasn't permitted, as she was just a farmer's daughter. She died in childbirth as did Ilam's mother.'

'Did the child live?' asked Eustacia.

'Oh yes. Michael is older than Gabriel by six months. He was packed off to another part of the country to save the family from embarrassment, but has always been supported by Ashbourne.'

'And did Lord Ashbourne show more interest in Michael than in Gabriel?' Eustacia asked, then almost bit her tongue off because she was being rather intrusive.

'Lord, how should I know?' asked her ladyship. 'Ashbourne has never taken me into his confidence, nor shown the slightest interest in me, either. He's a care-for-naught, and you'd do well to remember it.' When she next spoke, it was about a completely different matter, and Eustacia was left with the uncomfortable feeling that she had overstepped.

★ ★ ★

That wet day was succeeded by two more, but fortunately, the weather cleared on the evening that they were due to go to Illingham Hall for dinner. Lord Ilam sent a message asking whether they would like him to send the carriage, but Lady Agatha declined, telling his messenger, 'I have pattens for each of us, which will keep the worst of the mud off our hems.'

Eustacia was a country girl, so she readily agreed to this decision. Although she disliked wearing the overshoes which were clumsy and lifted her up to four inches off the ground, she saw the value of keeping the mud off her evening slippers, which were new and of white kid.

They were on the point of setting off when there was a knock at the door. 'Ilam has sent a servant to walk with us,' remarked Lady Agatha. 'That's good of him.'

Grimes opened the door to reveal not a servant, but Ilam himself, clad in evening attire, but with a pair of top boots on his feet. 'I thought you might like an arm if you're tottering along on those,' he explained.

Eustacia was torn between relief at not having to negotiate the drive on her clumsy pattens unsupported and vain annoyance at having Ilam seeing her in such unbecoming footwear.

'Miss Hope, good evening,' he said, bowing. 'You appear to have gone up in the world — at least three inches, I would say.'

'I hope you do not expect me to curtsy in these,' she retorted, then blushed because she had sounded very rude.

'Not at all,' he answered, rather taking the wind out of her sails. 'No doubt I should then be obliged to pick you up off the floor afterwards. Shall we go, ladies?'

Thanks to Ilam's strong support, the journey was accomplished without difficulty, and soon the ladies were in the entrance hall of Ilam's house being assisted to remove their pattens, whilst Ilam when upstairs to exchange his boots for shoes. The lace on one of Eustacia's slippers had worked itself into a knot, so while Lady Agatha exchanged a few words with Ilam's butler, Keithly, who was well known to her, Eustacia undid the knot, then proceeded to tie her lace once more. It so happened that she was rising to her feet as Ilam reached her side, having just come downstairs.

'Ah, that's better,' he remarked, smiling down at her.

'What do you mean?' she asked him, puzzled.

'I've got used to looking at you from this angle,' he replied.

'It isn't funny being so short, you know,' she answered him defensively. All through her childhood, she had waited to grow to her mother's height. At the age of fourteen she had stopped growing. Her nurse and even her parents had confidently assured her that she would grow taller soon, but it had never happened.

'I never said it was funny,' he insisted. He might have said more, but at that point, Lady Agatha finished her conversation with Keithly, and the butler led the way to open the door for them into a comfortable wood-panelled room with mullioned windows and a large stone fireplace with a screen in front of it, decorated with needlepoint embroidery of a hunting scene. A grey-haired man who was sitting in a chair by the window laid down the book that he was studying and rose to greet them.

'Miss Hope, you must allow me to present Dr Littlejohn,' said Ilam, when Lady Agatha and the older man had greeted one another.

'Miss Hope, I am very pleased to meet you,' said the former tutor, bowing courteously. He was a tall man, nearly as tall as Ilam, but with a slight stoop. He wore his own grey hair neatly tied back and his evening dress, of brown velvet with a frilled shirt, was in the fashion of about twenty years before. 'You remind me of someone, although I cannot imagine whom.'

'You will have all evening to think about it, Jonathan,' said Lady Agatha. 'Just don't stare at her while you do so, for she will find it very unnerving.'

'I wouldn't dream of being so unmannerly,' he replied. 'Although to look at such a pretty face would not be a hardship, I assure you.' He smiled at Eustacia in an avuncular manner, and she found herself smiling back.

'I would not object,' she replied. 'It would be quite a novelty. I usually find that the gaze of gentlemen passes over me quite rapidly,

139

and finds its way towards my mother.' She smiled as she spoke, and did not notice that Ilam was eyeing her rather keenly.

It was not long after their arrival that dinner was announced. Ilam offered Lady Agatha his arm, but she shook her head and turned instead to Dr Littlejohn. 'I can take your arm any day of the week, Gabriel. I have not seen Jonathan for a long time. You may give Eustacia your arm.'

'Youth must to youth,' Dr Littlejohn murmured, as he escorted Lady Agatha into the dining-room.

The meal began with soup, and was followed by a variety of dishes, including one of jugged rabbit, which Dr Littlejohn confided was his favourite. 'Gabriel always makes sure that it is served when I come,' he remarked, his eyes twinkling as he helped himself to more. Indeed, for a lean man, he seemed to consume an enormous amount of food, even surpassing the amount that Ilam put upon his plate — which was considerable.

During the meal, it became clear that the doctor was staying with Ilam for a few days. 'I have some reading to do and there is a fine library here with some volumes that I do not possess at home,' he said. 'Has Gabriel shown you his library, Miss Hope? Of course you only see part of it here. Some of the volumes are housed upstairs in the long gallery.'

'No, I have not yet seen it,' replied Eustacia, blushing as she remembered her visit to the long gallery, and how Ilam had found her looking at his father's portrait.

'It's an omission that I intend to rectify after dinner, sir,' said Ilam. 'With your permission, Aunt, I would like to show Miss Hope my garden plans.'

'Why don't we all repair there when we have finished?' suggested the doctor. 'I have no desire to sit over a glass of port, and you can bring one into the library.'

'An excellent suggestion,' put in Lady Agatha. 'You may bring me a glass as well, Gabriel. I see no reason why gentlemen should keep it to themselves.'

After they had finished the dinner, they all left the table together, and went to the library. It was a welcoming room, wood panelled like many others in the house, with chairs that looked comfortable rather than stylish, and curtains and carpet in shades of red. Eustacia looked around at the bookcases. Did Lord Ilam have a copy of *The Vindication of the Rights of Woman*? She doubted it.

Lady Agatha and Dr Littlejohn went to sit near the fireplace and chat, but Ilam put his hand under Eustacia's elbow and led her over to the library table, where the garden plans had already been set out.

'Ah yes,' she said, after she had looked down at them for a few moments. 'I remember seeing this motif in the ceiling of the gallery.'

'The maker of the original plan was thwarted a little in his ambitions by the parsimony of my ancestor,' remarked Ilam. 'He designed a fountain to go in the centre, and four more, one for each of the four segments.'

Eustacia wrinkled her brow. 'As far as I can recall, the fountain which is there at present is nothing like this one,' she remarked. 'I don't remember the others, either.'

'No, as you have obviously noticed, the only fountain is the one in the centre, and it's deuced ugly. In fact . . . ' He turned to Lady Agatha. 'Would you mind, Aunt, if I took Miss Hope outside to see the fountain?'

Lady Agatha waved her assent, and Ilam invited Eustacia to leave the library by the door which led into the drawing-room. Once there, he opened the French door and they stepped out onto the terrace. It was a beautiful summer evening after the rain. The sun was only just setting behind some of the bigger trees, and there was a wonderful smell of rain-moistened earth and fresh vegetation. Eustacia sniffed appreciatively. She glanced up at Ilam. Although he didn't say anything, she got the feeling that he, too, was enjoying the scent of the gardens after rain.

'Come to the end of the terrace,' he said. 'You can just discern the fountain from there.'

She walked beside him, and looked towards where he was pointing. 'No you can't,' she said. 'Not when you're my height.'

'It's too wet underfoot for your slippers,' he remarked. He turned to look at the stone bench which was just behind them. 'If you got up on there, you'd be able to see.'

Eustacia took his hand and, decorously turning her back on him, lifted her skirt so that she could climb up onto the bench. 'I see it now,' she said. 'It is ugly, as you say. What do you plan to do about it?'

'I've had a workshop near Derby recommended to me, and I plan to commission a new one, together with four smaller pieces, one for each of the segments. I don't think I want four more fountains, though.'

'You don't want to go on a Grand Tour to get some?' Eustacia asked him.

'I'd rather encourage British craftsmen. I'm not sure what I want yet.'

'What about statues depicting the four seasons?' Eustacia suggested.

He wrinkled his brow. 'Possibly,' he murmured.

She looked down at him. This new

perspective suddenly tempted her to tease him. 'Too orthodox for you, my lord? What about the four apostles? Or even the Four Horsemen of the Apocalypse?'

'Or I could be very daring and go for the four last things, couldn't I?' he replied, in a similar teasing manner.

'The four last things?' she echoed.

'Death, Judgement, Heaven and Hell, according to the church's teaching,' he replied, grinning. 'Wouldn't that make a fine display? Shall I help you down, now?'

'I don't know,' she answered him. 'I rather like being this tall.'

'What, seven foot?' he demanded.

'No, but you cannot imagine what a trial it is to be small,' she answered. 'It is impossible to see over the heads of people, and one gets overlooked.'

'Believe me, that's sometimes an advantage,' Ilam replied ruefully. 'If I misbehaved at school I was always spotted. There was no one to hide behind, you see.'

'No, but just a few more inches would be lovely,' said Eustacia regretfully. 'I suppose it is because Mama is so tall and elegant. I always feel little and insignificant next to her.'

'Comparisons are always odious,' he replied seriously. 'We'd all like to be other than we are. Shall I help you down, now?'

Suddenly she recalled his father's sneering remark about his 'coal-heaver's shoulders'. Was that what Ilam was thinking of? She put her hands on his shoulders and he put his around her waist so that he could lift her down. How strong he was!

Once down on the ground, she became conscious of her own diminutive size once again. 'Thank you,' she said, smiling up at him. The light was now beginning to go, and parts of his face were in shadow so that it was harder to read his expression. They paused briefly, his hands still on her waist, and hers on his shoulders. Then voices from inside told them that Lady Agatha and Dr Littlejohn were coming out to join them. They stepped away from one another, and walked towards the others; but the warmth of Ilam's touch at her waist stayed with Eustacia long after he had released her.

11

The following day was much improved and, mindful of the fact that Ilam had promised to go riding with her on the next fine day, Eustacia donned her riding habit. She was not to be disappointed. He appeared at nine o'clock with Butternut in tow, and threw her up into the saddle as before. With the memory of the previous night still in her mind, she was conscious of his strong hands on her waist as she had not been when they had ridden last, and she hoped that she was not blushing.

'I thought you might like to visit the Crossleys at Valley Farm today,' he suggested after he had climbed into the saddle himself.

Eustacia willingly agreed. 'I believe that you said they are tenants of yours,' she remarked.

He nodded. 'Some of the most hard-working and prosperous,' he told her. 'The family has farmed the land for several generations now.'

After they had been riding for perhaps half an hour, Ilam brought his horse to a halt at the top of a gentle rise and pointed to a group of farm buildings which nestled in the lee of a hill. 'Valley Farm,' he said. 'It's where I spent my childhood until I was sent to Harrow.'

As they made their way down the track that led to the farm, Eustacia reflected that the whole place showed signs of very good management. The outbuildings were in good order, the Derbyshire dry stone walls were well maintained, and all animals that were in the vicinity looked clean and healthy. The farmhouse itself, which they approached from the front but then skirted round the back, gave every appearance of being a gentleman's residence.

Their arrival in the yard seemed to be the cue for a number of different persons to descend upon them from various directions. A lad came running out to help Briggs take the horses saying, 'It's good to see you, m'lord,' with a broad grin on his face.

'How are you, Bert?' Ilam asked, clapping him on the shoulder, before turning to help Eustacia down from the saddle. Mr Crossley appeared from the side of the house with a dog at his heels, saying cheerfully, 'This is a fine surprise, and no mistake, my lord! And with Miss Hope as well. Has Mother seen you?'

Before Ilam could answer, a girl whom Eustacia recognized as Anna Crossley came out of what appeared to be the kitchen door with a bowl in her hands. Ilam was still speaking to his foster father when she emerged. Eustacia, however, saw the unguarded expression on the young woman's face, and knew her suspicions had been correct. Anna was deep in the throes of what was probably her very first romantic attachment. As if aware that she was observed, the farmer's daughter turned her head towards Eustacia. For a moment, the two young women's eyes met, and in those of Miss Crossley there was quite unmistakable hostility. Then the moment was gone as Gabriel turned to greet his foster sister and she put down the bowl and ran over to him with arms extended, clearly asking to be picked up.

'Gabriel!' she exclaimed. 'I didn't think we'd see you so soon after church!' Ilam lifted her as though she were no heavier than a feather — although she was quite a substantial young woman — and swung her around two or three times before he set her down.

'Forgive me for appearing unannounced, Uncle Tobias, but I thought as the day was fine I'd bring Miss Hope to pay that promised visit.'

'You're very welcome, Miss Hope,' said the farmer, with simple dignity. He was in shirt sleeves, with a leather waistcoat, home-spun breeches and stout shoes. Clearly he was dressed for work, but his clothes were clean, and of good quality, and his lack of embarrassment about his working attire impressed her. 'Anna, mind your manners,' he added sharply. 'You haven't greeted Miss Hope yet.'

'Pleased to see you again, miss,' said Anna, dropping a reluctant curtsy, but not looking noticeably gratified. Eustacia smiled at her, but although Anna smiled back, her expression was a little wary. Eustacia wondered how often they had visitors in this corner of Derbyshire.

'Is Aunt Bertha in the kitchen?' asked Gabriel. Anna nodded. 'Don't tell her. I'll surprise her.' The expression on his face was mischievous, delighted, almost boyish. He hurried inside, leaving Eustacia with Tobias and Anna. Moments later they heard a shriek proceed from the kitchen.

'He's managed to catch her unawares,' said Tobias, grinning. 'Next thing, she'll be out scolding us all for bringing you to the back door.'

'It was Gabriel who brought her to the back door, Father,' said Anna with a little defiant glance at Eustacia, as she used the viscount's Christian name.

149

'That's quite true,' agreed Eustacia. 'We are none of the rest of us to blame.'

Clearly Anna had no idea how to reply to this piece of banter, so it was as well that Mrs Crossley came hurrying out at that point. Like her husband, she was dressed for work in a starched white cap, her gown covered by a crisp, white apron.

'Miss Hope, what you must be thinking of me, greeting you at the back door; but there, his lordship, who *should* know better, is to blame!'

'We have just resolved that same thing, Mrs Crossley,' replied Eustacia, coming forward to greet her hostess.

'I do not see what can be done to remedy matters,' said Gabriel. 'If I take Miss Hope to the front door now, you will only reprimand me for trailing her through the farmyard.'

'Yes, but you should not have brought her to the back door in the first place,' Mrs Crossley pointed out.

'Gabriel could hardly be expected to be knocking at the front door of his own home,' put in Anna.

'That's enough from you, miss,' frowned Mrs Crossley reprovingly. 'Go inside and tell Lottie to put the kettle on. Miss Hope, please step this way; if you don't mind the kitchen that is. I don't know what his lordship can have been thinking, bringing you through the farmyard. Thank goodness it's not muddy, that's all I can say.'

Anna looked as if she might say something more, but in the end, she went back inside with something suspiciously like a flounce.

'I don't mind the kitchen at all,' said Eustacia cheerfully. 'I often go round the estate with my father, and we frequently end up in people's kitchens, and sometimes go home covered with mud as well.'

Perhaps by way of making up for the fact that Eustacia had been brought to the wrong door, Mrs Crossley hurried her through the immaculate kitchen into the passage as quickly as possible. From there, they entered the drawing-room at the front of the house. This was a fine, square room with thick green velvet curtains, a green patterned carpet, and chairs upholstered in a similar design. Looking at the well-polished woodwork and gleaming glass of the windows, Eustacia could see, if she had not been able to guess before, that Mrs Crossley was a meticulous housekeeper.

'Please to sit down, Miss Hope,' said the farmer's wife. She looked round and saw that the others had not followed. 'Now where have they got to?' she declared. 'Tobias always has to show his lordship the least little thing that's been done in the house; and here am I, still in my apron and without a chance of taking it off to entertain you properly.'

'You can take it off now, if you like,' suggested Eustacia.

'Take off my apron and cap in front of a lady?' replied Mrs Crossley in horrified tones, for all the world as if Eustacia had suggested showing her garters.

'It's very natural that your husband should want to show Lord Ilam what he has been doing,' replied Eustacia, in order to change the subject. 'I understand that he was brought up here.'

'Yes, he was,' agreed Mrs Crossley. 'I hope you don't think that any of us is too familiar with him, miss,' she added anxiously.

'I think it very natural that you should be quite informal with him when you know him so well,' Eustacia replied.

'Yes, but I know what's fitting, and so does most of the rest of the family. Sometimes I worry — '

'Worry about what, Aunt Bertha?' asked Ilam, strolling into the room.

'Sometimes I worry that Tobias will find so many things to show you that I shan't get to see you at all,' answered the farmer's wife. There was a glow in her eyes as she looked at him. In just such a way, Eustacia reflected,

152

might she look at a son of whom she was very proud. 'Now, if you'll entertain Miss Hope for a few moments, I'll go and make myself fit to be seen by decent people.' She cast a darkling look at Ilam before leaving the room.

His lordship chuckled. 'Aunt Bertha always has to find something for which to scold me,' he said. 'She'd feel that she was failing in her duty if she didn't.'

'Is the house much as you remember it from your childhood?' Eustacia asked, wandering over to the window.

'It sometimes seems to me as if the place and the people have changed remarkably little,' he replied, joining her. 'Uncle Tobias and Aunt Bertha welcomed me into their family as if I was one of them. They made no distinction between me and their own sons. I was here with the family on the night when Anna was born, and I was included in their celebrations.'

'Did you not spend any time at all with your father?' Eustacia asked curiously, turning to look at him.

His face lost the relaxed expression that it had worn since their arrival and took on the shuttered look that she had now come to expect to see whenever the earl was mentioned. 'Ashbourne came from time to time dispensing largesse,' he said scornfully.

'He usually managed to remember my birthday. No doubt Aunt Bertha prompted him. I spent more time at Illingham then later at Ashbourne after I started going to Harrow, but nobody could ever stop me from coming here.'

Eustacia wondered what it must have been like for a boy brought up to all intents and purposes as a farmer's son to go to Harrow and mix with those who had not had that experience. Had he been teased or bullied? She felt a sudden rush of sympathy which almost caused her to reach out and grasp hold of his hand. She was glad that she had not done so when, moments later, Aunt Bertha came back, this time without her apron and cap. She was closely followed by Anna, who had taken the opportunity of changing hastily into a different gown.

'Whyever have you put that on for?' asked Mrs Crossley. 'That's your party dress.' Eustacia could think of two possible reasons why the young girl had gone to change her gown. One might be that she did not wish to look unfashionable beside the family's lady visitor; the more likely explanation, Eustacia believed, was that she wanted to impress Gabriel.

Anna muttered something about the other one being soiled, whilst Gabriel said, 'I think she looks very pretty. You seem to have grown up all of a sudden, Anna. No doubt Uncle Tobias will soon have to look out for young men beating a path to the door.'

'I hope I would have more sense,' replied Anna, tossing her head.

At this point, Mr Crossley came in, having donned a coat, and a clean pair of shoes. His wife turned her head to make a brief inspection of his appearance, and whilst she did so, Anna took the opportunity to slip over to Ilam's side and tuck her hand into his arm. 'It's so good to have you home again, Gabriel,' she said, smiling up at him.

Eustacia casually took a step away to look carefully at them. Ilam was looking down at Anna indulgently, and he seemed to regard her as the young sister he had proclaimed her to be. She had already made a guess at Anna's feelings. The adoring way in which she was now looking up at his lordship would appear to confirm this opinion. Observing the two of them, she could only see heartache ahead. One swift glance at Mrs Crossley's anxious expression told her that the farmer's wife felt exactly the same way.

'Anna, what are you about?' said Mrs Crossley in a sharp tone. 'Let go his lordship's arm, and don't talk so familiar. 'Gabriel' indeed!'

Anna looked as if she might make some kind of defiant response. Fortunately before she could do so, a maid came in carrying a tray with a pot of tea and some warm scones. 'I hope you'll have some refreshment, Miss Hope,' said Mrs Crossley.

'Thank you, I should be glad of some tea,' replied Eustacia smiling. 'Did you make the scones yourself, Mrs Crossley? They smell delicious.'

'Aunt Bertha is one of the best cooks in the district,' Gabriel told her.

'Yes and many's the time I've had to count my baking and then count it again when you've been through the kitchen,' said Mrs Crossley scolding gently.

The rest of the visit passed very pleasantly, and at the close, Anna asked if she might take Lord Ilam to see the new chicks. A look passed between Mrs Crossley and her husband, whereupon the farmer said easily, 'I'll come along as well. I'm a little concerned about one or two of the birds.'

Eustacia made as if to go with them, but the farmer's wife said, 'Perhaps you would like to see some of the lace that my grand-mother made, Miss Hope. Tobias laughs at me for showing it off but it's very fine.'

The farmer's wife took her lady visitor across the hall and into the dining-room, which showed the same signs of excellent housekeeping as did the rest of the house. Mrs Crossley opened a drawer in the heavy oak sideboard that was set against one of the walls and took out some cloths to show her visitor. Eustacia was very ready to admire the fine workmanship, but before she could give voice to more than one sentence, Mrs Crossley spoke.

'Oh dear, I am so worried and I hesitate to burden you with it, only I think you see quite a bit of his lordship at present, and that's as it should be. I don't want you to think that I had any ambitions in *that* direction.'

'You are talking about Anna,' Eustacia surmised.

'You've seen it too, haven't you? The trouble is, she's been growing up without his realizing it, and although to him she's just a little sister and always will be, to her, well, she's getting foolish ideas, and I've had no idea of how to get her out of them — until today, that is.'

'Today?'

Mrs Crossley looked a little self-conscious. 'I hope you don't think I'm being over familiar, having just met you, Miss Hope, but you're the very first young lady that Gabriel — Lord Ilam, I should say — has brought here to the farm.'

Eustacia blushed. 'Oh no,' she exclaimed hastily. 'There is nothing of that sort between us, I assure you. I am a guest of Lady Agatha and Lord Ilam is taking me about just to be polite.'

Mrs Crossley looked doubtful. 'Well, if you say so, then it must be,' she replied. 'But it will do Anna no harm at all to see that he enjoys the company of ladies. I blame myself partly for this.'

'I am sure you have nothing with which to reproach yourself,' said Eustacia reassuringly.

'I do not mean to say that I have encouraged her,' said Mrs Crossley, taking the cloths from her so that she could put them away. 'It is just that we are a little isolated here, and she has few chances to meet any young men. I'm not much of a one for going out and about, and she has always been such an easy girl to have about the farm, doing her work and being no trouble, and so I suppose I did what was easy for me. But lately she's started going all quiet like, and she's been talking about his lordship quite a bit.'

'Are there no social occasions that she could attend so that she could meet some other young men?' Eustacia asked.

'His lordship always has a garden party at about this time of year,' said the farmer's wife. 'That'll be in a fortnight's time, and it's no doubt why he has come back. A lot of folk go to that. Then there's the ball at the Olde Oak, which always comes afterwards.'

'I think it would be a very good idea to take her to both of those events,' said Eustacia. They left the dining-room and went back to the drawing-room. The rest of the party had not yet returned.

'If you could contrive to hang off his lordship's arm, so that she will think that he is spoken for, I would be very grateful,' said the farmer's wife.

'No doubt he would think I'd run mad if I did,' replied Eustacia with a twinkle.

'Perhaps you could have a word with him about her,' the other ventured.

'Me?' squeaked Eustacia, her voice going up at least an octave.

Mrs Crossley sighed. 'She's only young, I suppose. They haven't much sense at that age. That's why we ended up looking after his lordship, Lord Ashbourne only being a boy himself when Lord Ilam was born.'

'How old was Lord Ashbourne when he married?' Eustacia asked curiously.

'He was not quite seventeen. The marriage was arranged by his father and I don't think he had much say in it.'

'Did you know his wife?'

At that moment, Lord Ilam came back in, followed by Anna, who was looking flushed and happy. He eyed Eustacia curiously for a moment before saying 'It is time we were on our way. Aunt Agatha will think I have made away with you otherwise.'

'Yes of course.' Eustacia got to her feet. 'Thank you so much for your hospitality, Mrs Crossley.'

'It was a pleasure, Miss Hope,' said Mrs Crossley beaming. 'I'll look forward to seeing you at his lordship's garden party.'

'If I'm invited,' Eustacia replied, glancing up at the viscount through her lashes. She could see out of the corner of her eye that Anna's face had now taken on a stony expression.

Ilam looked at her, his brows raised, for it was the first time that she had spoken to him in a way that was even remotely flirtatious. 'I can just imagine Aunt Agatha's expression if I were to exclude you,' he replied.

Mrs Crossley and Anna waved them off as they left the farm. 'It was a pleasure meeting you, Miss Hope,' said the farmer's wife. On her face was an expression which reminded Eustacia of the discussion that they had just had.

Eustacia's heart sank. Clearly Mrs Crossley hoped that she would speak to his lordship on the subject of Anna's infatuation. Yet how could she? She had known the man for only a week. To be advising him on his treatment of a young woman whom he had known all his life would be an unpardonable piece of presumption.

On the other hand, she knew all too well how painful it was to discover that one's hopes and aspirations did not match those of the man with whom one had thought that one had an understanding. If only Morrison Morrison had been honest with her earlier, then much of the pain and embarrassment could have been avoided. She did not think for a moment that Ilam was deliberately misleading Anna concerning his feelings, but the young girl was vulnerable through her infatuation. In such a state, she would see every smile, every friendly gesture as evidence of a warmer regard. It would be quite difficult for Lord Ilam to discourage her without being brutal. It behoved someone to make the situation plain to him. Mrs Crossley obviously thought that she, Eustacia, ought to be that person.

So deep in thought was she that she was not aware of how far they had travelled without speaking. Nor did she hear Lord Ilam speaking to her until he repeated his words. 'You won't find out very much about

Ashbourne from the Crossleys,' he told her. 'I shouldn't bother to quiz them again.'

'I wasn't quizzing them about your father,' replied Eustacia indignantly. Involuntarily she pulled at Butternut's reins, causing the mare to toss her head.

'Really?' said Ilam in disbelieving tones. 'I suppose I did not hear you asking Aunt Bertha about him after all. Doubtless I imagined it.'

'Doubtless you have turned the whole incident into something much more important than it really was,' she retorted swiftly.

'As you say,' he answered, inclining his head slightly. Eustacia was left with the distinct impression that he still did not believe her.

'For goodness' sake,' she said in exasperated tones. 'Why must you be for ever going on about your father and how handsome everybody thinks he is? Anybody would think that you were not exceedingly attractive yourself!'

For a moment, they stared at one another. Then a slow grin started to spread over Ilam's features and Eustacia turned bright red as she realized what she had just said. She was just wondering how she would ever get over this piece of awkwardness when Ilam took pity on her and said, 'Race you to that oak tree!'

After that, they talked of indifferent subjects until they reached the vicarage. Ilam lifted Eustacia down from Butternut's back. 'Thank you,' he said before releasing her. 'You have raised my self-esteem no end.' He refused to come in, pleading estate business. 'Pray send my duty to Aunt Agatha and tell her that I shall be consulting her about the garden party as usual.'

Eustacia promised to do so, and went inside and up the stairs to change out of her habit. She thought about what had just occurred. Ilam had seemed to be surprised to hear that he was an attractive man. Again she blushed at her own boldness. How Mama would scold her if she ever found out! Yet he was attractive. His face did not have the classic handsomeness possessed by his father and even, to a degree, by Morrison Morrison; but it had a certain rugged masculinity that, along with his fine physique, would always command female attention. Perhaps his conviction that his father was the kind of man whom women found appealing prevented him from acknowledging his own attractions; even caused him to think poorly of himself. That might explain in part why he did not realize that Anna fancied herself in love with him. He probably did not think that any woman would regard him in such a way.

Absurd, she exclaimed, wondering even as she said it whether she was condemning his low opinion of himself, or admitting how compelling she found him.

12

The following morning Eustacia went to the room which had been the Rev'd Colin Rayner's study, and was now referred to by everyone as the library, in order to answer a letter that had come to her from Miss Warburton. *Your Mama has been so kind* — wrote that lady — *and is treating me like an honoured guest.* Eustacia smiled. No one could be more gracious than her mama when she had a mind to it. Miss Warburton also went on to say that she had heard from Mr Lusty. *He has written me a very civil letter, telling me that he will do himself the honour of calling upon me as soon as his duties permit.*

'Ha!' Eustacia exclaimed. Then she looked round self-consciously, glad that no one else was present. She had almost sounded like her mama at that moment! 'As soon as his duties permit, indeed!' It did not sound very lover-like.

She had just taken up her pen to write an answer, when the doorbell rang. Shortly afterwards, Grimes came to say that Lady Agatha was receiving visitors and would be pleased if Miss Hope would attend her in the drawing-room.

'Who are these visitors?' Eustacia asked, as she laid down her pen and stood up, smoothing her gown. It was unusual for visitors to come to the rectory. Apart from Lord Ilam, and Mr Lusty, they had received no one, but then it was a small community, and Eustacia had learned that some families had gone to London for the season.

'It is Mrs Granby and her daughter, miss,' replied Grimes. 'They have just returned from London, I b'lieve.'

'Thank you, Grimes,' replied Eustacia, feeling pleased. Perhaps now there would be a female of her own age with whom she could associate, a commodity which had been sadly lacking in Illingham so far.

On her arrival in the drawing-room, she found Lady Agatha entertaining two ladies dressed in gowns which, whilst entirely suitable for the occasion, screamed expensive London fashion. The older lady, who was obviously a similar age to Eustacia's own mother, was in a bronze green walking gown, with a bonnet trimmed with ribbons in a similar colour. She was a fine-looking woman who had kept her figure, and who still had some claim to beauty. Her daughter, a ravishingly pretty blonde with sparkling blue eyes, was in a delightful shade of pink, trimmed with piping of a darker shade.

'Ah, Eustacia,' said her godmother upon her entrance. 'You have come at just the right moment. Mrs Granby, this is my goddaughter, Eustacia Hope. Eustacia, Mrs Granby.'

'Charming,' said Mrs Granby. Then she turned to her daughter with what could only be described as a slightly anxious look. 'Evangeline, do you not think so? Miss Hope, this is my daughter Evangeline.'

Evangeline looked at Eustacia in what could almost have been a measuring way. Then she smiled and said, 'Miss Hope, I am delighted to meet you, and I am convinced that we are going to be the best of friends.' There was an almost imperceptible sound from Mrs Granby's direction that could have been a sigh.

Eustacia smiled back. 'That is very kind of you to say so,' she replied. 'I will do my best to live up to your expectations.'

'Oh, I know you will,' replied Miss Granby. 'You are dark, and I am fair, so we will set each other off beautifully!' Eustacia tried to look gratified, but inside, she had come to the conclusion that here was another tall blonde beauty who, like her mother, would cast her into the shade.

'I have sent for refreshments,' said Lady Agatha. 'In the meantime, why not take Miss Granby into the gardens, Eustacia? Then Mrs Granby and I can have a comfortable chat.'

'That will be delightful,' said Miss Granby. She undid the strings of her bonnet.

'Evangeline, dear . . .' ventured Mrs Granby.

'I refuse to walk around the garden in a bonnet whilst Miss Hope is bare-headed,' Evangeline interrupted decidedly as she laid aside her head gear. 'It would make me look very foolish.' The two young ladies walked out of the French doors which led into the garden. There was a small terrace with two or three steps which took them down onto the lawn. 'I love this garden. Do not you?' asked Miss Granby, when they were walking beneath the trees.

'Yes, very much,' Eustacia replied. 'Do you live nearby, Miss Granby?'

'Yes, we live just outside the village, but we have a house in Town as well. We have been there for the season. Have you had a London season, Miss Hope?'

'No. My parents dislike London, so I have had to make do with York and Harrogate.'

Miss Granby's eyes widened. 'Not go to London? In your place, I would have made such a fuss that they would have been obliged to take me.'

'I don't think I would have been taken however much of a fuss I made,' said Eustacia ruefully.

'You are obviously not determined enough. One only has to drum one's heels on the carpet for the job to be done.'

'Did London live up to your expectations?' Eustacia asked, trying not to imagine what her mother would have done had she ever tried such a trick.

'Oh yes, very much so,' replied Miss Granby. 'I cannot think of anything better than a day spent shopping, then perhaps riding in the park, followed by dinner and a ball.'

'It certainly sounds exhausting,' remarked Eustacia.

'I cannot see any point in going to London and then doing things by halves,' declared the other. After a pause, she went on, 'I know what you are going to say next,' she declared. 'You are going to ask me if I attracted the attention of any gentlemen while I was in London.'

'I thought that that went without saying,' answered Eustacia with a smile.

'You are kind,' said Evangeline, tucking her hand into her companion's arm. 'As a matter of fact, I had a good many admirers.' She smiled secretively. 'One of them did please me more than any other, but I have not made up my mind. I only met him shortly before we came away, you see.'

'Does he have the approval of your parents?' Eustacia asked.

Evangeline shrugged. 'I dare say he might. He is an only child and his family have quite a good fortune. Mama wanted me to settle upon somebody, but I want to have another season next year.'

'Will she permit it?' Eustacia asked.

'Of course she will,' Evangeline responded, tossing her head. 'Mama dreads the possibility of one of my tantrums and Papa will do anything for his 'little angel', as he calls me.' She took one look at Eustacia's astonished face and giggled. 'You are thinking that I am dreadfully spoiled,' she said, correctly guessing what was in Eustacia's mind. 'I am their only child, you see. Besides, it is quite their own fault, you know. If they hadn't wanted me to be spoiled, they shouldn't have indulged me so much. Shall we go back to the house, now?'

'Yes, of course,' Eustacia replied, wondering whether the other young woman might stamp her feet and shout 'I won't' if she suggested that they walk to the other end of the lawn instead. 'Come this way, Miss Granby.'

'Please, call me Evangeline,' said the other. 'You know my darkest secrets, now, so we must be friends. Where is Miss Warburton, by the way?'

Even while she was giving an answer, Eustacia was thinking about what had just been said. Like Miss Granby, she was an only child, but she would never have dreamed of throwing a tantrum. Such tactics with Lady Hope would probably result in a day of bread and water in her room and possibly some rather nasty medicine as well. As for Papa calling her a little angel, he would be far more likely to tell her firmly to do what her mama bade her.

Inside the drawing-room, refreshments had arrived, and soon the two young ladies were being served with lemonade, whilst the older ladies enjoyed a glass of ratafia. 'I had ratafia in London,' said Evangeline, pouting.

Again, Eustacia noticed the anxious expression on Mrs Granby's face as she murmured 'Evangeline, dearest!' No wonder she had wanted to marry her daughter off this season. She could then have cheerfully consigned the control of that wilful young lady to her prospective husband.

'That may be so, Miss Granby,' answered Lady Agatha, quite unintimidated by the prospect of a storm to come. 'In my house, however, young ladies are served with lemonade.' Eustacia glanced at her in surprise. Her godmother was far more likely to serve her with drinks that her mama would not permit. It only took a moment or two for her to guess that Lady Agatha had made this pronouncement from sheer devilment, to see whether she could provoke Miss Granby into having a tantrum.

For a moment, the issue hung in the balance. Then Evangeline burst out laughing. 'Then lemonade it must be,' she responded. 'Thank you, Lady Agatha.'

'Your mama and I were just talking about the garden party at Illingham Hall,' said her ladyship to Evangeline. She then turned to her goddaughter. 'It is quite the social occasion in these parts. Some even go so far as to say that the Derbyshire set return from the London season simply in order to attend.'

'Yes, it is quite true,' agreed Mrs Granby. 'It is a very popular event.'

'I dare say you have been very dull up until now,' said Miss Granby sympathetically.

Eustacia could hardly agree, so she merely said, 'My godmother does her best to keep me entertained. Lord Ilam has been very kind as well.'

'Kind?' echoed Miss Granby in surprise. 'I would not have thought it of him. He always seems rather brusque to me.'

'Evangeline, dearest,' ventured Mrs Granby again.

Eustacia began to wonder whether these words might be carved on the woman's tombstone. 'Oh yes,' she said in response to Miss Granby's words. 'He has lent me a charming little mare and has taken me riding several times.'

'I know he is a very conscientious landlord,' said Mrs Granby.

'Sad stuff,' commented Evangeline. 'Let's talk instead about the garden party and the ball at the Olde Oak. Just think how much Eustacia will love them, Lady Agatha.'

'I am sure she will,' responded her ladyship, smiling.

The visitors left soon afterwards. 'She's as spoiled as a young woman could be,' commented her ladyship, 'but she seems to have taken to you, my dear. You'll have a livelier time with her about. No, there's no need to protest about it. I know it's been a little dull for you with only an old lady in mourning for company.'

'I haven't been dull, Godmama,' Eustacia protested, realizing as she spoke that it was true. This was in some degree due to her godmother's scheming, but she was forced to acknowledge that in part it was due to the presence of Lord Ilam. Would he attend the ball at the Olde Oak, she wondered, and if so, would he dance? Suddenly she realized that she was already reviewing the evening gowns that she had brought with her. Thanks to her mama, at least she would not be at a loss as to what to wear. She would hate to look dowdy in front of Evangeline Granby who, whatever her faults — and she certainly had a few — was certain to be fashionably dressed.

★ ★ ★

Miss Granby did not leave it very long to call again upon her new friend. Only two days later she arrived at the vicarage having been brought into the village by her father. 'Papa is going to enquire about the arrangements for the ball at the Olde Oak,' she explained when Mr Granby had brought her in and paid his respects to Lady Agatha. 'I thought that I would come and see my new friend at the same time.'

'You are very welcome, Miss Granby,' said Lady Agatha. 'Would you like to stay for luncheon? I am afraid that I cannot offer to send you home as I have no carriage.'

'Please, Papa?' said Evangeline meltingly.

'Anything for my angel,' he responded in doting tones. No wonder she was spoiled, concluded Eustacia. 'I will send the carriage round this afternoon.'

'Then may Eustacia come back and dine and stay the night?' asked Evangeline. 'I have so much that I want to tell her about my visit to London.'

'I could not leave Godmama all alone,' Eustacia protested.

'Nonsense!' her ladyship responded bracingly. 'I have Grimes and the other servants. I will not be at all lonely. In fact, I will be very happy to think that you are being so well entertained.'

Mr Granby declined the offer of a glass of wine, and left soon afterwards. Lady Agatha sent for refreshments for them all, and they were just sitting down together when the doorbell rang. 'I expect that that is Ilam,' said her ladyship. 'He is due to consult me about the garden party any day now.'

Sure enough, a moment later, Lord Ilam was announced, and he came in with his usual athletic stride. 'Aunt Agatha, Miss Hope, Miss Granby,' he said, bowing to the company. 'It's a pleasure to see you again,' he went on, addressing the other visitor. 'How was London?'

'Exciting: enthralling: wonderful!' she told him, her eyes sparkling.

'Busy, noisy and hot, is what I think you

mean,' he replied ironically.

'You don't care for the place, my lord?' Eustacia asked him.

'I can't abide it,' he admitted frankly. 'I have to go occasionally, but I get away again as soon as I can.' Noting his attire today, which comprised a comfortable coat and breeches and serviceable boots, she could well believe it.

'I can't understand it,' said Miss Granby in bewilderment.

'It is Doctor Johnson who says that anyone who tires of London has tired of life,' put in Lady Agatha.

'Is it he who wrote that dreary old dictionary?' asked Evangeline.

'The very man,' agreed Lord Ilam.

'I'm surprised that he said anything so sensible,' the young lady replied, with frank disregard for the doctor's scholarship.

It was at this point that the door opened and Grimes came in to say that Mr Lusty was in the hall. A look of consternation crept over Lady Agatha's face. It was as she paused to think that Ilam said 'Show him in then, man.'

'No, I will come out to see him,' she said hastily. Unfortunately, by this time, Lusty had heard what Ilam had said, and was on the threshold looking in at them.

Lady Agatha cast one anxious glance at her

176

goddaughter. It was at this moment that Eustacia remembered that her godmother did not want Mr Lusty and Lord Ilam to converse with one another. At about the same time, she recalled that as far as Lusty was concerned, she was supposed to be delicate. They all stood to greet the clergyman. Eustacia curtsied, rose, swayed, passing her hand across her brow. 'Oh dear,' she murmured, in fading accents. 'I do feel so . . . ' So saying, she closed her eyes and sank to the floor. The only thing that happened to change her plan was that she did not actually make contact with the carpet after all. Instead, she found herself caught by a powerful masculine pair of arms.

'Now, Lusty, only see what you have done,' Eustacia heard her godmother say. That lady's voice had regained all its customary confidence. 'Ilam, will you be so good as to take Eustacia up to her room? Grimes, show Ilam to Miss Hope's chamber and have her maid attend her.'

Eustacia allowed her head to loll back against Ilam's powerful shoulder as she felt him carry her out of the drawing-room, up the stairs and along the passage with effortless ease. She felt perfectly safe in his grip, just as she had when he had lifted her off the bench on the terrace. He would not let her fall. In fact, she decided, there was definitely something pleasant about the whole business.

'In here, my lord,' said Grimes. 'I will send for the young lady's maid.'

Lord Ilam set her gently down on her bed, and for a moment, before he eased his arms from beneath her and stepped away, his face was so close to hers that she could feel his breath on her cheek.

From beneath her lashes, she could see that Grimes had very properly left the door open. The butler's footsteps disappeared down the corridor. 'It's all right, Miss Hope,' said Ilam's voice. 'He's gone now. You can open your eyes.'

13

Eustacia's first feeling was one of disappointment that her performance had not been more convincing. When her mother had pretended to faint at her wedding, everyone had thought that her collapse was genuine. Now, quite obviously, Lord Ilam was not fooled. Had everyone in the drawing-room seen through her subterfuge?

Yet, she reflected, he might just be testing a theory. Slowly she opened her eyes. 'Oh dear,' she murmured in a thread of a voice. 'What happened? Did I faint?'

'I don't think so, ma'am,' replied his lordship. He did not sound annoyed, she decided. If anything he sounded a little amused. Before she could make any response to this remark, he said 'It's all right. I know why you did it.'

'You do?' she said cautiously. Accepting now that he really had detected her deceit, she sat up on the bed, swung her legs round over the side and stood up.

'Aunt Agatha told me,' he said, walking over to her from the window where he had been standing. 'That a man should jilt a woman is despicable enough; that a clergy-man should do it is beyond the pale. In my opinion, such a man should be drummed out of the church completely.' His expression was so grim that for a moment, she had a vision of him marching some fictitious clergyman, coincidentally resembling Mr Lusty, out by his ear.

Eustacia had temporarily forgotten about her godmother's fiction that she had been jilted by a clergyman. Really, she thought, it was quite difficult to keep track of which deceit she was supposed to be practising at which time.

'I hold myself entirely to blame,' Ilam was saying. 'I can only ask for your understanding and for your pardon.'

'Why should you blame yourself?' Eustacia asked, not at all sure what he was talking about.

'When your aunt said that she would see Lusty in the hall, I should have remembered your unfortunate experience,' he replied. 'Like a fool I said 'bring him in', or some such thing. What I can't understand, though, is why you didn't simply excuse yourself rather than pretend to faint.'

Since Eustacia could not understand why she should have done such a thing either, it was as well that Trixie came bustling in at that point.

'My Lord!' she exclaimed, her eyes sparkling. 'This is a fine thing, to find you in miss's bedchamber!'

'Which is why I shall be gone at once, now that you have come,' Ilam replied. He turned to Eustacia, his voice softening. 'May I call tomorrow to see how you do?'

'Yes, of course,' she murmured, feeling absurdly shy. It must be because he had picked her up and carried her, she decided. No man had ever done such a thing since she had been fully grown. So effortlessly he had done it, too!

'In your bedchamber, miss!' Trixie repeated after Ilam had gone. She looked rather pleased than otherwise.

'Trixie, do hold your tongue,' said Eustacia. 'Ilam is not a rake. He had simply carried me upstairs after I had . . . ' She paused, wondering what to say next. She usually told Trixie everything, but it occurred to her that the less people who knew that her faint had been a pretence, the better. ' . . . after I had fainted,' she concluded.

'Fainted?' exclaimed Trixie. 'Then you should still be lying down on your bed, Miss Stacia.' She took hold of her mistress's arm, seeking to guide her back to the bed.

'I don't want to lie down,' said Eustacia impatiently, pulling in the other direction.

Then she recalled that this was hardly convincing behaviour for one who had been unconscious just a short time before. She lifted one hand to her head. 'Perhaps I do still feel a little giddy,' she said in a softer tone. 'I think I might be better if I could sit down in this chair and have a cup of tea.'

'I'll fetch one right away, miss,' said Trixie eagerly, heading for the door.

'Trixie, will you find out if Mr Lusty is still there when you go downstairs?' Eustacia asked.

'I will, miss.'

Eustacia listened to Trixie's rapid footsteps as she hurried down the corridor. Then, only a short time later, she heard the more measured tread and the swish of silk that heralded the approach of her godmother.

'Eustacia, you clever girl,' said that lady, beaming. 'Imagine you thinking to faint! You fooled everybody. Lusty could not get away fast enough after I had castigated him for his insensitivity.'

'I didn't fool Lord Ilam,' replied Eustacia. 'He knew straight away.'

'You did not tell him?'

'He guessed. I suppose I didn't flop enough.'

'What did he say? What did you tell him?'

'He thought that it was because I was

disturbed by the presence of a clergyman when I had been jilted by one,' replied Eustacia. She remembered how kind Ilam had been, and felt strangely guilty. Her godmother laughed and clapped her hands. 'I do not know how you can be so pleased, Godmama,' Eustacia said reproachfully. 'He asked me why I did not simply excuse myself and leave, and I could not think of anything to say. Fortunately, Trixie came in before I could answer, but he is going to come back tomorrow to see how I do. I have no idea what I am to say to him, and it is thanks to you that I am embroiled in this deceit!'

'There, there, now, my dear,' said Lady Agatha, catching hold of Eustacia's hands, which the young woman had started to wring in her agitation. 'I will make it all right with Gabriel in the morning. In any case, you will not be here to face him tomorrow, because you will be at Miss Granby's house, so there is nothing to worry about.'

'Oh no, no, of course not,' murmured Eustacia. 'I had forgotten that I would not be here. I hope he will not think me terribly rude.'

'He will not do so when I explain,' answered Lady Agatha. 'Now come downstairs. Miss Granby is waiting.'

'Trixie was going to bring me tea.'

'We'll have tea together.'

Mr Granby sent his carriage that afternoon as promised, and after repeated assurances from Lady Agatha that she would manage very well on her own, Eustacia consented to go with her new friend.

'There is no need for your maid to come,' said Evangeline. 'My abigail can very well look after both of us for just one evening.'

Eustacia had to hide a smile. Trixie had been very excited about the outing and had then become quite sulky when she had discovered that she was to be excluded from the treat. She had been hoping for a chance to investigate any male servants employed in the Granby household.

'Now that we are alone together, you must tell me what you think of Ilam,' said Miss Granby, as soon as the carriage had turned out of the vicarage gates. 'Do you like him?'

'Do I like him?' ventured Eustacia cautiously.

'You know what I mean,' replied Evangeline with a touch of impatience in her tone. 'Do you *like* him?'

'Well, I . . . that is . . . ' stammered Eustacia.

Evangeline clapped her hands. 'I thought you did,' she declared, her eyes sparkling.

'What's more, I can tell that he is interested in you as well.'

'No, he is not!' declared Eustacia, conscious of going bright red. 'Is he?' she added more tentatively after a pause.

'You should have seen the way that he glared at Mr Lusty,' responded Evangeline. 'I quite thought that the poor man would flee the house immediately.'

'I expect he only glared at Mr Lusty because he was in the way, and because he wanted to put me down as soon as possible.'

Evangeline thought for a moment, then said, 'No, it wasn't that sort of glare. I did wonder whether you were just pretending to faint so that he would carry you upstairs. Was it very thrilling?'

'No; that is to say, I don't know,' stammered Eustacia. 'I was unconscious, remember?'

'What did he say to you when he had got you upstairs? Imagine having a man in your bedchamber!'

'He didn't say anything very much,' replied Eustacia, thinking that Miss Granby and Trixie had rather a lot in common. 'He left as soon as my maid came. Never mind all that. Tell me some more about your London season instead.'

This proved to be a very successful diversion, and in no time Miss Granby was chattering about her beaux, with Lord Ilam forgotten, at least for the present.

⋆ ⋆ ⋆

The following morning, Ilam called at the vicarage, to discover that only Lady Agatha was at home. 'Eustacia will be sorry to have missed you,' said her ladyship, as she invited him to be seated opposite her in the drawing-room. 'She has been spending the night at the Granbys'. I expect her home later today.'

Ilam was conscious of a feeling of disappointment which was out of all proportion to the event. 'Was this a sudden decision?' he asked. 'I had informed her that I would call upon her today to see how she did, and she gave no indication then that she might not be present.'

'It was not a long-standing arrangement,' replied her ladyship. 'I expect she had forgotten about it when you spoke to her. I think it will do her good to get away from here if only for a night. It is very unfortunate, but I am told that Mr Lusty bears a marked resemblance to the clergyman who let her down so badly.' Ilam opened his mouth to speak, but before he could say anything, her ladyship continued, 'No doubt you will be wondering why she pretended to faint when she could simply have excused herself. The fact of the matter was that in order to leave the room, she would have had to walk close by Lusty, and that she simply could not face.'

Ilam stared at her for a moment, then stood up abruptly, paced across the room and back again. 'Pardon me, ma'am, but this is absurd,' he said harshly. 'She cannot spend her life in fear of clergymen! Those who encourage her in this irrational fear do her no good at all! In any case,' he went on rather more slowly and in an altered tone, 'she attended church with no ill effects *and* it was Lusty preaching.'

'Yes, but a clergyman in a drawing-room is a very different matter to a clergyman in a pulpit,' Lady Agatha suggested.

He drew his brows together. 'Balderdash!' he exclaimed rudely. 'What game are you playing, ma'am? What's more, how is Miss Hope involved?'

Lady Agatha rose, straightening her spine. 'Game? How dare you accuse me of playing games, sirrah? Do not forget that I am your aunt and, as such, worthy of respect. Perhaps if you cannot be civil, then you had better leave.'

'Perhaps I had,' he agreed. 'Rest assured, ma'am, I shall be looking into this matter more closely.'

'Do so, by all means,' she replied, her head held high. 'My conscience is clear.'

Ilam threw her one more searching look before taking his leave.

'Drat the boy,' she muttered, before sitting down to read through some correspondence.

★ ★ ★

A brief stay with Evangeline Granby only confirmed Eustacia's view that the young lady was completely spoiled. The frightening thing was not that she threw tantrums, but that her control of the entire situation appeared to have gone beyond the point where she needed to do so. Mrs Granby's nervous suggestion that her darling ought not to wear one of her more elaborate evening gowns for a simple evening at home was met with a straight look and the firm statement that Miss Granby wanted to do so. No more was said on the subject.

'It is all very well for Mama to mutter about proper wear for the country, but I cannot see that it matters,' remarked Miss Granby as they were preparing to get ready. 'What is the point of having pretty things if one does not wear them? If I am not careful, all my things will be unfashionable before I get the use out of them.'

'I suppose so,' agreed Eustacia doubtfully, looking at the undoubtedly becoming but rather elaborate satin gown that Evangeline planned to wear. 'I shall look very drab next to you, I'm afraid.'

'Shall you?' asked Evangeline, wrinkling her brow a little.

'Oh yes. I haven't brought anything half so grand.'

At once the other young woman smiled. 'I'll wear something else, then,' she said. This exchange led Eustacia to think that although Miss Granby might be spoiled, she did seem to be good-natured.

Miss Granby promised to send her abigail along to Eustacia's room to do her hair after she had finished dressing her mistress, but in the event it was Evangeline who came, dressed much more suitably than she had originally intended in a white muslin gown sprigged with blue.

'I love doing people's hair,' she remarked, as she took up the brush and comb and got to work.

When Eustacia complimented her on her appearance, Evangeline said suspiciously, 'You've not been scheming with Mama, have you?'

'When would I have been doing that?' asked Eustacia, honestly bewildered. 'In any case, I hardly know your mama.'

189

'No; no, of course not,' agreed Evangeline. 'Your gown looks pretty too. Would you like your hair high up on your head, or more on the back of your neck?'

'Evangeline, my precious, you look enchanting,' was Mr Granby's first comment when they entered the drawing-room. 'Come, angel, and give Papa a kiss.'

Evangeline tripped across, beaming, to do as she was bid. Mrs Granby nearly spoiled the atmosphere by saying, 'Much better, my dear', but Eustacia intervened hastily, saying something about the room to which she had been allocated, the moment passed and with it the stormy look on Evangeline's face.

Given the fact that Miss Granby had clearly enjoyed a successful season in London, Eustacia fully expected all the talk to be of the previous weeks' triumph. Instead, much of the discussion concerned the forthcoming garden party and the ball that was to follow.

'The tradition of the garden party was begun some years ago,' explained Mr Granby in response to Eustacia's enquiry. 'The present Lord Ashbourne's grandfather had died the previous winter, and the garden party was a way of introducing the tenants and local residents to the new Lord Ilam. The event has carried on ever since, changing little over the years.'

'Is it well attended?' asked Eustacia.

'Oh yes indeed,' replied Mr Granby. 'Everyone has an additional incentive to go now, of course.'

'Which is . . . ?' Eustacia prompted him.

'Ilam must find a bride,' responded her host. 'He never goes to London; therefore it follows that he will probably look for a country girl.'

'All the young ladies will be looking out their best gowns and primping and preening so as to attract his attention,' remarked Evangeline, lifting her glass to receive more wine and quite ignoring her mother who was shaking her head. 'Not that it will do them any good. He takes no notice of any of them.'

★ ★ ★

'Have you known Lord Ilam all your life?' Eustacia asked Evangeline that night. They were both ready for bed, and Evangeline had wandered along to her guest's room to chat with her whilst sitting on her bed.

'Mostly,' the other girl replied. 'He came to live at a farm nearby not long after he was born, so he has always been around here on and off — apart from when he was away at school. I expect you know all about that already.'

'Yes, he took me to meet the Crossleys,' replied Eustacia.

'He really is quite eccentric, continuing to go there all the time,' Evangeline remarked. 'He's sometimes called a country bumpkin for that very reason. Yet he does not seem to want to cut the connection. I think it very strange.'

'Perhaps he feels that he owes them a debt of gratitude for bringing him up,' said Eustacia. She found Evangeline's remarks rather offensive, but did not want to start a quarrel with the young woman in her own home.

'That could easily be paid with a hamper at Christmas and a gift of money now and then,' pointed out the other carelessly. 'Mind you, he does make a terrible figure of himself at times. Would you believe he actually works alongside the field hands at harvest time?'

'It doesn't surprise me,' Eustacia answered, thinking of how absorbed he had been in all the farm concerns when they had been there.

'Anyway, he must be interested in you if he has taken you to the farm,' Evangeline remarked. 'Hardly any girls can boast that he's done that.'

'It's because we're almost related,' Eustacia replied, blushing.

'Oh, pooh!' responded Evangeline contemptuously. 'What does that signify if a man is attractive?'

'I thought that you said that you were not interested in him,' said Eustacia suspiciously.

'No, I'm not; but it doesn't mean I can't recognise a well-looking man when I see one.'

'What about the gentleman that you are interested in?' Eustacia asked her. 'Is he handsome?'

Evangeline refused to be drawn. 'I am hoping that he may come to the garden party and perhaps to the ball as well,' she answered, her eyes twinkling. 'Then you will see for yourself.'

14

The next time that Eustacia saw Lord Ilam, he was clearly a harassed man. 'It's this dam — dashed garden party,' he told his aunt, as they sat together in the vicarage drawing-room. 'I can't tell you the sleepless nights I've had over it.'

'It's not your first,' replied Lady Agatha. 'It shouldn't affect you like that.'

'It shouldn't, but it does,' he replied, running his hand over his lustrous brown hair.

'You must enjoy seeing people taking pleasure in your estate,' Eustacia suggested.

'Believe me, ma'am, at this moment, I would enjoy sending each and every possible visitor to perdition,' he replied frankly.

'That's not very civil of you, Gabriel,' said his aunt.

Realizing the implications of what he had said, he turned a dull red. 'Needless to say, I am not referring to present company,' he murmured.

'How could you be, when the only thing that makes the whole business bearable is the help that I give you?' said her ladyship reasonably. 'Do you have the list of tasks from last year?'

'I have it,' replied Ilam, drawing a sheaf of papers from inside his coat. 'Of course, what makes everything more complicated is the fact that the steward is newly appointed.'

'Bring it into the library and we'll have a look at it.'

During the next half an hour or so, Eustacia felt as much at home as she had ever felt since her arrival in Illingham. Her mother and father were hospitable people, and she had often been included in their conferences concerning similar affairs. She was therefore able to listen to Lord Ilam's and Lady Agatha's discussions with understanding, and she even felt able to contribute some suggestions of her own.

At last, they had gone through the whole list, and Lord Ilam's brow looked much lighter than when he had arrived. He willingly agreed to toast the success of the venture in a glass of wine, and before he left, his mood was so much improved that he bestowed a kiss upon his aunt's cheek, a thing that Eustacia had never seen him do before. 'Thank you,' he said, his cheerful expression making him look much more like his twenty-five years than usual. 'I do not know how I could have managed without you.'

'Remember that Eustacia has been of great assistance as well,' his aunt put in.

'I do not forget,' he replied, stepping forward, colouring and hesitating, before catching hold of her hand and raising it to his lips. She wondered whether he had wanted to salute her cheek instead. Of course, she was too much a lady to speculate as to whether she, too, would have preferred it!

To mask her embarrassment, she said 'Mary Wollstonecraft writes that many individual women have more sense than their male relatives.'

'Clearly she's a sensible woman herself,' observed Lady Agatha tartly.

'Does she so?' Ilam asked, wrinkling his brow. 'Is that in the *Vindication of the Rights of Woman*?'

'Why yes,' Eustacia replied in surprise. 'Have you read it?'

'It has not come in my way, but I found her *Vindication of the Rights of Man* persuasive,' he answered, surprising her.

Soon after this, he took his leave.

'Fancy the boy's kissing me,' Lady Agatha remarked. 'It almost makes me feel guilty for decciving him.' She did not sound particularly contrite. This impression was confirmed when she added, 'One good thing is that he'll be so busy organizing this affair to concern

196

himself with my dispute with the Church, at least for the present.'

★ ★ ★

Just as the whole village seemed to be looking forward to the garden party, the very future of the function was threatened by a fierce storm which visited the area just two days before the event.

'Wind's getting up,' Trixie remarked to her mistress as she helped to get her ready for bed. Sure enough, something woke Eustacia in the middle of the night, and she became aware of a roaring noise, which she identified as the sound of the wind as it howled around the house, and rushed through the trees. She thought of the huge fir tree that stood near to Woodfield Park and hoped that the storm would not go anywhere near her own home. She was glad that all the trees near to the vicarage were much smaller in size.

Conscious that she was beginning to worry to no purpose — for there was nothing that she could do to cause the wind to abate its fury — she lit her candle and took up her book, hoping for wise guidance from Miss Wollstonecraft. The lady did indeed have some good sense to offer.

In short, women, in general . . . have acquired all the follies and vices of civilization, and missed the useful fruit . . . Their senses are inflamed, and their understandings neglected, consequently they become the prey of their senses, delicately termed sensibility, and are blown about by every momentary gust of feeling.

The term 'gust' seemed particularly apposite. Unfortunately, the fact that Eustacia could and did castigate herself for being foolish did not put an end to her anxieties, and she put her book aside, unable to concentrate upon it.

Just when she thought the wind might go on for ever, it began to drop, but then the rain started lashing against the windows. As she was wondering whether anybody else in the house was being kept awake by the storm, Lady Agatha knocked on her door saying that she could not sleep and would Eustacia like a hot drink. The two ladies went downstairs to the kitchen only to find Trixie and one of the housemaids about exactly the same errand. The four of them sat in the kitchen enjoying a cup of warm milk before going back to bed.

The following morning, the wind had dropped. The rain continued with far less force, gradually petering out mid-morning, when the sun came out, making everything look fresh and new.

'It's almost as if nature had gone out of its way to give everything a wash just to oblige Gabriel,' Lady Agatha remarked when Eustacia said how lovely the garden looked. The two ladies had gone outside to inspect the vicarage garden for any damage. 'I do hope than none of the trees has come down in Illingham Park. Some of them are very old, and that would be an added task that he could do without at the moment.'

After lunch, as Lady Agatha did not need her for anything, Eustacia decided to walk into the village and see if the storm had caused any damage. She met the doctor who told her that as far as he knew, no one had been hurt as a result of the storm. 'Mrs Ross has given birth to her new baby early,' he told her. 'She vows and declares it was fright that did it.'

'But mother and baby are both doing well, I hope,' said Eustacia anxiously.

'Oh yes indeed, ma'am,' he replied. 'I have to say, it does worry me, though, the state of affairs that we are in with no vicar. Suppose something had gone wrong with the birth? Poor Mrs Ross might have died without benefit of clergy.'

'Oh,' murmured Eustacia.

'By the way, did you know that John Flew's cottage has been damaged?'

'Pardon?' said Eustacia, because she was thinking about the other matter. Then she said, 'I'm sorry, I don't know which cottage you mean.'

'The one at the far end of the village,' replied the doctor. 'It seems that a tree came down on it in the night.'

'Was anyone hurt?' Eustacia asked.

'No, thank God. His lordship will find Flew and his family somewhere else to live while the cottage is mended. It belongs to the estate. Well I'd best be on my way. Good day Miss Hope.'

After they had parted, Eustacia went straight to Mrs Ross's cottage to see the new baby. She was admitted by the Rosses' eldest daughter, who looked to be about twelve years of age. The cottage was spotless and Mrs Ross, tucked up in bed with her baby in her arms, seemed to be in good health and excellent spirits. She thanked Eustacia for her good wishes and told her that her husband would be pleased. 'He's our first boy, you see, miss. Sid loves all his children, and you couldn't have a better nor more helpful child than our Cissie what opened the door to you; but he's glad to have a boy this time. Do you want to hold him, miss?'

Eustacia took the sleeping baby with some trepidation, for she had never held such a small child before. 'What have you decided to call him?' she asked the child's mother.

'Edmund, after the saint that named our church,' replied Mrs Ross. 'I'm that thankful to have been preserved after last night. I do hate storms, miss. I quite thought that I would die of fright. But there now, all's well that ends well.'

Eustacia soon handed the baby back, and declined to stay for a cup of tea. 'I'll come another day,' she said. 'Apparently a tree has come down on a cottage and I want to report the matter to Lady Agatha.'

After she had left Mrs Ross, Eustacia set off to visit the cottage, her mind deep in thought. When she had first arrived in the village she had been shocked at Lady Agatha's determination to flout the wishes of the bishop. Then she had begun to find the whole business amusing and a harmless means of defying Lord Ilam after his earlier rudeness to her. Now, she remembered what the doctor had said about how Mrs Ross might have died without a clergyman to comfort her. Had that happened then she would at least have been partly to blame because she had colluded in Lady Agatha's plans, if only in a small way.

In some ways, to tell Lord Ilam about his aunt's plotting seemed disloyal, not only because her godmother had taken her in when she had needed a refuge, but also because she had compromised her own reputation for Claire Delahay years before. Now that she, Eustacia, had realized how the villages were being denied spiritual solace, she could not see how she could do anything else. It occurred to her that her godmother might be so annoyed at her perfidy that she would send her home forthwith, but that could not be helped.

Her parents' reaction held no terrors for her. They had always been prepared to listen to her and Lady Hope would be horrified at the deceit that her friend had practised. Her only fear there was that tales of hers might result in coldness between Lady Agatha and Lady Hope. She sighed. She had become rather fond of this place in a short period of time. If her godmother was particularly annoyed, she might even send her home before the garden party and the ball. She did not want to miss those. Then there were the people that she would miss: Evangeline Granby, the Crossleys, Lady Agatha, Gabriel. No, decidedly, she did not want to leave Gabriel. Then, as if forming his name in her mind had conjured him up, she saw him.

She had just turned a corner and come upon the damaged cottage. A number of men were working on clearing the tree and trying not to cause any more damage to the house in the meantime. The tree, a massive horse-chestnut, had broken through the thatched roof, and brought down part of the wall as well. A great carthorse with enormous hairy feet was standing by, harnessed to a pair of chains which at the moment lay slack on the ground, looking rather like sleeping serpents. Lord Ilam seemed to be directing operations, but by his appearance he had obviously been helping in very practical ways too. He had stripped to his shirt sleeves, and his linen was looking quite soiled. His boots were caked in mud, and his breeches bore several black marks. More of his hair had escaped from its confining ribbon than was still controlled by it, and there was a streak of mud on his tanned cheek. He looked active, absorbed and healthy. Point-de-vice he was not, but Eustacia thought that he had never looked more attractive or more manly.

As she arrived, Ilam and another man were finding the best way of attaching the chains to the tree in order to pull it away from the house. Three other men were helping in the task. One was on the portion of the roof that was still sound, sawing off some of the branches, whilst another held them steady and still another waited on the ground to take them and lay them down.

'Fine bit of firewood there when it's dry,' remarked an elderly man who, along with two or three urchins and a couple of women was standing and watching the proceedings. Two of the boys started rootling about amongst the fallen branches and soon found two smaller pieces with which they began to indulge in a mock sword fight. None of the adults present seemed to feel that it was their responsibility to draw them away so that they could play elsewhere. Presumably this was because the adults themselves did not want to miss anything. Eustacia would have liked to send the children out of harm's way, but did not feel that it was her place, especially when she heard one boy refer to one of the women as 'Mam'.

All went well until they got a little too near the horse and one of them caught him on the flank. The horse, an exceptionally quiet and placid animal, understandably took exception to this, and began to toss his head and stamp his feet.

'Someone go to Pluto's head,' shouted Ilam imperatively, 'and get those children away, for God's sake!'

There was a moment's hesitation, then the woman who had been called 'Mam' took hold of the two boys each by the arm and led them away. The other adults on the ground looked at each other then at the size of the horse. 'I'm not going near that gurt big thing,' muttered the old man. His words seemed to give voice to the general view.

Seeing that no one else was going to obey his lordship's commands, Eustacia walked quickly but calmly over to the horse, making sure that he could see her. Then, talking to him all the time, she caught hold of his bridle. Her arm was nearly at full stretch and, had he chosen to be recalcitrant, she would have been in great difficulty. Fortunately, such was his temperament that it only needed a word of reassurance and a gentle hand for him to calm down.

The chains were soon properly attached, and Ilam scrambled down athletically, followed by the other man. It was only when the viscount came to take hold of the horse that he saw who was holding him steady. A slow grin spread across his features. 'All's well, I see,' he said. 'Bruno could never move with your firm hand upon his bridle.'

Eustacia looked up at him. She could now see that his manual labour had wrought more havoc than she had thought at first. His shirt had been ripped down the middle, tearing off half the buttons, and revealing a broad expanse of well-muscled, hairy chest, gleaming with sweat and slightly marred by a small graze.

'You are hurt, my lord,' she said, looking at his injury, then looking away when she realized that in fact she was not really looking at his injury at all! He glanced down and began to brush the graze with his hand. 'No, my lord, you will make it dirty.' She fumbled at the fastening of her reticule with fingers that felt as if they were twice as large as usual, and eventually drew out her handkerchief.

'It's just a scratch,' he said. He put out his hand to prevent her from ministering to him, and as he did so, their two hands brushed against one another. He drew a deep breath before moving his hand away and saying 'It's not worth soiling your handkerchief. I'll put something on it when I get back. Stand clear, now, while we pull this tree away.'

Eustacia got right out of the way and made sure that the rest of the spectators did the same. Then she watched whilst Ilam guided the horse, and the tree was slowly pulled away from the cottage. All his concentration was now given to his task. She stood watching, telling herself that she needed to be able to give a full report to Lady Agatha. In reality, she knew that she was simply enjoying the opportunity to observe him at work. There at the horse's head, he was murmuring words of guidance and encouragement, his hand firmly on the horse's bridle. What a magnificent creature, she thought to herself; and she was forced to acknowledge that she was not referring to the horse!

Once the task was over, she turned round in order to walk back to the vicarage. She knew that she must speak to Ilam about Lady Agatha's schemes, but today was clearly not the day. She told herself that she must inform Lady Agatha about the morning's events, but when she reached the drive which led up to the vicarage, she walked past and carried on to the other end of the village wanting to clear her head.

She thought about how she had got out her handkerchief and blushed at her own boldness. 'Shameless hussy,' she told herself severely. Fancy pretending that she wanted to tend his wounds when if she was really honest with herself, she had simply felt a sudden and quite unexpected desire to lay a hand on his bare chest! Then, quite by accident, their hands had touched, and she had felt a shiver of excitement which had seemed to run all the way down to her toes. Evangeline Granby had challenged her about finding him attractive. The notion had taken her by surprise, but she now realized that his attraction for her had been growing ever since he had lifted her off the stone bench on the terrace behind Illingham Hall. The dreadful thing was that because of her reaction to him today, she was terribly afraid that he might have guessed it.

* * *

The day of the garden party dawned fine and bright, prompting Lady Agatha to remark that they were always lucky with regard to weather for this event. It had been decided that the two ladies from the vicarage would spend the day at Illingham Hall, to save time going back and forth to change. They would wear some older clothes for the morning, and would use rooms allocated to them by the housekeeper in order to prepare for the afternoon.

When they arrived, they found that the marquees had already been erected in the garden, and that tables were being carried into them and put in place. They were just wondering what would be the most useful thing for them to do when the viscount appeared, striding towards them across the grass. Like his two lady helpers, he was in working apparel. His head was bare, the sunlight revealing copper hints in his hair. He was also in shirt sleeves with the neck open, and without the usual concealment of a coat, the muscles in his thighs were very evident. At least his shirt was properly fastened on this occasion, Eustacia thought, then she blushed as she remembered his dishevelled appearance outside Flew's cottage, and her response to the sight of his naked chest.

'You're very welcome, ladies,' said Ilam, sketching a bow. 'I'm hoping you'll direct the arrangement of the flowers and tablecloths.'

'That doesn't sound very testing,' remarked Lady Agatha.

'No; that's why I think Miss Hope ought to be able to manage out here, while you go into the house to work alongside Mrs Davies.'

Lady Agatha nodded and was about to leave them when suddenly Anna Crossley came running across the grass. Unlike those already present, she was clearly attired in one of her best gowns. She looked happy and pretty and eager, and her eyes were fixed upon Lord Ilam. 'Good morning, Gabriel,' she cried, hurrying over to him, her hands held out. 'What a beautiful day for your garden party! I've come to help you. Give me any task you like.'

Only an absolute churl would have refused

to take the hands that she offered to him so trustingly. 'Anna, my dear,' he responded, smiling back at her. 'This is very good of you.' He let go of her hands after a brief moment or two. 'You will wish to greet my aunt and Miss Hope,' he added after a tiny pause.

'Oh, oh yes,' Anna replied, colouring and making her curtsy.

'Are your family well, Miss Crossley?' asked Lady Agatha.

'Yes, very well thank you, your ladyship,' answered Anna.

'You are hardly dressed for helping,' Gabriel said gently.

At this, Anna did not appear to know what to say. Fortunately, Lady Agatha had a solution. 'I am going to the house now,' she said. 'If you come with me, I am sure that Mrs Davies will be able to provide you with a big apron to protect your gown. Then you can come back here and help Eustacia with the flowers.'

For a moment, Anna hovered in indecision. Clearly, she wanted to remain with Ilam, but she certainly did not want to have to attend the garden party that afternoon in a soiled gown. On the other hand, she had not gone to the effort of looking her best for her pretty gown to be smothered with an enormous apron. Common sense won the day, and she accompanied Lady Agatha into the house.

Ilam watched them go. 'She's a dear child, but as to why she decided to come this morning, I haven't the least idea.'

Eustacia looked at him incredulously. 'For goodness sake, Ilam, can you not see what is staring you in the face?' she exclaimed, quite forgetting to be cautious. 'The girl is besotted with you.'

He stared at her. 'Little Anna? Don't be absurd. She's only a child. Anyway, she's like a sister to me.'

'I'm sure she is,' Eustacia replied. 'But she's no longer a child. She's a young woman. Does she still see you as a brother? I doubt it.'

'And you have made this judgement on the basis of three meetings?' His tone was calm, but his brows were slightly raised.

Eustacia coloured. She knew that to mention Mrs Crossley's fears would give strength to her argument. Mrs Crossley had not given her permission to refer to her opinions, however, and she did not want to repeat anything that might cause difficulties between Ilam and his foster mother. 'I . . . that is, I have thought a good deal about it,' she said eventually.

He sighed. 'Miss Hope, I will give you credit for being well meaning, but you must allow me to know Anna far better than you do.'

'Yes, perhaps,' Eustacia agreed, 'but you are a man and see things differently. On the other hand, I am a woman, and — '

'That fact had not escaped me,' Ilam interrupted, with a brief, rather insolent up and down glance. 'Now, there is much to do, and I do not have time to stand here bandying words about a situation that you know nothing about.'

'Lord Ilam — '

'Miss Hope, I have given you credit for your good intentions, but my patience will rapidly come to an end if you do not leave this subject alone. There is much to do. I will be very much obliged to you if you will occupy yourself with your own affairs and leave other people to manage theirs.'

He paused for a moment as if he would say something more, then turned and strode away, affording Eustacia an excellent view of his broad, well-muscled back, if she had been in any mood to appreciate it. She had done her best, she thought with a sigh. She had warned him. If he did not heed her warning, then it was his own fault.

She did not really expect Anna to return to help her in the marquee, and was not surprised when she found herself supervising the placing of floral arrangements unaided. Later in the morning, when everyone stopped work for a glass of wine or beer and some rout cakes, she caught sight of the girl lingering about near where Ilam was talking and laughing with a small group of workers. There was no sign of the big apron that she was supposed to be wearing. As for Ilam, he looked very much at ease among ordinary people. When he had directed operations at the cottage, those who had been working with him had taken instructions from him quite naturally, as if they had often done so before, and had confidence that he knew what he was about. Was he just as comfortable with his peers in a London club, for example, or at Tattersall's?

Suddenly, she wondered whether she and Mrs Crossley had not made a big mistake in regarding a match between Ilam and Anna with disfavour. After all, the girl was of respected farming stock. *She* would not refer to him as an eccentric or as a country bumpkin as Miss Granby had done. She was in addition well educated, and if she did not have any worldly airs and graces, what of that? Ilam clearly preferred country life to the fashionable world. It was true that Anna was only seventeen, but Ilam himself was only twenty-five. Far more unequal matches were promoted in London every day. He had said that she was only a child. What a dreadful irony it would be if he began to think of Anna as a woman because of what she, Eustacia, had said.

Eustacia felt a horrible sinking feeling in the pit of her stomach, and a sudden, unreasonable desire to escort Anna firmly to the fish pond and push her in. Never before had she been a prey to jealousy, but she recognized it for what it was. Recently, she had been forced to acknowledge that she found Ilam exceedingly attractive. Now she realized that she did not want Anna to have him because she wanted him for herself. What was more, for two pins she could feel herself to be quite capable of trailing around after Ilam and staring at him adoringly just as Anna was doing; for, incredible though it seemed, she did not just want him, she was actually in love with him.

She thought about her feelings for Morrison. They had been pale, puny things compared with the strength of feeling that she now felt as she thought about Lord Ilam. She wanted to work by his side as he redesigned the gardens. She wanted to help him come to a better understanding with his father, if that were possible. She wanted to be here every year, to help him with the garden party, to stroll around the gardens and welcome their guests. She wanted to wave them all goodbye, then go upstairs with him and discover whether the rest of him was as splendid unclothed as was that magnificent chest of his.

She came to with a start, looking round and blushing at the shocking nature of her own thoughts. She was glad that Ilam was not nearby to see how flustered she looked. The housemaid who had brought her the glass of wine asked if she was all right, and she murmured something about the day being rather hot.

When lunchtime arrived, Anna, who was still at Ilam's heels, was invited to join the viscount and his two lady helpers for a light meal. Before she could accept or refuse, however, her brother came striding towards her across the grass. He made his bow to Ilam and Eustacia, then turned to his sister. 'There you are,' he said. 'You'd better come home straight away. Mother's none too pleased with you, I can tell you.'

'But I left a message,' Anna protested. 'Besides, Gabriel has just invited me to stay for lunch.'

'I didn't realize that Aunt Bertha hadn't actually given permission for you to be here,' said Gabriel gently. 'Perhaps you'd better do as your mama bids you.'

After one stormy look, Anna said, 'Oh I wish everyone would stop treating me as if I were a child,' before running in the direction from which her brother had come.

'Perhaps you'd better stop behaving like one, then,' he responded, perhaps unwisely, before offering Ilam a brief word of apology and going after her.

After watching them for a moment or two, Gabriel sighed and turned to Eustacia. 'Shall we go inside? I am sure my aunt is ready for some luncheon, and I think the preparations are complete out here.' They walked towards the house. When they were halfway there, he said, 'I fear I was rather abrupt with you earlier. I think that perhaps I owe you an explanation of Anna's conduct. She is like a little sister to me, as I've already told you. She has grown up fast, and she has always been affectionate towards me. It never occurred to me that that affection could so easily be misinterpreted.'

Eustacia could almost feel her sigh of relief turning into a gasp of dismay. He had not understood at all, then. 'But . . . ' she began, wanting to protest against his mistake.

He raised his hand. 'It's all right, Miss Hope. I agree that she should be much more guarded in her manner towards me. I'll make a point of taking her on one side this afternoon and warning her how her behaviour could be misunderstood.'

With that, Eustacia had to be content. At least he was now aware that there was a problem, even if he had not grasped the nature of it.

Luncheon was a very simple repast, and she was surprised and pleased to discover that Dr Littlejohn was present. 'I've been keeping well out of the way this morning, I must confess,' he said. 'However, ladies, I will do myself the honour of taking a turn about the garden with you this afternoon, if I may.' Both ladies professed themselves delighted.

After the meal, Lord Ilam and his lady guests repaired to their chambers to wash, change and repose themselves, whilst Dr Littlejohn returned to the library. Eustacia thought that Lady Agatha was looking a little pale, and she was glad that there would be time for a lie down. The vicar's widow always seemed absolutely indomitable. It was strange to imagine that she might need to rest during the day.

Eustacia herself was not tired at all, and in no mood for a nap. Trixie, who had come with them to Illingham Hall, had put her gown out ready and was soon helping her into it. 'It's going to be a big do,' said the maid as she was fastening Eustacia's primrose yellow gown, trimmed with cream lace. 'Everyone in the village is invited.'

'Yes, I know,' agreed Eustacia. 'Are you looking forward to it?'

'I should say,' Trixie responded with enthusiasm. 'There's a groom here who is a bit of a rogue, so who knows what may happen?'

'Oh Trixie, you and your rakes!' exclaimed Eustacia. 'Just be careful, and remember what Mama would say.'

'Of course, miss,' replied Trixie demurely, but she had a twinkle in her eye.

When Eustacia had changed she wandered downstairs. She would have liked to explore, but did not want Ilam to think that she was being nosy. Nevertheless; she decided that to make her way to the ground floor via the most circuitous route need not make her look anything other than a little foolish to get lost.

Before arriving on the ground floor, she found herself at one end of the long gallery and, on impulse, she walked its length in order to take another look at Lord Ashbourne. Now that she knew Lord Ilam better, she could see that there were more likenesses between father and son than were at first apparent. That arrogant tilt of the head, for example, was very like one of Ilam's gestures, seen when Lady Agatha had challenged him about his rudeness towards her goddaughter. As Eustacia looked at the picture, she remembered Ilam taking up almost the exact same pose when they had been talking about the arrangements for the garden party.

As on a previous occasion, she became aware of being observed and turning she saw without surprise that Ilam was standing watching her. Without thinking, she said at once 'You are very like him in some ways, you know.'

His face stiffened, and he made a bow that was curt in the extreme. 'Thank you, ma'am,' he said in tones that matched his demeanour. 'You have now set the seal on what promises to be an excessively tiresome day.' He turned on his heel and left her.

She sighed. She had not forgotten that she still needed to speak to Ilam about his aunt's battle with the Church of England. These quiet moments before the guests began to arrive might have given her an opportunity, but she had squandered it through her thoughtless words. She turned to go, hesitated, then turned back again to look at the picture. For a moment, she could have sworn that Lord Ashbourne's painted face was grinning.

'You're right, there is a likeness between

them, but you must never ever remark upon it.'

She turned round to see Dr Littlejohn coming into the room. 'Lady Agatha said much the same thing to me,' she agreed, as they began to make their way outside.

'I hold the previous Lord Ashbourne very much at fault,' said the doctor. 'He was quite implacable, utterly unforgiving of his son's mistakes and determined never to let him share any responsibility. Consequently, Raphael doesn't know how to do anything but play.'

'He was called Michael, wasn't he?' Eustacia was remembering that Lady Agatha had described her father in just the same way.

'Yes, he was. It's odd, you know, but amongst the angels of Ashbourne, the Michaels always seem to have that hardness in them. They are the most difficult to love.'

'You've known the family for a long time, I gather.' By this time, they were emerging into the sunlight. The gardens were beginning to fill up nicely.

'My father had a living in Ashbourne's gift, and I took it over when my father died. I've known them all my life. A hugely privileged family, but one in which love is strangely absent. If you find Gabriel to be a little prickly at times, it's partly to protect himself from being hurt.'

No wonder Ilam found himself drawn to the warm and friendly Crossleys. 'I would not see him hurt for anything, Dr Littlejohn,' murmured Eustacia, aware that she might be giving her feelings away, but somehow sure that her confidences would be safe in this scholarly man's keeping.

'No, I thought that might be the case,' he replied. 'The relationship between Ilam and his father has never been good, but an incident took place about five years ago which made it far worse. It's had the result of making him very defensive about all kinds of relationships.' They walked for a little longer, then Dr Littlejohn continued, 'There was a young woman whom Ilam met in London. He was very much attracted to her and she seemed to show a similar interest. When he invited her and her family to visit him here, they accepted willingly. The young woman's father indicated that a match between the two young people would be welcome. In preparation for an engagement to be announced, they all went on a visit to Ashbourne.' He paused.

'Oh no,' breathed Eustacia.

Littlejohn nodded. 'The family were quite innocent, but the young woman had only been using Gabriel as a means to get to Ashbourne. Raphael went upstairs and found her in his bed, quite . . . ' — he mopped his brow with his handkerchief — 'unclothed. Unfortunately, Gabriel saw his father escorting the young lady back to her room and came to the very worst of conclusions. There was a dreadful scene, Ilam left, and the young lady's parents who, I'm thankful to say, had rather better morals than hers, removed her the next day. It wasn't Ashbourne's fault, but Gabriel would never believe him. Now, he cannot hear a good word spoken about his father, and I do not believe that he has fallen in love since.'

'What a dreadful story,' murmured Eustacia.

'Yes indeed. If I could bring the two of them together I would, but it is beyond my powers, I fear. Perhaps someone other than myself will have better fortune. Now, my dear young lady, what would you say if I suggested that we should go and have one of Ilam's ices?'

15

It seemed as if Trixie had been right when she had stated that the world and his wife had decided to come to his lordship's garden party. Miss Granby had predicted that those inhabitants of the fashionable world who lived in the vicinity would put in an appearance. Eustacia could see that a good many of those present were dressed in the latest styles, and she was glad that she had chosen to put on one of her prettiest gowns in a fashionable design. None of these notables was known to her, but they were all happy to be introduced by Lady Agatha, and were disposed to be gracious.

The Granbys arrived in good time, and Evangeline was eager to share the gossip with Eustacia. 'Miss Wing,' she said, indicating a plump young lady with a rather pasty face, 'has just got engaged to Lord Durose. Imagine! Her mama is as proud as a peacock. Heaven knows why, for the man is nearly sixty! But I suppose she could not attract anyone else, poor thing. Oh look, there is Mr Berry with an acquaintance. Is he not handsome? Have you met him?'

Eustacia had not met the young gentleman or his companion, Mr Lloyd by name, so for half an hour or so, the four young people viewed the gardens together, chatting easily of this and that.

As well as the fashionable folk, it seemed that every inhabitant of the village and the tenants and workers from the surrounding farms had turned out, dressed in their best. Lord Ilam spent a fair amount of time walking round with Lady Agatha who was acting as his hostess, and trying to exchange a few words with each guest.

He contemplated the assembled throng with some irritation. Half of them, he knew, had only come to gape. A large number of the wealthier folk were simply continuing their favourite London activity of seeing and being seen. There were always a few who were hoping to marry him off to their daughters, even though privately they might think of him as something of an oddity. Of all the people present, he had the most patience for the hard-working folk, who well deserved this brief time away from their daily toil. He always made sure that he spent as much time making them feeling welcome as he did talking to the notables.

He had wondered whether Miss Hope might find herself without company, and he had promised himself the pleasure of spending some time with her. Glancing across the lawn, he could see her walking with that effeminate dandy, Roland Berry. Even while he was watching, the young man leaned down to whisper something in Miss Hope's ear which had her laughing in what he considered to be quite an immoderate way. Where upon earth had Evangeline Granby gone? She had been with them a few minutes ago.

'Gabriel, take that scowl off your face, for goodness' sake,' said Lady Agatha, interrupting his thoughts. 'Everyone will think that you do not want them to be here.'

He looked down at her, grinning. 'Heaven forbid,' he replied.

★ ★ ★

Anna had not been at all pleased to be dragged away from Illingham Hall, but upon reflection she had decided that it might be for the best. She had not considered how much she would appear to disadvantage in a gown that she had been wearing to work in, even if half of it had been hidden by an apron for some of the time. The return home would give her a chance to change into another becoming gown, for her mother, despite her tiresome tendency to forget that a female of seventeen was a grown woman, liked to see her family well dressed and was generous with regard to new clothing.

After scolding her for leaving the farm without her mother's expressed permission, her brother David kept quiet as they travelled back in the gig, thus allowing her to think about Gabriel. How handsome and manly he had looked in his shirt sleeves; and what a lovely smile he had given her. It was a smile which seemed to her to speak about the strong bond that there was between them. Of course, he had not had time to take a lot of notice of her that morning. He had been busy, and he had had his aunt to attend to, as well as Miss Hope who was Lady Agatha's goddaughter, and was therefore almost like a cousin to him.

David had been so rude, trying to drag her off like a child, but Gabriel had smiled at her, as if to say that they would be able to spend some time together that afternoon. What if he were to propose that very day? She let out a gasp, and David, who had been thinking about meeting Rachel, the doctor's daughter, turned in surprise and had to give some attention to his horse, which had responded to the change of pressure on the rein.

So wrapped up was she in dreams of

romance that she paid very little heed to the scold that her mother offered for leaving the farm unbidden. Instead, she offered a serene apology and went upstairs to change, prompting Mrs Crossley to say to her husband that in some ways, little Anna appeared to be growing up at last.

When the family eventually set off, it was in the wagon rather than the gig, for not only was the whole family going, but also Lottie the kitchen maid, and Bert, the lad who helped with the horses. The cowman and his wife stayed behind, neither of them being enamoured of social occasions.

Anna very much regretted the indignity of this mode of travel. She would have preferred to arrive in the gig with David; for however disagreeable her brother might be at times, there was no doubt that today he looked the gentleman in his tan-coloured breeches and grey coat. Bundled in the back of the wagon with David, Elijah, Lottie and Bert, she did not feel as if she cut the kind of elegant figure that would make a splash at Illingham Hall.

She was hoping to be able to scramble down and go off on her own to find Gabriel, but Mrs Crossley knew her duty. 'I'm not having you dashing all over the gardens like some kind of romp,' said that lady firmly. 'David, you must look after your sister and make sure she behaves like a lady. Elijah, you're to stay with me and your father, until I give you leave. Bert, you're to look after Lottie. I don't want to hear anything about the behaviour of any of you that will put me to the blush. Now off you go and enjoy yourselves.'

'I hope you're not referring to me, my dear,' said Farmer Crossley, as he offered his wife his brawny arm.

'Give over with you, Tobias,' smiled his wife. 'Well this is very agreeable to be sure,' she went on, looking at the marquees, and the bunting, and the happy smiling faces. 'I feel a little guilty taking a day off, but we work hard the rest of the time, don't we?'

'Aye,' replied her husband smiling back at her. 'As for a day off, there's nobody deserves it more than you, my dear.'

★ ★ ★

The garden party at Illingham Hall was normally an afternoon and evening affair. Plenty of food and drink was provided. No person was told where he might or might not go, but the usual pattern was for the quality to congregate near the house and eat the food that was laid out in the marquee on the lawn outside the drawing-room. The less exalted members of the company tended to take their food from another marquee that was situated further from the house. Ilam, his aunt, and those persons who were easy in any company drifted between the two. In the afternoon, a game of cricket would take place in the field beyond the ha-ha. Those who did not care to watch or take part continued to wander about the gardens, consume the food of his lordship's providing, or repose themselves under the trees.

After the game of cricket was over, there would be a treasure hunt for the children, in which they searched for coloured pottery eggs which had been hidden in the parterre. The child who found the most eggs without pushing — for a careful watch was kept, and unmannerly children were disqualified — received a prize, but all the children who took part were given a shiny sixpence.

Once the treasure hunt was complete, a small band usually played on the lawn, and a few energetic souls usually had a dance or two. No one was told to leave, but after this, people tended to drift away, a good time having been had by all; all, that was, apart from the master of the house. He approved of the tradition, for he knew that it provided much needed diversion for people who worked hard all through the year. If he was honest with himself, however, he found the whole business awkward in the extreme, because he did not really know where he belonged.

Thanks to his father's virtually disowning him in his childhood, he had spent more time with a working family than would normally have been the case for someone of his rank. That experience meant that he had an intimate understanding of the concerns of ordinary folk, and had no difficulty talking with them and even working alongside them.

At the age of thirteen, after some coaching from Dr Littlejohn, he was sent to Harrow. Those first weeks and months until he had established himself had been sheer torture. Some of the boys who already attended the school conducted themselves like little princelings, and seemed to feel that it behoved them to persecute anyone who did not conform to what was expected of them. He never told anyone about the torments that he endured, not even Aunt Bertha, who wrote to him every week, no matter how busy she might be on the farm. He certainly did not inform his father, who occasionally swept into the school grounds tooling his curricle, and bore him off to a local hostelry for an awkward lunch, during which neither of them could find anything much to say.

It had never occurred to Gabriel that his father's appearance at school could have had anything to do with the lessening of his torments, but such was the case. The truth of the matter was that the then Lord Ilam, at a little over thirty years old, was considerably younger and more dashing than any other parent, and was, moreover, an acknowledged leader of the ton. His arrival in style did much to raise his son's credit with his school fellows.

Gabriel's early life on the farm had meant that he was accustomed to physical exertion, and he had gained height and weight earlier than some of his peer group. Swift retaliation over some insult or other earned him a beating or two, but with time he learned to keep his feelings and his temper under control. Meanwhile his formidable inches meant that bullies became wary of him

Gradually, he made friends, choosing as his companions those who proved loyal to him, rather than those who wanted an introduction to the ton through the son of Lord Ilam. It was those friends who helped him through the social pitfalls at Oxford and in London when he visited there, which was as seldom as he could manage.

Thanks to his early upbringing on the one hand, and his school and university life on the other, he had learned to move in two worlds. For the most part, he managed this without any difficulty. The problems rose when his two worlds came together, as they did at the garden party. Then he found himself wondering who he really was and where he belonged. This feeling, which was for the most part a vague sensation of unease, was always at its most acute when the Crossleys arrived. It was then that his two worlds really did collide.

As if this were not awkward enough, Eustacia Hope had pointed out to him that he was not the only one who was confused. If she thought that Anna might have romantic designs upon him, then no doubt others might be thinking the same thing, and that would never do. For one thing it would be damaging to Anna's reputation, and might perhaps keep away some of the sons of farmers, any one of whom would be a suitable match for her. For another, whilst Anna was hero-worshipping her adopted big brother, he might be prevented from fixing his interest with the lady to whom he really was attracted.

Again, his eye was drawn to Eustacia Hope, as she stood talking to Miss Granby. He admired her style of beauty. Her dark hair and eyes seemed full of life and her complexion was charmingly healthy. She was not tall, but her figure was excellent, and her dress sense was superb — unlike that of Evangeline Granby, who was, as usual, tricked out as if she were attending a function graced by royalty. As for her height, she might deplore her lack of inches, but to him she seemed to be exactly the right size.

Miss Hope's manners were good, too. His invitation to her to visit the Crossleys with him had been an impulse of the moment. Her behaviour at the farmhouse had been faultless, neither proud, nor condescending, but friendly and unpretentious. She seemed to have the ability to move between his two worlds.

He recalled the moment when he had gone to Bruno's head and had seen that she was there holding the horse already. Her gown had been stretched tight by the movement and he had been able to appreciate the outline of her excellent bosom. Then she had glanced down at the graze on his chest. Until that moment he had not realized the extent of his dishevelment. She had made as if to reach for her handkerchief and he had thought to himself, *Oh no, if she touches me now I'll be all to pieces.* Then their hands had brushed against one another and he had felt a surge of excitement flood his whole being.

At that moment she turned her head, saw

him and smiled. His heart, normally a very sensible organ, began to beat in thick, heavy strokes. He turned away from a lady and gentleman with a brief 'excuse me' and began to walk towards her. He was still a dozen paces away when he heard his name called, and with a sinking feeling, saw that Anna was hurrying in his direction, closely followed by her brother David.

'Anna, my dear,' he said, putting out his hands to prevent her from throwing herself into his arms. At the same time, he glanced across at Eustacia. He still did not think that she was right, but there was something here that needed nipping in the bud.

'Anna, I told you not to go running off,' scolded David. He made his bow to Ilam. 'I'm sorry, my lord,' he said, 'but you know what she's like.'

'None better,' answered Ilam cheerfully. 'Anna, you're looking very pretty today. Shall we take a little stroll about the garden?' He offered her his arm. She took it, throwing a triumphant smile in David's direction. What would they all say when she was Lady Ilam, she wondered.

David, mindful of his manners, turned to Miss Hope who was standing near by, and asked her if she would like a glass of lemonade. 'Thank you, Mr Crossley,' she replied. 'That would be very welcome.'

Walking with Gabriel between the flower beds and under the trees, Anna was in seventh heaven. When he suggested that they should find somewhere quiet for a little talk, her cup of happiness almost overflowed. It must be that he intended to propose, she told herself. That a man of Ilam's character would never, ever press his suit upon a seventeen year old girl even supposing that he had her parents' consent did not occur to her. She was too lost in her dreams of a rosy future.

Once they were sitting down in a little arbour, well within sight of other people but out of earshot, Gabriel looked at the girl next to him, unsure of how to begin. How could he make his meaning plain without hurting her and damaging their relationship?

It was Anna who spoke first. 'Do you really think my gown is pretty, Gabriel?' she asked him softly.

He cleared his throat. 'Yes, certainly; it makes you look very grown up,' he replied, feeling as if he sounded like a man twice his age.

'I'm seventeen, now.'

'I know — almost a woman.'

This remark did not seem to her to be so promising. 'Some people get married when they are seventeen,' she pointed out.

'You have no plans to get married yet, have you?' he asked, a little startled.

'Not as yet,' she replied demurely, looking at him through her lashes. 'I am waiting for the right man to ask me.'

'Very sensible,' he said, lightly patting her hands as they lay in her lap. 'The right man is worth waiting for. In the meantime, my dear — '

'Yes? In the meantime?' she prompted him eagerly.

'In the meantime, it might perhaps be better if you did not run across the lawn and throw yourself into my arms. To those who are watching, your gesture might be misinterpreted.'

'You mean it might make me look childish?'

'Something like that,' Gabriel agreed, not wanting to explain any further. 'You would not want that right man to catch you acting like a child, would you?'

'No, of course not,' Anna replied looking at him, her eyes glowing.

Gabriel got to his feet. 'I have other guests that I must attend to,' he told her. Then he added in a hearty tone, 'I must not be seen monopolizing one of the prettiest young ladies here, must I?'

'All right, Gabriel,' Anna answered. 'I'll just

stay here for a while.'

She sat and watched him as he walked with long easy strides to greet an old-fashioned-looking clergyman. Of course, he would always do what was right and proper! She sat and thought about what he had said. He thought she looked pretty and grown up. He had not actually said that she was too young to marry and he had commended her plans to wait for the right man. He had even told her to be more circumspect in her behaviour towards him. He could hardly have been more plain!

She left the arbour in a happy dream, and Eustacia had to speak to her twice before she realized that she had been addressed. 'Are you having an agreeable day, Miss Crossley?' Eustacia asked her.

'A wonderful day,' replied Anna, her face aglow. 'The most wonderful day of my life. Oh Miss Hope, I'm so happy!' She scampered away, in hot pursuit of two young ladies of her own age who were standing next to the food tent.

Eustacia looked after her, astonished. She had seen Ilam take Anna on one side, and had assumed that he had been going to speak to her about being more circumspect in her manner towards him. Anna's behaviour seemed rather to suggest that she had received a proposal of marriage, or at any rate something very like it. Again, she felt a sharp stab of jealousy before she recalled that he had described Anna as being like a little sister to him. No doubt he had warned her off so gently that she had completely failed to grasp his meaning!

Ilam was still talking to the clerical gentleman. He turned his head and looked at her for a long moment, then placed his hand under his companion's elbow, and walked with him towards the house. She had just watched them out of sight, and was reprimanding herself for standing so long admiring the length of his lordship's muscular legs and manly stride, when someone caught hold of her arm.

'Eustacia, my dear, have you seen Gabriel?' Lady Agatha was looking as alarmed as her goddaughter had ever seen her. Her hands fluttered restlessly, now clasping at each other, now smoothing her gown. Her eyes did not meet those of Eustacia as she turned her head first one way then the other, trying to discern where her nephew might be.

'He's just gone into the house,' Eustacia replied. 'Have you seen Miss Granby? I promised that I would take a turn with her later.'

'No, I haven't,' replied Lady Agatha

impatiently. 'Was he alone?'

'He had someone with him,' replied Eustacia. 'A clergyman, I think.' Her gaze locked with that of her godmother. 'Oh good God, no,' she exclaimed.

'Yes,' answered Lady Agatha. 'The bishop has caught up with him, and now there will be all hell to pay! Come on!'

'Come on where?'

'Into the house, of course! If the bishop is blackening my name, I want to be there to defend myself.'

16

'What do you mean?' Ilam asked the bishop, drawing his brows together. 'How has my aunt been obstructive?'

'Rather ask, how has she *not* been obstructive!' the bishop replied. He was of medium height with a slight stoop, and plainly dressed, his clerical wig proclaiming his calling. 'She has continued to occupy the vicarage for far longer than would normally have been expected. Mind you, I do not hold back from saying that I blame you for that, my lord, at least in part.'

'Blame me?' echoed Ilam in completely baffled tones.

'To be plain with you, her ladyship has implied that she will have nowhere else to go if she is forced to leave the vicarage,' responded the bishop in blunt tones. 'The church is not in the business of putting people out into the street.'

'Neither am I,' Ilam informed him. 'Despite what you may have been told, my aunt could easily find a home, either with me or on her brother's estate. May I pour you a glass of sherry?'

'Thank you,' the clerical gentleman replied. 'I can see that there is more than one piece of confusion that may need to be sorted out. Talking of Lord Ashbourne — '

'Were we?' murmured Ilam.

'I believe so. I understood from your aunt that he was travelling in Greece and therefore could not be approached, but that he would unhesitatingly support her because her knowledge of local interests would be superior to his.'

Ilam gave a crack of laughter. 'Do you know Lord Ashbourne?' he asked.

The bishop's face stiffened. 'Only by repute,' he answered.

'Then you will be unaware that the only notice that his lordship would take of his sister would be to do the opposite of what she wanted. By the way, he isn't in Greece, he's in Italy. Incidentally, why the deuce haven't you been applying to me? You must know that in his absence I deal with all matters pertaining to the estate.'

The bishop's pale cheeks flushed. 'Her ladyship gave me to understand that as far as you were concerned the church could go hang.'

'Did she indeed?' asked Ilam, his eye kindling.

'Not only that, but she has threatened one

of my priests and offered him physical violence.'

'That would be Lusty, I suppose,' said his lordship.

'That insect!'

The two men turned to where Lady Agatha was standing on the threshold, awesome in her righteous anger.

'Ah, Aunt Agatha,' exclaimed Gabriel, in tones of assumed affability that fooled no one. 'Please come and join us. I am finding out all sorts of interesting things, and am discovering how much wool you have pulled over my eyes.'

'None at all,' responded her ladyship. 'The church is seeing fit to throw me out of my home; my home, Ilam, to which your uncle brought me thirty years ago. In order to do so, it has sent that insect Lusty to do its dirty work. The man would not leave my premises when I asked. How else was I to effect his departure save by throwing him out?'

'My lady, they arc not your premises,' answered the bishop. 'They belong to the church.'

'The church of which my sainted husband was a vicar, and where he remained appointed until the hour of his death,' answered her ladyship. 'He was never relieved of his position. Therefore he is still the vicar in principle and I am still entitled to reside in the vicarage.'

'Balderdash!' exclaimed Ilam. 'My grandfather was Lord Ashbourne and died in that office. That does not mean that he continued to be Lord Ashbourne after his death.'

'He died in the performance of his duties,' insisted Lady Agatha.

'He fell into a newly dug grave on his way back from the vestry having over-indulged in communion wine,' answered Ilam brutally.

Eustacia gasped audibly. 'Lord Ilam, how can you be so brutal?' she demanded.

Ignoring her interruption, he went on. 'Aunt, you are not entitled to be there; and whilst you have been occupying that house illegally, the people of this village have been denied the pastoral care that was their right.'

'That is not true,' his aunt insisted, flushing. 'See if you can find anyone who has been sick who has not received a visit from the vicarage. I defy you to do so.'

'Tom Seppings was like to die last week,' said Ilam quietly. 'He wanted to see a priest. There was none. Luckily he rallied, but what if he had not? And what of Mrs Ross?'

For the first time, Lady Agatha's gaze dropped from his. She walked slowly away from the entrance to the room, and towards a chair, with Eustacia holding her arm.

'I'm all right, child,' said the older lady. 'No doubt these two *gentlemen* will acknowledge your presence in their own good time. Fetch me a glass of sherry, will you?'

'I beg your pardon, ma'am,' said Ilam to Eustacia, inclining his head. 'This is my aunt's goddaughter, Miss Hope,' he told the bishop. 'Miss Hope, this is the Bishop of Sheffield.'

'Ah, this is the young lady who has . . . has suffered a severe disappointment, and is somewhat delicate in health,' said the bishop, his tone dropping and becoming warmer. 'Pray sit down, my dear, and do not fear my clerical attire. I will not do you any harm.'

Ilam gave another crack of laughter. 'Save your sympathy, Bishop,' he said. 'The young lady is in as excellent health as I am.'

'You are very arrogant in your pronouncements, Ilam,' replied Lady Agatha.

'Am I?' he asked quizzically. 'I don't think so. I'm willing to hazard a guess that Miss Hope has not been jilted by a clergyman, or indeed by anyone at all. I don't believe that she's suffered a day's illness in her life. In fact, I am convinced that she is nearly as deeply involved in this matter as are you, Aunt.'

'I have not been jilted by a clergyman,' Eustacia agreed, blushing, 'but — '

'Eustacia has been all that is kind and helpful,' interrupted Lady Agatha, sitting up straight in her chair. It was as if the attack on her goddaughter had put spirit back into her. 'I regret to have to say that she has proved to be far kinder to me than my own nephew. Do not dare to pour scorn upon her misfortune. It was for that reason that her mother sent her to me.'

'And because of Lord Ashbourne's interest in her and concern for her well-being,' the bishop put in helpfully.

'Indeed,' put in Ilam, staring at her for one long moment.

'No indeed,' retorted Eustacia, turning bright red. 'Lord Ashbourne has nothing to do with it.'

'But my lord, I am completely at a loss,' said the bishop in baffled tones after a short pause. 'What is this all about?'

'Have you not realized, even now?' demanded Ilam scornfully. 'My aunt, who is so devious a person that she might give Beelzebub a run for his money, has been bamboozling you from start to finish, and so has the innocent-seeming Miss Hope. She has no right to be in the vicarage and no reason to stay there.'

'Ilam!' exclaimed her ladyship in outraged tones.

'And Lord Ashbourne and his concern for the young lady's condition?' enquired the bishop. Deathly silence fell as the implication of his words sank in.

'I do not have any condition,' exclaimed Eustacia, her voice trembling.

'No, no, of course not, my dear young lady,' declared the bishop hastily, drawing out his handkerchief and mopping his brow. It was his turn to go red. 'No one would dream of thinking it.'

'Of course not, my dear,' added Lady Agatha soothingly.

'Judging by her evident talent for scheming, I would have said that anything was possible,' Ilam drawled. Eustacia looked at him. He was leaning negligently against the table in the centre of the room with his legs crossed and his arms folded and one brow slightly raised. In that moment, he was the image of his father. She walked across to him, drew back her arm and slapped him hard across the facc. Then, amid horrified exclamations from Lady Agatha and the bishop and a hastily repressed oath from Lord Ilam, she gathered her skirts and ran out of the room.

She had not gone very far when she heard footsteps behind her. Then she felt her arm being seized, and turning, she found herself facing the viscount. He looked furious, an expression which was accentuated, if anything, by the red mark on his cheek.

'No you don't,' he said in minatory tones.

'How dare you! Let go of me!' she demanded.

'Not until I've had my say. I know that my aunt is not the most truthful of people — '

'An understatement if ever there was one,' Eustacia interjected, shaking her arm. Now, he did release her.

'But I had thought better of *you*,' he went on, as if she had not spoken. 'I was told you had had your heart broken by a clergyman and this is now revealed to be untrue. I've also been told that you were ill, and that, too, has been proved to be a lie. Nor are you the impoverished young woman that rumour has reported you to be. Instead, I find that you are aiding my aunt in her unprincipled deception of the church and the bishop.'

'That isn't fair,' Eustacia retorted. 'I didn't tell you any of those lies.'

'Didn't you? What about fainting in my presence?'

She stared at him, blushing. She had forgotten that. 'I didn't set out to deceive you,' she protested in a small voice.

'Perhaps not; but you could have sought me out at any time, and told me the truth.

Why did you not do so?'

'I was going to,' she told him. When he looked doubtful, she added, 'It's true. I was going to, but at first . . . '

'Well?'

She looked down. 'I didn't think it mattered,' she replied. 'You annoyed me and I wanted to get my own back. Anyway, I thought it was just a game.'

There was an ominous silence. 'A game? To deny the villagers the spiritual guidance and solace to which they are entitled? How old are you, Miss Hope? I thought that you were a grown woman, but you seem to me to have been behaving in as childish a fashion as . . . as Anna.' She did not answer him, but hung her head instead. 'Now, if you'll excuse me, I have a cricket match to take part in. You know about cricket, don't you, Miss Hope? It's a game in which there are rules, in order to ensure fair play.' So saying, he turned on his heel and left her.

She did not head for the garden. It was full of people and her emotions were so jumbled up that she had no desire to confront anyone at that moment. The door by which she had left the room gave onto a corridor, at the end of which was a flight of stairs. She ran up to the next landing, turned to the left, and more by luck than by good judgement, found

248

herself in the passage that led to her room. She went inside, shut the door and sat down on the bed. She felt she needed a time of quiet reflection so that she could recover her composure after the awful scene that had just taken place.

How she wished now that she had made more of an effort to speak to Ilam and explain things. Of course he had a right to be angry. She had put him into a most awkward position, but she had to admit that although the confrontation had been unpleasant, she was glad that Ilam now knew the truth. He had also discovered it in a way that had meant that she had not had to betray Lady Agatha. She would be able to stay in the village; except for the fact that Ilam's disapproval might now make that impossible.

She would have liked to go straight back to the vicarage, and would have done so but for two considerations. The first was that she had no intention of allowing Ilam to think that he had intimidated her. The second was that it would be a shockingly disloyal act towards her godmother. She would just have to endure the day as best she might; and to think that she had been so much looking forward to it!

She felt her heart sink right down into her sandals. She could not delude herself. He could be as angry as he pleased. He might even make her just as angry in return. It did not alter the way that she felt about him. Thinking about that made her realize that there was another reason for staying; he might seek her out and forgive her.

★ ★ ★

By the time Eustacia had composed herself sufficiently to come outside and rejoin the company, most of those who had come to the garden party had already gathered to watch the cricket match. This took place on one of the fields just beyond the ha-ha. Lord Ilam captained one of the teams, and the other was led by Mr Granby who, apart from his sentimental approach to his daughter, whom he always addressed as angel, my precious, or something similar, seemed to be a very sensible man.

The game was already underway, Mr Granby having won the toss and chosen that his team should be the first to bat. Eustacia looked round for her godmother and found her sitting on a chair in the sun. She opened her sunshade and sat down next to her.

'Are you all right, my dear?' asked her ladyship quietly. 'I declare I could murder my nephew after the things he said!'

'He wasn't very polite,' Eustacia agreed.

'Polite? I've never heard anything so rude. His insinuations about you and Ashbourne were quite unforgivable, and so I told him.'

'What did he say?'

'Nothing much. He ran after you moments later. I don't suppose it was to apologize?'

'No, it wasn't,' Eustacia answered. She would have liked to ask if the late vicar had indeed perished in the manner in which Ilam had described, but she did not know how to approach the subject. Perhaps she would ask Trixie to find out later.

At that moment, Ilam came running in to bowl to Mr Granby, who looked quite menacing, bat in hand. 'Good,' said her ladyship fiercely. 'I hope he knocks his block off. Call himself a nephew! Judas is what *I* would call him.'

Glancing round hastily, Eustacia saw with some relief that no one else was sitting near them. She was glad that her aunt had regained her customary self-possession. She had been rather anxious when Lady Agatha had asked for a glass of sherry when Ilam had confronted her in the house. For the first time since Eustacia had met her, the vicar's widow had looked old.

In order to divert her thoughts, she tried to concentrate on the game. It seemed as if Mr

Granby had not knocked Lord Ilam's block off. On the contrary, he was having some difficulty in dealing with the ball which his lordship had just delivered.

Eustacia had had the opportunity of watching cricket being played at home, and had never previously taken any interest in it, always thinking it a rather dull game. She could vaguely remember her father trying to explain the rules to her, and they had seemed to her to be impossibly complicated. Even when Morrison had been playing, her only wish had been that he might finish his turn very quickly so that he might sit with her. Never had she gained any pleasure from watching him as she did now from watching Ilam.

As a diversion from her romantic feelings towards his lordship, however, it could not have been said to be entirely successful. The energetic nature of the game meant that those involved were obliged to take off their coats and, if applicable, their waistcoats and cravats. She was therefore treated to the rather distracting sight of Ilam's shirt being moulded to his form by the action of the breeze. She was also able to observe the ripple of the muscles in his thighs as he ran forward in order to propel the ball in Granby's direction.

At that point, a particularly fine delivery on his lordship's part knocked the stumps behind Mr Granby clean out of the ground. A cheer went up from the viscount's side, and Granby left the field looking rueful. Ilam's face was lit up by a broad grin, and as Eustacia looked at him, he turned his head and their eyes met for a brief instant. It was a moment or two before the smile died out of his eyes. He looked at her for a little longer, then turned away. Suddenly, she felt very hot. 'Godmama,' she asked, 'do you mind if I go and sit in the shade?'

Her godmother looked at her, frowning. 'You are a little flushed. Run along. As you see, Dr Littlejohn is now coming to join me, so I shan't be alone.'

She walked to the nearest clump of trees, where Anna Crossley was sitting with two or three other girls of her own age. They were clearly listening avidly to what she had to say, but when Eustacia approached, they all fell silent. She did not make the mistake of supposing that they had been talking about her. Given Anna's infatuation, she was sure that the girl had been regaling them with her dreams about Ilam. She had met them briefly earlier on in the day and now asked if they minded if she joined them.

They willingly assented and made space for

her on the rug on which they were sitting. Eustacia deliberately sat so that she could not easily see the play without turning her head. Anna was facing her, and was therefore able to look her fill at Lord Ilam without turning her back on her companions.

Both of Anna's companions looked at Eustacia with unconcealed admiration. She was older than all of them by at least three years. Add to that the fact that thanks to Lady Hope, her outfit was both summery and stylish, and she became a person well worth cultivating.

'Miss Hope,' began one of Anna's companions, 'have you been to any weddings recently?'

Suppressing the urge to say 'Only my own,' Eustacia answered 'Not very recently, no.'

'We were just wondering what brides are wearing at the moment,' said the same girl, whilst the other one giggled.

'Why? Is there to be a wedding around here?' Eustacia asked.

'Maybe,' said the giggling girl.

Anna frowned at her two friends. 'I don't actually know of one,' she said with dignity.

'But there *might* be one,' added the girl who had just spoken.

'Oh do hold your tongue, Susan,' said Anna firmly. 'Miss Hope, do they play cricket where you come from?'

Her words and expression made it sound as if Eustacia must, at best, come from some outlandish and probably primitive country on the other side of the world, or at worst from a very distant planet or possibly the moon.

Eustacia answered her question politely, but inside, her mind was seething. About whose wedding had they been speaking? No one was due to get married, were they? Their general demeanour confirmed Eustacia's earlier opinion, namely that Ilam had been so gentle in his conversation with Anna that she had completely failed to grasp what he was trying to tell her. She felt her heart sink. She really must speak to him again, before Anna said so much that she made a fool of herself. The only trouble was, he had not received her first attempt at raising the subject of Anna's infatuation very well. Then she had slapped his face and that awful scene had ensued. He would not be very likely to listen to her now.

After the conversation had limped along for a short time, Anna said 'Shall we stroll about a little? I'm getting tired of sitting in one place. Will you join us, Miss Hope?'

Her two friends obediently got up, and turning, Eustacia was not surprised to observe that Lord Ilam had ceased bowling and had retreated well away from them in order to take his turn retrieving the ball on the other side of the pitch. She had no wish to look as if she were pursuing him around the field, so she declined Anna's invitation and instead went to see if she could help those who were hiding the pottery eggs.

Thanks to a little confusion over whose task it was this year, the job had not been completed, and her offers of help were greeted with grateful thanks. After the busyness of the morning preparations, the need for company manners as she greeted many acquaintances, and the disturbing nature of her encounter with Lord Ilam, a task which involved nothing more testing than hiding pottery eggs amongst the vegetation was very much to her taste. Consequently, by the time childish voices were heard as they approached the parterre, she was feeling very much more at ease.

The cricket match was not a long affair, and after Lord Ilam's team had emerged the winner — by only a mere handful of runs — everyone wandered over to observe the treasure hunt, or to wait for the band to start to play. Young Elijah Crossley was an enthusiastic participant in the treasure hunt, and some of those who joined in were very much the same age as Anna Crossley. Indeed, her two friends were not above participating, even if they did proclaim themselves to be helping the giggling girl's younger sister. One of them cried out in triumph as loudly as any ten year old when she located one of the better hidden eggs, and Eustacia liked her the better for it. She noticed that Anna carefully edged through the group of observing adults in order to get nearer to Lord Ilam. In the meantime, her brother David, watching her movements, was clearly intending to head her off.

Soon the treasure hunt was over, and people began to gather on the lawn to listen to the band and then to make their farewells. The musicians struck up with a country dance, and Ilam began the proceedings by leading his aunt out to take a few steps. Either they had made up their differences, or they were putting up a very good front, Eustacia decided as she accepted an invitation from a Mr Percy, a landowner from the next village.

'Your first affair of this kind, Miss Hope?' Percy asked as they waited their turn at the bottom of the set.

'It's not the first garden party I have attended, but I have not been to one here before,' she replied.

'Oh, they're always big affairs. Mind you, I suspect Ilam doesn't enjoy them above half.'

'Really?' enquired Eustacia, who had her own reasons for suspecting that he hadn't enjoyed this one.

'Oh, he does his duty, and all that,' replied Percy. 'Look at him now; plenty of pretty girls around, but he'll only dance with his aunt.'

'Indeed?' murmured Eustacia, wanting to vary her responses.

'Oh yes. He never dances with anyone else. If you ask me, he'll be glad to see the back of us.'

When the dance was concluded, Ilam led his aunt to one of the chairs that had been set around the grassy area at the foot of the terrace, on which the band had set up their instruments. Eustacia could see that Anna was rejecting an invitation to dance, and looking hopefully in his lordship's direction. Perhaps earlier in the day she, too, might have hoped for an opportunity to dance with him; but not now. She had had enough of the day, and would have been glad to go home with Trixie who was saying farewell to a wiry-looking lad from one of the farms. Unfortunately, she could not leave without telling her aunt, and she would not approach her because Ilam was standing behind her chair. It was not that she was nervous, she told herself stoutly; she was just very unsure of her welcome at present.

She drifted away from the dancers and wandered into the house, quite unaware that she was observed. There were a few servants about, and one or two guests talking quietly, but no one appeared to take any notice of her. She found a candle and wandered upstairs. After going through two or three rooms and crossing another small landing, she found herself, by a strange quirk of fate, to be yet again in the little room which housed the portrait of Lord Ashbourne.

She recalled the lie that her godmother had told about Ashbourne's interest in her, and Gabriel's insinuations about a possible relationship with his father. She stared up at the painted face. She had never even met the man, and he had caused her nothing but trouble.

'You, my lord, are exceedingly tiresome,' she told him wearily. 'As for your wretched son, I would very much like to push him into his own stupid fountain, because he is just as tiresome as you are.'

'I'm obliged to you, ma'am,' said Ilam grimly from the other entrance. 'I might have guessed you would come here.'

She jumped as he spoke. He had appeared noiselessly, and, moreover, she had assumed him to be outside with his aunt. 'Oh, might you? Well, I can assure you that it was a complete surprise to me for I arrived here entirely by chance,' Eustacia answered, colouring a little because he had overheard her saying that she wanted to push him into the fountain.

'You'll allow me to keep to my own opinion on that matter,' his lordship replied.

'Well, I suppose I had better do so, even if it is a completely stupid opinion,' Eustacia replied. 'As a matter of fact, I came up here to get away from people, not to be pursued by . . . by — '

'You don't need to say any more,' replied Ilam suavely. 'Your destination tells its own tale.' He glanced up at his father's picture.

'Oh, for goodness' sake,' Eustacia began.

'The first time I saw you, you had laid flowers before his picture,' Ilam interrupted.

'No I hadn't. I put them there by accident.'

Ilam laughed. 'A fine story,' he declared. 'I wouldn't be surprised if you came here quite deliberately, hoping to meet him, as I had assumed originally.'

'I certainly did not,' retorted Eustacia indignantly, turning quite pink. 'I do not go running round throwing myself at men.'

They stared at each other. Up until now the air had been filled with fury. Now it seemed to crackle with tension of quite another kind.

'No, you place flowers beneath their portraits instead. Don't try to deny your interest in him. Remember that I heard you quizzing Aunt Bertha about him. This is not the first time that I have found you sighing over his picture. God Almighty, I have even had you defend him to my face!' His voice had risen during this speech. Now, he made a perceptible attempt to pull himself together, and went on in a calmer manner. 'I am well aware that your mother was pursued by my father and in your eyes he must have acquired an aura of glamour. Believe me, Miss Hope, you are far from the first to be captivated by his charms.'

'Ooohh!' Eustacia made an infuriated sound which was something between a growl and a scream. She looked around for something to throw at him, failed to find anything and eventually resorted to seizing hold of his coat and attempting to shake him. 'For the thousandth and what I hope will be the last time, although somehow I doubt it, I do not know your father, I have never met your father, I have no desire to meet your father, and *I do not find your father attractive!*'

''Methinks the lady doth protest too much',' Ilam quoted softly.

With a squawk of rage, Eustacia tugged hard at his coat once again, and this time, whether because she tugged harder or because he chose to give way at that moment,

261

she succeeded in pulling him down so that his face was close to hers. This proximity was so unexpected that she was taken completely by surprise, and therefore acted without thinking. Recalling the incident afterwards, she decided there could be no other way of accounting for it, for she took a deep breath, and kissed him full on the mouth.

His lordship did not respond by taking her in his arms, but he did not pull away either. When Eustacia drew back, the enormity of what she had done swept over her and she felt herself turning bright red.

Ilam stared down at her for a long moment. 'I think you've made your point,' he said, his voice sounding very quiet.

Before either of them could speak, or do anything, they heard the sound of footsteps in the passage, and a footman appeared with the message that Lady Agatha was now ready to leave.

'Allow me to escort you downstairs, Miss Hope,' said Ilam, politely making way for her, then giving her his arm the length of the long gallery. They were both silent, each lost in thought.

As they made their way into the garden, Ilam said, 'Believe me, Miss Hope, this conversation is very far from finished.'

Eustacia watched him as he exchanged a

few words with his aunt before their departure. She thought about how *she* had kissed *him* — and it had undoubtedly been she who had kissed him, not the other way round. She began to feel hot at the very thought; and not entirely from embarrassment. What would everybody think if she ran to him now and planted another kiss upon his lips? What would it be like to be pulled into his arms and enfolded in his powerful embrace? She was sure it would be powerful. His arms were so strong and muscular. Involuntarily she gave a little shiver.

How could she have been so unprincipled and vulgar, she asked herself. He had accused her of running after Lord Ashbourne. She had not done that, but she had behaved in just the kind of way that some female in pursuit of a notorious rake might be expected to conduct herself. It was high time she exercised a little more control.

That, she had found, was a good deal easier to say than to do. Quite recently, she had been afraid that he might have guessed that she was attracted to him. Now, the situation was infinitely worse, for she was in love with Lord Ilam, and thanks to the shameless way in which she had kissed him, he probably knew that as well.

17

When Ilam arrived at the vicarage the following day, hoping for private words with his aunt and with Eustacia, he found that at least half-a-dozen persons had arrived and were cluttering up her ladyship's drawing-room. Now that many people had returned from London, and marked their presence by their attendance at the garden party, it seemed that at least half of them wanted to pay their respects to Lady Agatha who, after all, was Ashbourne's sister. Lady Agatha had her own reasons for wanting to avoid a tête-à-tête with her nephew, so she made no effort to see him on his own.

Eustacia, too, was much occupied, though not by her own design. Miss Granby appeared with two other young ladies, and all three of them wanted to discuss the garden party in detail as well as the forthcoming ball at the Olde Oak.

'What are you going to wear, Miss Hope?' asked Miss Barclay, one of the two. A slender, brown-haired young woman of about the same height as Eustacia, she spoke in rather a breathless voice.

'Yes, do say,' said the other newcomer. She was about the same height as Miss Granby, but with darker hair and prominent features. 'Evangeline tells us that you are very stylish, despite never having been to London.'

'Why do you not take the young ladies up to your room?' suggested Lady Agatha. 'Then you will be able to show them what you plan to wear.' After Eustacia had shown them her gown, which was yet another item from her trousseau, they seemed to want to examine every piece of clothing in her possession.

Later, as they descended the stairs, Miss Granby encouraged Miss Barclay and the other young lady, Miss French, to go on ahead. 'Come and take a turn with me in the garden,' said Miss Granby under her breath. 'I have something very exciting to relate.'

As they reached the bottom of the stairs, the two other young ladies entered the drawing-room and Eustacia could see that Lord Ilam was in there. He glanced up, and their eyes met. She paused briefly, but then Miss Granby pulled at her arm and said, 'Do come on. I must talk to you in private.'

Eustacia acknowledged his look with an inclination of her head, and hoped that he realized she was already committed to Miss Granby for the time being. She did not know whether to be glad or sorry. Part of her longed to speak to him, even if he wanted to reprimand her again. On the other hand, part of her dreaded the next meeting because of her brazen behaviour towards him.

'Ah, that's better,' said Miss Granby. 'I didn't want to speak in front of Amy Barclay. If you tell her anything, you've told the entire village.'

'I'm glad you consider me a safe confidante,' answered Eustacia. 'What is it you want to tell me?'

Evangeline waited until they were well out of earshot and said, 'Do you recall that I told you about a certain gentleman who attracted my interest whilst I was in London?'

Eustacia nodded. 'Well he is definitely coming to the ball. He wrote me a letter telling me so.'

'He wrote you a letter?' Eustacia repeated, reflecting that she had never received a letter from a single gentleman, even from Morrison when they were engaged.

'You are thinking that Mama would have wanted to read it,' answered Evangeline carelessly, as if she could guess her thoughts. 'Mama never interferes in my correspondence. I would not permit it. Anyway, he is coming, and I shall have a chance to see whether I like him as well as I did in London. It will make my life a lot easier, though, if you

266

say that you know him or are acquainted with his family. Mama thinks that you are the model of a well-brought-up young lady, and if you say that your family approves of him, or something like that, then she will not make a fuss, and that will make my life a lot easier.'

At this, Eustacia could feel her heart sinking down into her boots. More intrigue! What had she done to deserve this? 'Evangeline, I don't see how I can,' she answered. Then, when Evangeline looked mulish, she said craftily, 'Your mama is aware that I have lived a very quiet life and never been anywhere. She will want to know how on earth I came to be acquainted with him — especially if he lives in Town.'

'He doesn't live in Town all the time,' answered Evangeline. 'His parents have an estate somewhere in the far North of England. Please help me,' she went on in the same sort of wheedling voice that Eustacia had sometimes heard her use with her father.

'We'll see,' temporized Eustacia, feeling a strong sense of kinship with Mrs Granby. She knew she was being weak, but she could not face making anyone else angry at the present time. 'The most I will promise to do is to say that I don't know anything against him.'

'Well I suppose that that will have to do,'

replied Evangeline. Her tone reminded Eustacia very much of that of her music teacher at school on those occasions when she had not found enough time to practise before her lesson.

By the time they got back indoors, Ilam had gone.

'He barely had a chance to exchange a single word with me,' Lady Agatha said gleefully after the visitors had all gone and they were both sitting down to luncheon.

'Did he say that he wanted to see me?' asked Eustacia, trying to sound casual.

'He did make an enquiry, but I managed to brush him off,' said her ladyship in satisfied tones.

Eustacia laid down her fork. 'Ma'am, do you think that perhaps it might be time to enlist Lord Ilam's help?'

'His help?'

'In resolving the problems concerning your living quarters,' answered Eustacia measuring her words carefully. 'After all, he now knows about your plans . . . ' she allowed her voice to tail off delicately.

Suddenly Lady Agatha looked rather weary. 'Yes, you do not need to tell me that. Of course Ilam will side with the church. I suppose I should not be surprised, when I consider that his half-brother is a clergyman.'

'A clergyman!' exclaimed Eustacia.

Lady Agatha gave voice to a brief laugh. 'Ironic, isn't it?'

'Was it his own decision to enter the church?' Eustacia asked curiously.

'I've no idea,' replied Lady Agatha. 'Anyway, to get back to Ilam, he may support the bishop, but he won't see me without somewhere to live.' She looked about her and uttered a heartfelt sigh. 'I suppose I always knew that I would have to leave this place. I just wanted to put it off for as long as possible. It can be rather a dull existence here, you know. A fight with the church provided me with a little sport.'

Eustacia reflected that this was yet another piece of information that she would not be passing on to her mother. It occurred to her, however, that Lord Ilam might be the very man to provide his aunt with some kind of occupation which might give her talent for scheming and planning an opportunity to flourish in a legitimate manner.

As for his attitude to herself, though, that might be a different matter. He knew his aunt and all her foibles, and would doubtless forgive her. What would be his attitude to her goddaughter?

She was soon to have her answer. That afternoon, while Lady Agatha was busy with her correspondence, Lord Ilam returned. 'I didn't manage to speak to you this morning, and very much wanted to,' he said to Eustacia after Grimes had shown him into the drawing-room. 'May we talk now?'

'I don't know,' Eustacia replied, recalling all that had happened on Saturday. She took a few steps away from him, then turned to face him. 'Are you going to talk, or will you shout at me again?'

'I wasn't shouting, I was raising my voice,' he replied.

'That's what men always say,' she retorted.

'You knowing so many,' he murmured.

'There is no need to talk in that kind of sarcastic way,' she told him. 'In any case, you cannot go round implying that I do not know any men, when just a short time ago you have been harbouring improper suspicions with regard to your father and myself.'

He flushed. 'Improper and reprehensible,' he acknowledged. 'Forgive me. My only excuse is that I am so used to imagining the worst about Ashbourne's behaviour. If it is any consolation to you, I would only ever have supposed you to be a victim.'

'That's very kind of you, but it does make me sound a little pathetic.'

He laughed. 'I apologize for that too.'

'Perhaps none of us can ever look at our

parents' behaviour in an unbiased manner,' she suggested.

'Or even our aunts' behaviour. There is one aspect of my aunt's schemes that I would like to ask you about; and that is why you ever allowed yourself to become embroiled in them.'

'I'm truly sorry for that,' she told him sincerely. 'There is very little excuse for me. I know how important a parish priest is to his people. I hardly knew Lady Agatha when I arrived, and as a guest in her house, I wanted to please her.'

'Well yes, but — '

'There is another reason.' She told him about how she suspected that Lady Agatha's friendship with Claire Delahay had damaged her reputation. 'So you see, I owe her a good deal on my mother's behalf, as well.'

'I see what you mean,' he agreed, 'although I think that my aunt always was the mistress of her own destiny. You must not make yourself responsible for the consequences of her actions. However, I do understand your motives better, now.'

'I hope you will believe me to be guilty of thoughtlessness rather than of deliberate malice.'

'I couldn't ever believe you to be malicious,' was his reply. He looked at her steadily, and said, 'Did anyone tell you yesterday how lovely you looked in that gown?'

'Possibly,' she replied airily. 'One amongst the many men of my acquaintance must have said something.'

He stepped a little closer and caught hold of her hand. 'Forgive me; I don't have Ashbourne's facility for flattering the opposite sex.'

'I've no particular desire for flattery, my lord,' she answered, feeling a little breathless at his touch. At that moment, she heard Lady Agatha's footsteps as she came back towards the parlour.

Ilam heard them too. He glanced round swiftly at the direction from which they came, and added in a low tone, 'Then let me offer you a home truth. To me, you were the loveliest woman present, and if we were sure of not being interrupted, I would return that kiss with interest.'

When Lady Agatha appeared in the doorway, Ilam said, 'Forgive my returning so soon, but I wanted to ask Miss Hope if she would honour me with a dance at the ball.' He turned to Eustacia, who had half turned away from the door so that her godmother would not see her blushing at Ilam's audacious words. 'What do you say, ma'am?

Will you dance the first dance with me at the Olde Oak on Thursday?' He was still holding her hand.

She looked up at him. The echo of the last words he had spoken before Lady Agatha came in seemed to hang in the air. 'Thank you, my lord, I would like it of all things,' she said as he raised her hand to his lips.

18

The ball at the Olde Oak was due to take place on the Thursday of that week. Unlike the garden party, it would not attract attendance from the whole village, but many of the farming families would be invited. Eustacia knew that Anna Crossley would be there, and she very much wanted to warn Ilam to be on his guard before the young girl had a further opportunity of making a fool of herself and perhaps exposing herself to the ridicule of her friends. She knew that she really ought to have spoken to him about the matter when he had visited the rectory, but his remark about wanting to return her kiss had driven everything else out of her mind. Even if the subject had occurred to her, she admitted to herself that she would have found it difficult to raise it. She would not have wanted to destroy this rapport which had sprung up between them and which seemed to promise so much more.

She had only one other opportunity of speaking with Ilam before the ball, but the circumstances of their meeting — in the village street, whilst she was walking with

Miss Barclay and he was on horseback, ready for a journey — meant that there was no possibility of private conversation. A little discreet enquiry revealed the fact that he had gone to Ashbourne on a matter of business.

'He wants to pack me off to the dower house,' Lady Agatha told her in long-suffering tones. 'I expect he's gone to make arrangements.'

'Has he said so?' Eustacia asked curiously.

'Not in so many words,' answered her godmother, 'but there's nowhere else he can put me. I shall be bored out of my skull and shall probably take to low intrigue in order to entertain myself.'

Thinking of the deceit in which she had found herself embroiled since her arrival, Eustacia barely repressed a shudder.

*   *   *

Despite the anxieties that hovered at the back of her mind, however, Eustacia found herself preparing for the ball on Thursday with a fair degree of excitement. It would after all be the first such event for some time that she had attended as an unattached young lady. She had been aware that several young men had been eyeing her with interest at the garden party. Such interest could not help but increase her self-esteem which had taken something of a battering through Morrison's defection.

It was not of any of those young men that she was thinking as she got ready, however, but of Gabriel. If she were honest with herself, she had not really stopped thinking about him since the moment when she had realized that she was in love with him. Unfortunately, although he had made it clear that he desired her, she had no idea whether he returned her feelings. What made the whole business worse was that since she had had no opportunity to talk to him about Anna, she would have to try to do so tonight. Then, he would probably think that she was just making up excuses to find a reason for pursuing him. The forthcoming evening seemed to be likely to provide a large number of opportunities for her to embarrass herself.

Still, she reflected, as she surveyed her reflection after Trixie had finished getting her ready, she would at least look her best. Her gown was of a dusky raspberry shade, cut low and trimmed with floss of the same colour. Around her neck was a fine string of pearls which had been presented to her by her father on her eighteenth birthday. Her hair shone with copper lights, and Trixie's clever fingers had contrived a dainty head dress of pink and white flowers and seed pearls.

When she entered the drawing-room, her godmother, who was dressed regally in purple satin trimmed with black lace, eyed her with approval. 'Claire always did have good taste;' she said. 'Come along now. The carriage is at the door.'

Gabriel was walking that evening, but he had sent his carriage for their use. It did seem a little strange to be going in the carriage to the inn down the road, when Eustacia walked more than that distance every fine day, but as Lady Agatha said, it was no good arriving at a ball with muddy shoes and dirty hems and neither lady wanted to appear in pattens before the quality of Derbyshire.

The Olde Oak was a handsome timbered building, constructed in the late sixteenth century. For much of the time, it was larger than the needs of the village warranted, having a handsome upstairs room that was only suitable for large gatherings. On an occasion like this, however, it was felt to be the ideal place. Illingham Hall, of course, had a gallery that was even bigger, and would also have been appropriate, but tradition dictated that as the garden party was hosted by Lord Ilam, the ball should not be his responsibility as well.

On entering the upstairs room at the inn,

the ladies from the vicarage noticed that the landlord must have put in every effort to make the place look its best. There were flowers arranged in pedestals at each end of the room, plenty of candles made everything look bright and cheerful, and the furniture and panelling shone with the effects of copious amounts of beeswax.

A number of people were already present and the members of the small orchestra, assembled at one end of the room, were trying out various melodies and tuning their instruments. A quick glance around the room assured Eustacia that neither Anna nor Ilam had yet arrived. She joined her aunt as they chatted with some of the other guests, and tried not to look as if she was waiting for someone. She knew that Ilam would arrive soon because he had asked to have the first dance with her. Almost certainly, Anna would insist on arriving at the beginning of the event as well. Perhaps, she thought, she could flirt outrageously with Ilam in front of the younger girl. After the conversation that she had had with him at the vicarage, she felt that he just might respond. The idea made her feel rather excited.

By the time the dancing was due to begin, the room was quite full. There were chairs placed around the edge so that those who were not dancing could sit and talk. Drinks were available in a small room which opened to one side, and refreshments were to be served downstairs in a large dining-room at the back of the inn. Eustacia had attended similar local events near her home, and it seemed to her that everything had been arranged very well. Certainly all those who were arriving seemed prepared to enjoy themselves. She knew that a number of them had only lately arrived from London, and were accustomed to attend this event on a regular basis, so she felt sure that the standard of the entertainment and catering would be high.

A burst of masculine laughter from the doorway drew her eye, and she saw that Lord Ilam had arrived and was exchanging a laughing comment with two other gentlemen who Eustacia knew had but lately arrived from town. They were both dressed very stylishly in knee breeches, white stockings and dance pumps. Their linen was snowy white, and their coats — one blue, one black, fitted their shoulders without a crease.

Eustacia was accustomed to seeing Ilam striding about his acres or ready for riding, in serviceable boots, and a coat cut for comfort rather than fit. Tonight, dressed similarly to his companions, but in a coat of rich midnight blue, and with his hair shining in the candlelight, he looked as fine as any London beau, and he almost took her breath away.

Perhaps something caused him to be aware of her scrutiny, for at that moment, he turned his head and looked at her, laughter dying out of his eyes. She smiled and dropped a small curtsy. He inclined his head in acknowledgement, and excused himself to his companions before walking towards her. She had seen him stride hastily, even impatiently at times. Tonight, he seemed to prowl towards her like a great cat, and for a moment, she felt an absurd urge to scurry away into the nearest corner.

Before she could do any such thing, or he could draw close enough to speak to her, Anna Crossley, who had also just arrived accompanied by her brother and another lady, intercepted him, tucking her hand in his arm. Dressed in white muslin, she was looking remarkably pretty. 'Gabriel,' she said smiling. 'You're very grand.'

'Thank you,' Ilam replied. 'You're looking attractive too, Anna.' He took hold of her hand, gave it a little squeeze and disengaged himself, before turning to Eustacia. 'Good evening, Miss Hope,' he said, bowing again. 'I trust that you are feeling strong enough for our dance.'

'I trust so, Lord Ilam,' Eustacia answered demurely.

She turned to Anna and was about to greet her, not yet having spoken to her that evening, when Anna said to the viscount pleadingly, 'You will dance with me, too, won't you?'

'I can't dance with you both at the same time,' Ilam answered playfully.

'No, but later,' Anna persisted.

'My dear Miss Crossley, it really isn't done to seem too eager,' Eustacia put in, anxious to preserve the girl from exposing herself further. 'It makes the gentlemen far too conceited.'

'But . . . ' Anna began. What she might have been about to say was lost as the music began.

'I'll see you later, Anna,' said Ilam. 'At the moment, I am promised to Miss Hope.'

Anna's face brightened. 'All right,' she said, scampering off the floor.

'I suppose that I am rather late in admitting it, but it seems that you were right and I was wrong,' said Ilam, as they took their places. 'How could I have been so obtuse?'

The movements of the dance separated them for a time. Eustacia noticed that her partner was frowning over the difficulty in which he now found himself.

'Lord Ilam, I believe you ought to smile,' Eustacia suggested, when she was next able to speak to him. 'People will be wondering what I have said to make you look so displeased.' Instantly, his expression lightened, and the next time they took hands to go down the set, he showed every evidence of being in an excellent humour. 'You weren't being obtuse,' she assured him. 'I believe that you know her so well that it was difficult for you to perceive that she had begun to see you as something other than an older brother.'

'Yes, you are right,' he answered ruefully. 'The devil of it is, I *am* fond of her, and I really don't want to hurt her. I'll just have to break it to her gently.'

'Forgive me, my lord, but have you not tried to do that already?'

He grinned. '*Touché*, Miss Hope. How do you contrive to be right so often?'

'By constant practice; but I do have a natural aptitude,' she replied, as they honoured one another at the end of the dance.

'Baggage,' he said, grinning, as he took her hand to lead her off the floor. 'And now, I am going to take you into a corner and monopolize you.'

Eustacia glanced around and saw that Anna was watching them. 'A very good notion, my lord,' she agreed.

Seeing the direction of her gaze, he smiled down at her. 'That was exactly my view; but not just for that reason. By the way, do you think we might drop this 'my lord-ing' and 'miss-ing'? My name is Gabriel. I would be honoured if you would use it.'

'And you may call me Eustacia, or Stacia if you prefer. What other reason did you have in mind?'

'I'm simply consulting my own preference,' he murmured. 'Could you doubt it? By the way, may I also have the supper dance?'

'Yes of course,' Eustacia replied, feeling absurdly shy.

Soon after this, one of the London gentlemen to whom Gabriel had been talking approached her with Lady Agatha and after being introduced as Mr Wragley, craved permission to lead her into the next dance. Eustacia accepted with pleasure, and discovered Wragley to be an accomplished dancer, light on his feet, and ready to guide his partner expertly through the steps.

'Is this your first visit to Illingham, Miss Hope?' he asked in a light, cheerful voice.

'Yes it is,' Eustacia replied. 'We do not live very far away, so it makes it all the stranger that I have not been to see my godmother here before.'

'Perfectly natural, I would have said,' he replied. 'Take me, for instance. My estate's less than ten miles from the sea. Do I ever go there? Never. Then there's my sister with whom I'm staying at present. She comes to see me two or three times a year. What must she do every time she arrives, but go off and take a look at it.'

Eustacia laughed and agreed that it was strange. Altogether, they had such a pleasant conversation that she was surprised when the music came to an end.

The next dance was claimed by David Crossley and for the fourth she was solicited by the other London gentleman, Sir Brian Millet by name. It really was a delightful evening, she reflected. In fact, it was almost perfect. Then the whole thing was spoiled as she looked across towards the entrance and saw Evangeline Granby coming in, her parents behind her and her hand resting on the arm of Morrison Morrison.

19

She stumbled, and Sir Brian, thinking that she had hurt herself, led her solicitously to the side of the dance floor. Ilam, who had been observing her enjoyment of the evening with mixed feelings, did not see the stumble. He did see the handsome, elegant baronet lead her off the floor, however, and he scowled, causing Lady Gilchrist, with whom he was dancing at the time, to reprimand him for his disagreeable expression.

'I beg pardon, ma'am,' he replied politely, and endeavoured to give his attention to his partner.

'No doubt Miss Hope will be much happier now that her fiancé has arrived,' she observed.

It was Ilam's turn to miss his step. 'Her what?' he demanded.

'Her fiancé,' replied Lady Gilchrist, reflecting that her revenge upon Ilam for his inattention was turning out very satisfactorily.

'When heard you this?' he asked in rather peremptory tones.

'My husband is a distant connection of her father, Sir Wilfred Hope,' she replied. 'Come to think of it, I'm sure that the wedding should have taken place by now. Who do you think cried off?' Ilam merely grunted in response. 'I wonder how happy she will be to see him hanging upon Miss Granby's arm. Do you think there will be a fight? I should so love to see the fur fly.'

Pulling himself together, Ilam said 'I am sure both ladies have too great a sense of decorum, ma'am. By the way, when do you expect to see Sir Philip return?'

Deciding to relent, for after all he was a very striking young man, as well as being from one of the most significant families in the district, Lady Gilchrist allowed him to change the subject. Were the viscount questioned later, however, he would have been quite unable to have given any information with regard to the whereabouts of the dashing lady's husband. Instead, he was thinking about the relationship between Eustacia and the young man who had entered the room with Evangeline Granby.

His aunt had told him that Eustacia had been jilted by a clergyman, but then his aunt had told him a lot of other tarradiddles as well. Could she have been jilted by the handsome young man, whose practised smile and elegant movements reminded him ever so slightly of his father? It had seemed to him, foolishly perhaps, that she had been showing a fondness for him. Certainly his own feelings for her had been growing stronger by the day. Had he only been the means for her to convince herself that she was still desirable after the desertion of the man she really loved, and who might even now be returning to her?

Lady Gilchrist halted in the middle of a lively account of Sir Philip's travels, for once again Ilam was glaring in the direction of Miss Hope. 'Then without more ado, I garrotted the first highwayman, slit the second from his neck to his navel, and allowed the third to have his way with me in the bushes,' she said in matter-of-fact tones.

Ilam's head swivelled back in her direction, a startled look on his face. Lady Gilchrist let out a peal of laughter. 'I wondered what it would take to get you to remember with whom you were dancing,' she said, the laughter still in her eyes but a hint of challenge in her voice.

'I beg your pardon,' he replied. Then he started to grin. 'How intrepid of you, Lady Gilchrist,' he remarked. 'What did you do with him then?'

'What do you think I should have done with him?' she asked provocatively.

'I suppose that would depend on the

prickliness or otherwise of the bushes,' he answered her. They both laughed.

It was very unfortunate that when Sir Brian led Eustacia from the floor, it was in the direction of the Granby party. Evangeline looked flushed and triumphant, and Eustacia could not be in any doubt that Morrison's was the arrival that she had been awaiting with such excitement. It had never occurred to Eustacia that the gentleman in question might be Morrison. After all, there was no reason why it should.

Given the smallness of the gathering, it was almost inevitable that Eustacia and Morrison should meet. In this encounter Eustacia had the advantage, for she had seen him first. When he looked around the room and caught sight of her, his face took on a shocked expression and lost a little colour, whereas she was able to appear calm and composed. This was as well, for Evangeline was looking straight at her, rather than at Morrison.

'I told you that he would be here,' said Evangeline with more than a hint of smugness. 'Eustacia, may I present Mr Morrison to you? Mr Morrison, this is my newest and best friend, Miss Hope.'

'Mr Morrison and I are already acquainted,' replied Eustacia calmly, making her curtsy, before introducing Morrison to Sir Brian, who was still hovering at her elbow.

'You didn't say so,' said Evangeline in surprised tones.

'You didn't mention his name,' replied Eustacia. 'How are your parents, Mr Morrison? Have you seen them recently?'

'No not really,' answered Morrison, still looking very uncomfortable.

At that moment, the dance came to an end, and Evangeline said gaily, 'Come, Mr Morrison, you promised me the first dance.'

'Of course,' replied Morrison with a smile. 'Perhaps Miss Hope will honour me later?'

'Perhaps,' replied Eustacia, adding with a hint of waspishness. 'I may already be engaged.'

She turned away, feeling very shaken despite her calm demeanour. Somehow, seeing Morrison again had brought back all the unpleasant feelings that she had experienced on her wedding day. After exchanging a few words with Mr and Mrs Granby, Sir Brian had left the group in order to join some other gentlemen, and Evangeline's parents followed him. Eustacia looked around for someone to speak to and was in time to see Ilam and Lady Gilchrist standing at the edge of the dance floor, laughing into one another's eyes. Suddenly, she felt very much alone. When Gabriel looked around, he was in time to see her retreating figure heading for the ladies' retiring room.

★ ★ ★

By great good fortune, the room was empty when Eustacia arrived, and she was able to sit down and think about what had just happened. How on earth had such a mischance occurred? Of all the places that Morrison might have chosen to make an appearance, why did it have to be here? What was more, how had he and Evangeline met? It was barely a month since she had left Woodfield Park and that had only been a matter of days after she had been jilted. She could only think that he must have gone straight to London, possibly hoping to purchase his commission. No doubt he had met Evangeline at some social occasion then. He had obviously begun a new romance very quickly.

She realized that had this happened a comparatively short time ago, she would have been distressed about the matter. Now, her chief feeling was one of anger at Morrison, that he should have put her into such an impossible position.

Conventional form dictated that an engagement, once entered into, was almost as binding as a marriage. A man's honour demanded that he should see it through, no matter what his feelings might be. Eustacia had never been entirely convinced of the rightness of that view. She could think of nothing worse than being married to a man who would much rather be somewhere else. In her opinion, the most honourable course would be to tell the other person involved that one's feelings had changed. Only an utter poltroon would leave a woman standing at the altar as Morrison had done.

How would Gabriel have behaved in similar circumstances, she wondered? She was as sure as she could be that he would not have followed Morrison's example. His reaction to his discovery of his aunt's scheming gave added support to that view. Probably that aspect of his nature would mean that he would rather confront the lady concerned than live a lie. One thing was certain. Had it been Gabriel who had failed to marry her and then turned up today she would not be sitting here dry-eyed. The feelings that she now had for him far exceeded the mild inclination that she had felt for Morrison. In fact, she asked herself sternly, why was she wasting her time thinking about Morrison at all when Gabriel was probably out there whispering improper suggestions into Lady Gilchrist's ear?

She was on the point of leaving the room when she paused, struck by a sudden thought. How serious was Morrison in his intentions towards Evangeline? Was this now true love, or was there any chance that he might prove to be a jilt yet again? Miss Granby ought at least to be warned of the possibility. After all she had proved to be an agreeable friend, even if she was rather spoiled.

What should she do? If Lady Agatha had been anything like a responsible older relative ought to be, then she could have asked her advice, but Lady Agatha, vicar's widow though she was, seemed to lack any proper moral sense. Ilam's advice would be good, she was sure. When she thought about asking him, however, she shrank from describing exactly how Morrison had humiliated her. It made her sound so undesirable, and she knew that she did not want to appear to him in that kind of pitiful light.

Suddenly she became conscious that she had been in the room for rather a long time, whilst other ladies had come in and gone out again, some of them eyeing her rather curiously. She wondered how close it was to the supper dance, which she had promised to Gabriel. Coming out of the ladies' room, she walked straight into Morrison Morrison, who seemed to have been hovering in wait for her.

'There you are at last,' he said peevishly. 'I've had the devil of a job making sure that I didn't miss you. What on earth have you been doing in there all this time?'

'That is a most improper question for you to ask,' Eustacia replied indignantly, 'and even if it were not, you have long since forfeited any right to ask me any questions with regard to my whereabouts.'

'All right, all right, there's no need to take on so,' he grumbled, taking her by the arm and pulling her onto the landing so that they could sit on a seat set into a recess in the wall.

'That's an interesting point of view,' she replied, shaking off his hand but going with him none the less. 'I would have thought that I had ample reason for 'taking on' as you put it. What do you want?'

'I only want to talk to you,' he replied, brushing the tails of his coat back before seating himself next to her. She could well understand why Evangeline was so enchanted with him. He was a very handsome young man, she thought dispassionately. He was well turned out in a plum coat and tight-fitting knee breeches, although it seemed to her now that he was a little too slim for her taste. Since he was not in uniform, he had evidently not yet purchased his colours.

She would have liked to say that she would prefer not to exchange another word with him ever again, but that would not have been true. After all, she wanted to find out about his intentions towards Evangeline, and she would rather like to know how long she would be obliged to endure his presence in the neighbourhood. 'Well I'm here,' she said. 'What do you want to say? I can't spare very much time. I'm promised for the supper dance, which can't be long now.'

'I just want to make sure you don't spoil things for me with Evangeline,' he said. 'I think she likes me and I don't want you to put her off.'

'By telling her how you left me at the altar?' Eustacia asked sweetly.

'Oh come now,' he replied in tones of false heartiness. 'It wasn't as bad as that.'

'I beg pardon, but it was exactly as bad as that,' answered Eustacia. 'I have the dust from the church floor on the hem of my wedding gown to prove it.'

He turned pale. 'Oh Lord,' he exclaimed. 'I never thought of that. You mean the lad came to the church? He was supposed to go straight to your house, the silly clunch. You can scarcely blame me for *that*.'

She stared at him aghast, unable to speak

for several moments out of sheer astonishment at his insensitivity. 'It did not occur to you, then, that you might have averted this whole catastrophe if you had simply sought me out and told me plainly the change in your sentiments?'

He coloured and looked down at his hands, clasped between his knees. 'I dared not,' he said. 'There'd have been such a rumpus.'

'There *was* a rumpus; one which you, by great good fortune, were able to avoid.'

'All right all right, you've had your say,' he said wearily. 'Can't we just leave the matter be and get back to what you're going to say to Evangeline?'

'Not yet, I'm afraid,' replied Eustacia. 'There is just one thing that I am waiting to hear from your lips. It's something that is long overdue.'

He looked at her with a puzzled expression on his face, before saying eventually, 'You're expecting me to apologize,' as if the idea had only just occurred to him.

'Personally, I think that that is the least that the lady might expect under the circumstances,' said Ilam as he strolled into view. 'When you jilt the lady you're engaged to, I would have thought that it was obligatory.' Evangeline's hand rested on his arm. Her face was looking rather set.

Morrison sprang to his feet. 'Have you been eavesdropping?' he asked in scornful tones.

'Certainly not,' Ilam replied haughtily. 'This is a public area, open to all. Miss Granby enlisted my help in finding you as you are her partner for the supper dance. I was looking for Eustacia for a similar reason.'

'Who gave you permission to call her by her given name?' Morrison demanded belligerently.

'I did, if it is any business of yours,' Eustacia replied, getting to her feet.

Morrison opened his mouth to speak again, but before he could do so, he was silenced by a ringing slap dealt him by Evangeline. 'How could you?' she demanded furiously. 'How could you jilt my dear Eustacia? To think that I put other gentlemen off for you! Poltroon! Scoundrel!'

'Oh I say, Miss Granby,' cried Morrison, his hand going to his cheek.

'And don't think that you will be welcome in our house after Mama and Papa hear how you have behaved,' she added.

'If you take my advice, Morrison, you'll leave of your own volition,' Ilam advised him. 'If Miss Granby doesn't throw you out, I certainly will.'

Morrison took due note of Ilam's powerful

frame. The viscount topped him by several inches and was broader than he. After one fulminating glance around the group, he made a bow which was commendably dignified under the circumstances. 'I shall go and make my farewells,' he said. 'I'll instruct my servants to remove to an inn in the next village.'

'That will be far enough — for tonight,' Ilam replied, with an ominous smile that did not reach his eyes.

'Evangeline, would you like to sit here with me for a while?' Eustacia asked the other girl after Morrison had left them.

Now that the drama was all over, Evangeline looked much younger and rather forlorn. 'No thank you,' she answered, with more dignity than Eustacia would have expected from the spoiled young woman that she knew her to be. 'I think I will go to the ladies' room for a while to compose myself, until I am sure he has gone.'

'Would *you* like to remain here?' Gabriel asked Eustacia after Evangeline had left them. 'I'm sure that you have no more desire than Miss Granby to see that fellow again. Did it distress you very much to see him?'

Eustacia sat down again. 'No it didn't distress me, precisely,' she told him. 'I was shocked to see him, of course.' For a time they sat in silence.

Eventually Gabriel exclaimed, rather unwisely, as if the comment had been torn from his lips, 'I can't imagine what possessed you to go apart with him. Had you taken leave of your senses?'

Eustacia took a deep breath, reminding herself the while that this was the man who had just sent Morrison packing. 'Lord Ilam, I am grateful for your intervention, but — '

'Gabriel,' he corrected.

'Gabriel, then, I am grateful for what you did, but who I do or do not choose to go apart with is surely no concern of yours,' Eustacia replied with dignity.

'It most certainly is,' he replied. 'My aunt is your godmother. That makes me in some sense your older cousin.'

'Oh pooh,' Eustacia replied. 'If you had been as close as that, you'd have been at the wedding.'

'I gather you really were jilted,' Gabriel observed. 'I thought it must have been something that my aunt made up.'

'No, it wasn't made up; well, the bit about my bridegroom being a clergyman was.'

Looking down, Eustacia saw Ilam's fist clench on his powerful thigh. 'If I had been there, I would have gone after him and knocked his teeth down his throat,' he said.

'You could have done it and welcome,' she replied frankly. 'The difficulty would have been that nobody knew where he had gone.' She paused. 'To be honest with you, I would have released him, had he asked. I cannot think of anything worse than being married to a man who had changed his mind.'

'The blackguard really allowed you to go to the church and receive the news there?'

'He actually allowed me to get right to the altar,' Eustacia admitted.

'Then blackguard is too good a word for him,' said Ilam in disgusted tones.

'I suppose it had its funny side when you come to think about it,' she reflected. She began an account of the day, leaving nothing out, from the note brought by the small boy to her mother fainting followed by her own escape out of the vestry door.

'Fancy sending a small boy to do his dirty work,' Gabriel exclaimed.

'Yes, he did,' Eustacia assured him. 'It was the absurdest thing. This child came clattering down the aisle in a pair of working clogs and stood there holding out a piece of paper and asking which one of us was the bride.'

The laughter which she had felt welling up inside her on the day and to which she had never given voice, suddenly came back as she was finishing her account. Laughter is very infectious, and in the end, they were both overcome by quite uncontrollable mirth.

When at last they began to regain control of themselves, they found that they were looking into each other's eyes. Without unlocking his gaze from hers, he edged closer, took hold of her hand and raised it to his lips. Then moving closer still, he pulled her into his arms, and lowered his lips to meet hers.

Whilst she had been engaged, Morrison had kissed her on more than one occasion. She had found it pleasant, but no more preferable to any other agreeable occupation such as drinking tea or reading a good book. By way of contrast, Ilam's kiss was a revelation. She had kissed him once before, but that had been half in anger, to prove a point. Now, held firmly in his embrace with his mouth covering hers, his tongue gently but insistently probing between her lips in order to explore inside, she could not imagine anything that she would rather be doing. She began to do a little experimenting of her own, caressing the hair which grew at the nape of his neck just beneath his queue. She loved the feel of it, and the appreciative growl that he made deep in his throat indicated that he enjoyed the sensation of having her hands caress him in that way.

It was the sound of a gasp that caused

them to spring apart. They looked up and saw Anna, a stricken expression on her face, her hands to her mouth. Moments later, she whirled round and turned to go down the stairs.

'Anna!' Ilam called out. 'Wait!' He stood up and made as if to follow her.

'Gabriel, no,' said Eustacia urgently, as she also rose to her feet and caught hold of his arm.

'Someone must go after her,' he insisted.

'Yes, but it must not be you after what she has just seen,' she told him. 'Her feelings for you are still too raw. Send her brother after her.'

He hesitated. 'Yes, you are right,' he agreed. 'I'll find him.'

'I'll go and see if Evangeline is all right.' Before she could turn away, he caught hold of her hand and raised it to his lips. Then he straightened his cuffs, smoothed his hair and headed for the ballroom.

His actions reminded Eustacia that she, too, might be looking a little untidy after their recent embrace. Even if she had not decided to speak to Evangeline, she would have needed to go to the ladies' room on her own account. No doubt any interested observer of her actions would conclude that she was spending an inordinate amount of time there.

She found Evangeline perched on a little fireside chair, her handkerchief in her hand. 'Are you feeling any better?' Eustacia asked her.

'A little,' replied the other wanly. Eustacia pulled up another chair and they sat together in silence for a short time. 'Did he really jilt you?' Evangeline asked her, all unconsciously repeating the thought if not the exact words of Lord Ilam just a few minutes before.

'Yes, he really did,' Eustacia replied. She took Evangeline's hand. 'Did you like him so very much?'

'I hadn't known him for long,' Evangeline admitted. 'But he is very handsome, isn't he?'

'Yes, he is,' Eustacia agreed. 'How did you meet him?'

'It was not at a ball, or anything like that. Perhaps that's why he seemed to stand out from the rest. My maid had accompanied me to Bond Street to visit the modiste's. When we came out, our carriage had had to pull a little way down the road, so Millie and I walked to where it was. There were too many packages for Millie to carry so I had three, and I dropped one. The next thing I knew, this handsome young man came running up, and presented it to me. Suddenly it came on to rain, and as Millie was with me, I offered to take him up in the carriage, and it went on from there.'

So it was very much as Eustacia had concluded. Frightened by what he had done, he had run away to London to hide. 'Did he say anything about having been engaged or about his home or anything?'

Evangeline shook her head. 'He said nothing about an engagement, although he did talk a little about his home and his parents. He mentioned something about a little awkwardness — strained relations with a neighbour or something — that meant that he felt it advisable to get away for a while.'

'Strained relations!' exclaimed Eustacia indignantly. 'I should say so! Why, my father was ripe for murder after what he did.'

'So I should think! I wonder whether I should send Papa after him to challenge him.'

'Do you think he would go?' Eustacia asked her.

'Oh yes, he would go if he thought that I wanted him to,' responded Evangeline. 'He would do anything for his little angel, you know.'

'Perhaps he would get hurt,' Eustacia suggested. 'Remember that Morrison is much younger than he is, and he is fit. You wouldn't like that would you?'

'No,' Evangeline agreed regretfully. 'But I certainly don't want to stay here. Those two cats, Miss Wing and Miss Barclay will be crowing all over me. I shall insist that Mama and Papa take me away somewhere — perhaps to the seaside.'

'Do you think they will do so?'

'Oh yes. I have only to threaten a tantrum and they will do whatever I ask.'

Soon after this, they left the room in order to rejoin the company. Eustacia wondered whether Ilam might be waiting for them, but she was not really surprised when the passage was empty. He was not the sort of man to be caught loitering outside the ladies' room.

It was not necessary to pass through the ballroom in order to go down to supper, since they were in a central corridor which ran between the ballroom on one side and a number of bedchambers on the other. The corridor itself had stairs at either end, one flight leading down into the entrance and the other leading to the dining-room. They did go via the ballroom, in case anyone should be there waiting for them. It was almost deserted but Ilam was there, talking urgently to David Crossley and Miss August, the village schoolmistress, a sensible lady in her forties.

Ilam had his back to the door, but upon hearing them come in, he turned towards them, his face hard and anxious. 'Anna's gone,' he said bluntly. He looked at Eustacia with what seemed to her to be accusing eyes.

'I was going to go after her but you stopped me. Now, thanks to . . . ' He had half said the word 'you' when he corrected himself. 'Thanks to that circumstance, no one knows where she is.'

20

Ilam knew he had spoken unfairly as soon as the words were out of his mouth, but Eustacia had turned away before he could take them back. David Crossley put his hand on the viscount's arm. 'No need for that, my lord,' said the young man. 'It's no one's fault but her own. She's been fancying herself as her ladyship for a while now.'

'Yes, and I, fool that I am, did not realize it,' Ilam interrupted bitterly.

'Even if you had done so, I doubt anything you could have said would have made a difference,' David assured him. 'The main thing now is to find her.'

'I will go to the supper room and see if any of her friends have left,' said Evangeline.

'That's a good thought,' said Ilam. 'You go too, David.' When the young man seemed about to protest, Ilam added, 'Miss Granby has been away in London, remember. There might be people that your sister knows that Miss Granby may have forgotten about.'

'Miss Hope and I could make discreet enquiries of the landlady,' said Miss August.

'Perhaps one of the servants might have seen her.'

'Perhaps,' Ilam agreed. 'In the meantime, I'll go outside and take a look around. We'll meet back here in, say, a quarter of an hour?'

Miss August took the lead in questioning Mrs Venables, whilst Eustacia stood by and tried to give her full attention to what was happening. Gabriel's accusations had been unfair, but she knew that he had spoken out of anxiety. After all, they had both been taken aback by Anna's sudden appearance. She still believed that Ilam would have been quite the wrong person to go after Anna at that moment. Nevertheless, it would have been much better for the wrong person to pursue her and catch her than for her to disappear in this way. If anything had happened to the girl, then she would find it hard to forgive herself for holding Ilam back.

Even whilst Eustacia was racking her conscience, Ilam was going through the same kind of exercise. He knew that he could easily have ignored Eustacia's advice and run down the stairs after Anna. The fact was that he had not wanted to leave the woman who had been in his arms so recently, and whose kisses had had such a powerful effect upon him. He, who had prided himself on being cast in a different mould to his father, had allowed his desire for a woman to cloud his judgement!

Determinedly, he turned his mind to the matter in hand. The night was fine, and the moon was full. It was, in short, the perfect night for driving, riding, or even for walking, were one in the kind of mood to do such a thing. He made a sweep of the area around the front and the back of the inn, but found no one. Two grooms were about and he engaged them in casual conversation, trying to discover whether either of them knew anything. Neither of them did. He went back to the rendezvous anxious about Anna, but still feeling guilty about the way that he had spoken to Eustacia.

None of them had anything useful to contribute. Mrs Venables had not noticed anyone leaving in a hurry. She was not able to speak to all of the servants straight away, but promised to send anyone to the ballroom if she discovered anything.

On looking carefully at those consuming supper, Evangeline and David had come to the conclusion that all of Anna's friends were still present. None of them looked anxious or preoccupied.

After Ilam had disclosed his own lack of success, they stood for a while wondering what to do. 'Some of us, at least, ought to go down to supper,' said Miss August. 'The absence of such a large group will be bound to cause the kind of gossip that we are surely most anxious to avoid.'

'I'd like to take a look outside myself,' said David anxiously. 'She's only a child, after all.'

'I'll come with you,' said Ilam. 'The ladies should all go downstairs, I think.'

Eustacia was very reluctant to go, but could not think of a way of suggesting that she should help search outside without it sounding as if she wanted to sneak into a dark corner with Gabriel. Miss August and Evangeline made their way towards the supper room, but she hesitated. Before she could follow them, one of the servants came upstairs from the tap room. 'Begging your pardon, my lord,' he said, 'but missus said to remind you that a young man that came with Mr and Mrs Granby left sudden a little while ago.'

'Morrison!' exclaimed Ilam, his expression hardening. 'By God, if he's harmed her!'

Eustacia hurried back to his side. 'Morrison would not harm her,' she said positively.

'He did *you* enough damage,' he retorted.

'Yes, but that was through thoughtlessness. He would not deliberately harm a young girl in any way. Truly, he would not.'

Gabriel stared at her incredulously. 'I'm amazed that you can defend him after what he has done,' he said.

'I've known him for over half my life,' she replied simply.

'Never mind that,' interrupted David Crossley. 'You told him to go to the next village, my lord. If Anna found out where he was going she might have begged a ride. Remember that my older sister is married to the doctor who lives there.'

'I'd forgotten that,' said Ilam, his expression lightening. 'I'll wager that's where she's gone. Come. With any chance we'll be back here with her even before we're missed.'

They strode to the door. Gabriel turned in the doorway, looked back towards Eustacia, hesitated, then in response to David's urgent summons, he was gone.

Eustacia stood in the centre of the deserted ballroom, lost in thought. The two men might think that Anna had gone to her sister, but she did not believe it to be the case. Anna's chief emotion would be grief from what she believed was a broken heart. Coming a close second to that, however, would be a strong feeling of humiliation and shame. She had obviously been boasting to her friends about how she would be marrying Ilam. Now that she had seen him kissing someone else, the last thing that she would want would be company. She would want to lick her wounds in private. Furthermore, she was certain that no young woman brought up by Mrs Crossley would get into a carriage with a young man whom she had never met before, however upset she might be.

Where would she go? A sudden inspiration caused Eustacia to look discreetly into the other chambers on the same floor in case Anna had hidden in any of those. This search unfortunately yielded no results.

Where else might the girl have gone? All at once she remembered how Anna and Gabriel had sat together in the arbour at the garden party. She was sure in her mind that it had been on that occasion that Ilam had attempted to tell Anna that he was not for her and the girl had completely failed to understand his meaning. If he had been very tactful indeed — and from her experience of him, Eustacia found this very hard to imagine — she might even thought that he was hinting that he was just waiting for her to grow up so that he could propose. Would Anna have gone there to sob her heart out? Eustacia felt that it might be possible.

At that moment, she heard the sound of people coming back up the stairs after their supper. Quickly, before she could be turned from her course, she snatched up her shawl, which she had placed on the back of a chair, and hurried down the stairs and out of the front door. As she stepped outside, she heard the sound of horses clattering down the street. That must be Ilam and Crossley leaving, she decided. On an impulse, she went back inside the inn and sought out the landlady.

'I have an idea that the young lady may have gone to the arbour in the grounds of Illingham Hall,' she said. 'Will you please tell his lordship where I have gone when he returns?'

Thankful that it was such a bright night, she walked briskly up the main street to Illingham Hall. The main gates were closed and she did not try them, choosing instead to enter by a smaller one to the side. Thankfully, like everything else at Illingham Hall, it was well maintained and did not creak. It was only once she was well inside the grounds that it occurred to her to wonder whether there might be any dogs roaming free, in order to deter housebreakers. She stood quite still, listening, but no sound of barking or pounding paws disturbed the night. The only dog-like creature she saw was a fox, but he was about his own concerns. After a long unwinking stare at her, he slunk off on his way.

She was not sure how easily she would find the arbour at night, but as she stepped onto the lawn, the few clouds which had briefly obscured the moon drifted away, leaving the scene almost as brightly lit as it had been a few days ago when the company had danced by torchlight during the evening. Suddenly aware that she might be observed by some servant up late, she hurried to the edge of the grass and worked her way around so that she could approach the arbour from the side. As she came near, she could hear the murmur of a human voice. At first Eustacia thought that it must simply be Anna crying. As she drew closer, however, she realized that the voice was that of a man speaking. Who could it be, she wondered? Was he with Anna, or was some other couple enjoying a tryst in the moonlight?

Her question was answered when she heard Anna's voice. 'I can't go home, I just can't! Everybody will laugh at me!' She sounded as if she was crying.

'I doubt that very much, my dear,' a second voice answered. It was a male voice, cultured and slightly familiar in its intonation.

'But I have made such a fool of myself! I didn't realize how big a fool until I saw — ' She broke off. Eustacia raised her hands to her cheeks in the darkness. She could well imagine what it was that Anna had seen that had so discomposed her.

313

'You saw . . . ?' prompted the male voice.

'I saw Gabriel and . . . and . . . They were embracing!'

'Indeed?'

'It just isn't fair!' Anna declared. 'I love Gabriel, and if she hadn't come along, he would have been mine!' She burst into noisy sobs.

'Come come, my dear,' said the man, his voice full of compassion. There was a short period during which the only sound was Anna's muffled sobs, as if she might be crying into her companion's shoulder. Then, as the sobs subsided, he said, 'Here, take this.' Eustacia guessed that he had handed her a handkerchief.

Eventually, the man said 'You've known Ilam for a very long time, remember.'

'All my life,' Anna agreed. 'Please don't tell me that I cannot possibly love him for that reason. People do marry when they have known one another all their lives. Look at my mother and father.'

'Yes, they do,' her companion agreed. 'Your mother and father were childhood sweethearts. There is a difference between them and yourself and Ilam, however.'

'You're going to say that I'm just a farmer's daughter and he's the heir of an earl, aren't you?'

'I wouldn't dream of saying anything so blindingly obvious,' the gentleman replied. 'The fact is that your parents married, having known one another all their lives, never having been anywhere else or ever having had any intention of doing so. Ilam, on the other hand, has experienced a far wider selection of people than you have encountered.'

'Other people do come here sometimes,' Anna countered swiftly. 'Miss Hope did.'

'Precisely. She, like Ilam, has had the advantage of a wider society. It is not surprising that they should have been drawn together.'

'But if she had not come — '

'It pains me to be brutal, my dear, but if she had not come, I do not think that he would have turned to you.'

'I was so sure that he loved me!' Anna's voice broke on a sob.

'Why, so he does,' said the man.

'But as a sister, not as a wife. It's so unfair.'

'There's love for you,' replied her companion. 'If you've found that out, you've learned a valuable lesson. I don't suppose it's much consolation to you at the moment, but it does work the other way, you know. I wouldn't be at all surprised to learn that there were several young men sighing over you this evening and wishing that you would look their way, even whilst *you* were sighing over Ilam.'

'Do you really think so?' Anna asked, sounding a little more cheerful.

'Undoubtedly. You're a very pretty girl, you know. Why don't you permit me to escort you back to the ball? You might still be in time to have a dance or two. I might even dance with you myself. Now wouldn't that be a coup?'

Anna gave a watery chuckle, then there was a rustling sound, as if the two were getting up. They moved out into the moonlight. Eustacia stepped back, hesitating. She would have liked to reveal her presence and walk back with them, but she was not sure how her appearance would be received by Anna. The girl seemed to have come round to a more reasonable way of thinking, but Eustacia feared that she might decide to flee again if she thought that she had been overheard by her rival.

'I must look a mess,' said Anna anxiously, as the couple began to walk away from the arbour, with Eustacia following at a short distance, still in the shadows.

'Not at all,' replied the man, who was now revealed to be tall, probably as tall as Ilam. Eustacia still did not recognize him. 'The walk to the Olde Oak will enable your complexion to recover. However, I would

316

advise a visit to the ladies retiring room. Your hair rather gives the impression that you have been abroad in a high wind.'

Anna chuckled again as the man gently tucked a strand behind her ear. It was at this unfortunate moment that Ilam came striding towards them across the grass. In the bright moonlight, he must have seen exactly what the man had been doing.

'Get your hands off her, you depraved lecher,' he said in threatening tones.

'And good evening to you too, Ilam,' said Anna's companion suavely. 'I see that your manners are much as they have ever been.'

'Damn you to hell, Ashbourne,' uttered Ilam, in the same murderous tone as he came ever closer. So this was Lord Ashbourne, Eustacia thought. She ought to have guessed. She became conscious of another figure running across the grass in their direction and surmised that it must be David Crossley. Dear heaven, she thought, there will be murder done if nothing happens to prevent it! Lord Ashbourne might be all that he was said to be and worse, but on this occasion he had behaved like a true gentleman, and she was a witness to the fact. She prepared to emerge from the shadows, but even as she did so, Anna took a step forward.

'No, Gabriel, it wasn't like that,' she said

317

urgently. 'He was comforting me.'

'Oh yes,' replied Gabriel with heavy sarcasm. 'And what else was he attempting to do?'

At this point David Crossley arrived on the scene, somewhat out of breath. 'Gabriel . . . My lord, wait!'

'It's young Crossley, isn't it?' said Ashbourne, for all the world as if his son and heir was not breathing murderous threats at him. 'It must be some time since I've seen you. Are you well? And your parents?'

'Yes, very well, thank you, my lord,' replied David, making his bow as he had been taught. Then he turned to Ilam again. 'My lord, please.' He laid a hand on Gabriel's arm, but Gabriel shook him off.

'You don't know what he's like,' he said, his eyes never leaving Ashbourne's face. 'God knows what he would have done to Anna if we hadn't chanced along.'

'It's not true,' Anna protested vehemently. 'He was going to take me back to the Olde Oak!'

Gabriel laughed derisively. 'Is that what he told you?' he said. 'A likely story.'

Why doesn't Ashbourne say something in his defence? Eustacia asked herself, before stepping forward and saying out loud, 'It is quite true, Gabriel. I came to find Anna and

318

overheard part of their conversation.'

Ashbourne turned and saw her. Immediately she recognized the man from the portrait. 'I doubt if anyone will have the manners to introduce us, so I must assume that you are Miss Hope,' he said, making a courtly bow.

Eustacia, well taught by her mother, curtsied in response. As she rose from her reverence, the incongruity of this behaviour, given their present situation, suddenly struck her, and she felt a giggle rising in her throat, in response to which Lord Ashbourne grinned.

Unfortunately, this little exchange was noticed by Ilam. 'My God is there no woman you will not attempt to despoil?' he exclaimed, throwing himself forward, his fists raised. Yet again, David caught hold of Ilam's arm. Young Crossley was accustomed to farm work, and this time he held on tight. Gabriel, however, filled with ungovernable fury against his father, pulled himself free, turning at the same time so that the movement carried his arm round with some force. In the meantime, however, Eustacia had stepped between father and son, and so it was that Gabriel's powerful clenched fist made contact with the side of her head and she fell senseless to the ground.

21

For a moment nobody moved. They stood staring down at the still, crumpled figure lying on the grass in the moonlight.

Ilam was the first to speak. 'God, what have I done?' he exclaimed, distraught, sinking to one knee. 'Eustacia! My darling!' She did not move.

David Crossley took hold of her wrist, and bent to listen to her breathing. 'She's only stunned,' he said.

'Little though I wish to disturb your emotional transports, I must insist that we get her out of the night air and have the doctor attend her,' Ashbourne said to his distracted son in urgent tones that nevertheless still held a hint of his usual society drawl.

'I'll fetch the doctor,' said Crossley, making as if to start across the grass.

'Tell him to come to the rectory,' the earl instructed. 'She'll be happier if she wakes in her own bed.'

'The Hall is nearer,' ventured Ilam.

'Yours is a bachelor household,' Ashbourne reminded him. 'Go, Crossley. Ilam, you had better run to the rectory and make sure that they are ready to receive her. Then find your aunt and tell her to go home.'

'What of Eustacia?'

'I'll bring her.'

'If you harm her — ' Ilam began menacingly.

'Strive for a little sense, Ilam,' said Ashbourne in much his usual tone. 'I shall have Anna to act as chaperon, shall I not, my dear? No doubt her presence will force me to restrain my rakish impulse to ravish an unconscious and possibly concussed female.'

'Very well,' replied Ilam reluctantly, 'but you'll answer to me if you drop her.'

'I see.' Ashbourne grinned in the darkness. 'You are obviously wondering whether carrying Miss Hope is within my powers. I can assure you that it is. Where do you think you got your coal-heaver's shoulders from, Ilam?'

* * *

Eustacia never really remembered any of that night's events clearly after the moment when she had interposed herself between Lord Ashbourne and his son. She was quite unaware of being carried by the earl, whilst Anna walked alongside, opening gates and warning of obstacles as and when the need arose. She vaguely recalled being laid upon something soft and warm amid the murmur of voices. Then there was nothing until late the following morning when she came round, aware of an unpleasantly aching head.

'Trixie?' she breathed in a thread of a voice.

'Oh, heavens, miss, you've come round,' said Trixie. 'I'll go and tell her ladyship.'

Eustacia drifted off to sleep again. When she awoke, the pain in her head was a little less, and Lady Agatha was sitting at a table by the window, writing. 'Letters to the bishop,' murmured Eustacia.

Lady Agatha got up with a rustle of her black silk skirts and walked gracefully over to the bed. 'No, not on this occasion,' she said with a chuckle. 'Not but what it would be an excellent scheme. I could say that you had developed brain fever and could not be moved. Are you feeling a little better, my dear?'

'A little,' Eustacia replied. She was somewhat confused about the detail of what had occurred the previous night and was hoping that her godmother might enlighten her. She was not to be disappointed.

'Such a drama we were treated to last night,' said the older lady, sitting down on the bed, after she had helped Eustacia to have a drink of lemonade. 'You must not think, by the way, that I was unaware of what was happening earlier. I discovered from Mr and Mrs Granby that the young man with them was called Morrison Morrison. There can only be one set of parents who would name their son in such a stupid way, so I guessed at once who he must be. By the time I found out about him, however, Ilam had success-fully ejected him and you were soothing Miss Granby.

'It was Miss August who told me about the search for Anna Crossley. She was much inclined to blame herself for losing sight of you. She thought that you might have gone with Ilam and David Crossley to find Anna. I told her that you would not come to any harm, especially if you were with Ilam. Then, of course, Ilam gave the lie to my words when he arrived looking absolutely ashen and saying that he had hit you over the head.'

'Gabriel hit me,' Eustacia murmured, a wisp of recollection returning.

'I could hardly believe it, even though he himself had said it,' Lady Agatha confessed. 'Then Ashbourne, of all people, arrived, carrying you in his arms, and along with him was the wretched young woman who had caused all the trouble in the first place! 'She has sustained a blow to the head', was all he told me. It was Anna who blurted out 'Ilam hit her, but I don't think he meant to'.'

'I remember, now,' said Eustacia slowly. 'Ilam was angry with his father because he thought that he was seducing Anna.'

'Absurd!' declared her ladyship. 'Ashbourne has his faults — plenty of them — but he's never been a despoiler of young virgins. Besides, he wouldn't foul his own nest. You're looking tired, now. Shall I leave you to rest?'

Eustacia tried to nod, but the pain came back into her head again. Instead, she simply whispered, 'Yes, please.'

After her aunt had gone, she lay there in bed with slow tears rolling down her cheeks. The scene in the garden had now come back to her with distressing clarity. All Gabriel's fury had been on Anna's behalf. He had intended to knock his father down because of her. No doubt Anna's sudden perceived danger had made him think of the girl in a new light. She recalled how she and Ilam had kissed. Would they have done so if she had not told him the sad tale of her jilting and made him feel sorry for her? She remembered how just before their embrace he had clenched his fists and declared that had he been at the wedding he would have knocked Morrison's teeth down his throat. He was obviously the kind of man whose chivalrous impulses would cause him to leap to the defence of any female whom he perceived was being badly treated. Probably he had kissed her out of pity. This was such a lowering reflection that she began to cry in good and earnest. Mercifully, the weakened state of her constitution meant that she had soon cried herself to sleep.

★   ★   ★

When she next awoke, it was late afternoon. She was aware of the sound of voices and opened her eyes to see Dr Bennett standing next to Lady Agatha at the foot of the bed. 'How are we now, young lady?' he asked in a voice that was naturally deep and booming but which he had lowered in the sick room to what, if Eustacia's mother had been speaking, her daughter would have referred to as 'front stalls'.

Eustacia thought carefully. The pain in her head had subsided considerably, and was now only at the level of a mild headache. She passed this information on to the doctor.

'Excellent,' he said. 'You must look more carefully where you are going in future. Running into a branch, indeed!'

'Yes,' agreed Eustacia, not feeling well enough to dispute this point.

'See how she is in the morning,' said the

doctor, turning to Lady Agatha. 'She should have a good night's sleep after one of these powders, but I would not advise getting up, at least until the afternoon, and then only to sit in a chair up here. And no visitors, apart from yourself, of course, my lady.'

The following morning, Eustacia woke up with the pain in her head completely gone. Indeed, she felt so much more herself that she tried to persuade Trixie to allow her to get up.

Trixie shook her head. 'Her ladyship was most strict,' she said. 'You're not to come down today, or even to get out of your bed until this afternoon.'

'Surely I can just get out of bed and sit by the window in my dressing-gown?' coaxed Eustacia. 'I'm so tired of lying in one position.'

'I suppose it can't do no harm,' said Trixie fetching the dressing-gown in question. 'If you show any signs of faintness, though, it's straight back to bed with you.'

Eustacia stood up cautiously, and found that there were no ill effects. With a sigh of relief she sat down at the window. She did not want to say too much for she was not sure which version of events Trixie knew: the true version, or the one which involved the branch of a tree. She was aware that if she just kept quiet, Trixie would soon reveal all she knew.

As soon as Eustacia was settled, Trixie began to tidy up the bed, pulling the sheets tight and shaking up the pillows. 'It's been very busy downstairs this morning,' she said. 'All sorts of folks coming to ask about your welfare. That Lord Ashbourne came,' she said with a gleam in her eye, hugging a pillow to her before putting it down. 'He's a proper rake, he is, as anyone can see. Fancy him carrying you up here and placing you on your bed! What a pity that you weren't awake to enjoy it! I wouldn't've minded a chance to dally with him but I had to come back up here — no blame going to you for that, miss, of course! He brought those flowers over there.' She pointed to a vase in which were displayed some magnificent lilies. 'Aren't they a picture? They smell as good as they look, but beware of the pollen.'

'They are lovely,' agreed Eustacia. Then, after a pause, she asked, 'Have there been any other visitors or . . . or enquiries?'

'Miss Granby came,' volunteered Trixie. 'The schoolteacher looked in as well.' Then after a long pause she said 'If you must know, that Lord Ilam came — curse him! Hit you on the head! I'll hit *him* on the head!'

'How did you know?' asked Eustacia curiously.

'Miss Anna spilled it out as Lord Ashbourne was laying you down on the bed,' said Trixie, her voice softening at the mention of his lordship and the word bed in the same sentence. 'Her ladyship says it's to be a secret. I didn't see why it should be, since if he's hit a young lady over the head everyone should know, in my opinion. Then Lady Agatha said that it was to protect your reputation, otherwise everyone would know that you'd been out with a man in the moonlight. So I agreed to hold my peace, but for your sake, not his.' She paused. 'He did bring some flowers when he came this morning. I put them in the passage.'

'I'd like them in here if you please,' said Eustacia.

Trixie sniffed. 'They're nothing special,' she said, before going into the corridor and coming back with a vase of golden roses. 'He brought them when he came with Miss Anna.'

'He came with Anna?' echoed Eustacia.

Trixie came over and sat next to her. 'Look, miss, to bring another young lady on an errand like that says something, doesn't it? They've known each other all their lives. A bond like that isn't broken so soon. If you ask me, the sooner we leave here and get home the better.'

Eustacia thought about what Trixie had said after she had gone. Ashbourne had not appeared to think that Gabriel and Anna's closeness was of the kind that would lead to love. The fact was that Ashbourne was estranged from his son and therefore might not be the most likely person to know. It was true that Gabriel himself had told her that he did not love Anna in a romantic way as they were dancing, but that was before Anna had disappeared. The anxiety of that moment might have caused him to think about his childhood friend in an entirely different way. If he had had a romantic reason for visiting her today, why bring Anna? The more she turned the whole matter round and round in her head, the more she came to the conclusion that Trixie was right. It was time they went home.

★   ★   ★

The following morning, Eustacia was halfway down the stairs when the doctor appeared at the bottom of the flight. 'And where do you think you're going, young lady?' he asked her. This time, his voice was nearer to back of stalls level.

'I felt so much better,' she confessed. 'You did not say that I must stay in my room today, so I thought that I might come down.'

'Not until I've had a good look at you first,' he said. 'Back upstairs with you.'

After Trixie had been sent for, the doctor examined Eustacia and asked her a number of questions, the answers to which involved, among other things, saying the Lord's Prayer, and telling him who was king and what season of the year they were in. After he had done all this he pronounced her completely recovered. 'No more running into branches, mind,' he warned her. 'I am sure you will not experience any giddiness, but if you do, just sit down for a time until it passes. Try to avoid getting over excited.'

She thanked the doctor, and asked Trixie to show him out. Then she waited for the maid to return so that she could put her hair up again, since the doctor had been obliged to disarrange it during his examination.

'There's a fine to-do going on downstairs,' said Trixie looking excited. 'Her ladyship's arrived.'

'Which ladyship?' Eustacia asked her, mystified.

'*Our* ladyship,' said Trixie impatiently. 'Lady Hope.'

'My mother!' Eustacia exclaimed.

'Well haven't I just been saying so?' sighed Trixie in a long-suffering tone. 'She's saying something about that Morrison being at that ball the other night. You didn't tell me about that, miss.'

'No, I know I didn't,' replied Eustacia. 'Such a lot seemed to have happened since then you see. I wonder what brought her here?'

'I don't know; But it sounds as if there's hell to pay.'

Although Eustacia was feeling perfectly well, she really did not want to face a scene. She therefore told Trixie the whole story, judging that by the time she had finished, Lady Agatha would also have completed her own account. After Trixie had finished exclaiming over Morrison's perfidy, Eustacia decided to make her way downstairs.

Her mother was sitting in the drawing-room with Lady Agatha. Both ladies rose at her entrance and Lady Hope glided over to embrace her daughter, bestowing a scented kiss upon her cheek. 'Eustacia, my love!'

'Mama, this is a surprise,' Eustacia replied. 'What brings you here?'

'A most unpleasant rumour,' her mother replied. 'Fortunately Agatha has been able to put my mind at rest over the matter.'

'And what rumour was that, Mama?'

'That Lusty fellow came over to see Miss Warburton, and he told me that Rake Ashbourne had made a kind of pet of you

— *and* when I had told you not to have anything to do with him.'

'But . . . but that's nonsense,' Eustacia exclaimed, colouring. 'I had not even met Lord Ashbourne until two nights ago.'

'I told your Mama all about it,' put in Lady Agatha. 'That Lusty is a fool and a troublemaker.'

'He should be drummed out of the church, and so I shall tell the bishop when next I see him,' said Lady Hope decisively.

'Oh, pray do not,' cried Eustacia, not wanting to see the poor man condemned simply as a result of Lady Agatha's scheming. 'I am sure that he is just unhappy because Jessie prefers Lord Ashbourne to himself.'

'What a charitable child you are,' said her mother. 'And when I think what a wretched time you have had of it!'

Eustacia looked from her mother to her godmother and back again. 'But I have not, truly,' she replied. 'Lady Agatha has been so kind and I have made some new friends.'

'I am pleased to hear it, my love,' said her mother. 'Of course Agatha's kindness goes without saying. What I am referring to are your experiences of the last few days. First, your encounter with that Mo-rrrrison, then the disgraceful affair of Ilam's knocking you down.'

'Mama, please, it was not his fault.' Eustacia protested. 'He did not mean to hit me. It was an accident.'

'An accident?' exclaimed her ladyship. 'How could the man strike you down by accident?'

'He was trying to hit someone else,' said Eustacia. 'I got in the way.'

'Eustacia Mary Louisa, it sounds as though you were in the middle of a brawl,' said Lady Hope sternly. 'How came this about?'

'It was not a brawl,' said Eustacia, very well aware that the more she tried to explain the events of the previous night, the worse they would sound. She would very much have liked to pretend to faint again, but her mother would not be fooled for an instant. 'Lord Ashbourne and his son had a disagreement and I thought that Lord Ilam was going to hit his father so I rushed between them.'

'It was gallantry of no mean order,' said a new voice from the doorway. They all turned and saw Lord Ashbourne standing on the threshold. From the foaming lace at his throat and wrists to the mirror-like gloss of his boots, he looked as if he had been poured into his clothes. His jet black hair was caught at the back of his neck with a ribbon. His brows, of the same shade as his hair, soared in the arc that was so accurately depicted in his portrait. His eyes surveyed the company with lazy disdain. Naturally enough, he looked older than he did in his portrait. There was a touch of grey at his temples and faint lines on his countenance which might indicate dissipation, but these did not by any means diminish his air of fascination. Eustacia was not surprised that he turned Trixie weak at the knees. He almost did the same to her.

He moved away from the door, and bowed to the assembled company. Nothing in his manner betrayed any doubt of his welcome. 'Agatha, my dear, it's good to see you looking well after your recent excitement.'

'Yes, I am well, and now you've found that out, you might as well take yourself off back to Italy, or wherever it was you were wallowing in debauchery,' his sister replied forthrightly.

'Oddly enough, that is not how I spend all my time, Sister mine,' he replied before turning to Eustacia's mother. 'Lady Hope,' he murmured, raising her hand to his lips. 'If anything, you contrive to look even lovelier than I remember, were that possible. How do you do it?'

'By the same means as you manage to be as much a scoundrel as ever you were,' Lady

Hope replied, taking back her hand as soon as possible. 'No doubt we're both as nature intended us.'

He laughed softly then turned to Eustacia. 'Miss Hope, our greeting was brief the other night, but I believe I must count you as my friend. You are as lovely and as gallant as any child of Sir Wilfred Hope and Claire Delahay could hope to be.'

Eustacia's mother straightened her spine. 'You forget, sir, that I am no longer known by that name. I am Lady Hope, and I will thank you to stay away from my daughter.'

'That will be a little difficult when she is my sister's guest and I am honour bound to call and see how she does.'

Eustacia glanced at Lady Agatha. She had resumed her seat and was observing the encounter as if it were the performance of a play to which she had been given a front-row seat.

'I am not referring to this morning,' said Lady Hope. 'I am referring to the night when, as far as I can see, you allowed my daughter to become embroiled in some kind of drunken brawl. I suppose I cannot expect any better from Ashbourne and his heir.'

'I'm quite prepared to take the blame for my own misdeeds, but I do not see why all of Ilam's failings should be laid at my door,' complained the earl.

'Ilam does not have any failings,' protested Eustacia. She coloured, suddenly aware of how that must sound. Then all at once her head started to swim and she remembered the doctor saying that she must avoid getting over excited. Luckily, Lord Ashbourne was close enough to catch hold of her by the waist. Amid exclamations of concern from Lady Hope and Lady Agatha, who had got to her feet, he steered her solicitously to the nearest chair.

It was at this unfortunate moment that Ilam came in. 'What the deuce are you doing to her now?' he asked.

'That sits rather oddly on the lips of the man who knocked her down,' remarked Lady Agatha, staring coldly at her nephew.

'It was a mistake, for which I have come to apologize,' said Ilam, still staring at his father, who had settled Eustacia in her chair and was now straightening up.

'I take it that this mannerless oaf is your son,' said Lady Hope coldly.

'He is my son,' agreed Ashbourne. 'I would have introduced him as soon as he entered the room, but as you know I was a little preoccupied, and while he may be a mannerless oaf, I am the only one who is entitled to call him so.'

'You would defend him?' exclaimed Lady Hope incredulously, whilst Ilam directed a look of surprise at his father.

'I would expect you to be prepared to give him a hearing.'

Lady Hope stared at him for a long moment before saying, 'If only Charlie were here, he would soon avenge any insult to his sister.' She strode to the window and stood gazing into the middle distance.

After a pause, during which for a brief moment both men forgot their hostility, and their eyes met in bafflement as they wondered to whom Lady Hope could possibly be referring, Lady Agatha said, 'Would you be so good as to ring the bell, Ashbourne? I think that Eustacia could do with a glass of wine and I'm sure that the rest of us could as well.'

As soon as his father had walked to the bell rope beside the mantelpiece, Ilam approached Eustacia's chair and took her hand. 'Are you all right?' he asked her. 'I would never forgive myself if — '

'Unhand my daughter, sirrah!' exclaimed Lady Hope, whirling back from the window.

Ilam straightened. 'My lady you must allow me to apologize to her for what I did. Natural justice demands it.'

'Does it indeed? Let me tell you, young man, that the authority of a parent demands that you tell me what you were doing out with my daughter in the dark.'

The butler came in with wine, which he then poured out at Lady Agatha's signal. Ilam tried to take a glass to Eustacia before he was forestalled by Ashbourne. The earl turned to carry it to the young woman, but found Lady Hope in his way, her hand outstretched. Eustacia, who was now beginning to feel much better, barely restrained herself from laughing at this piece of farce.

'Well, sir?' said her ladyship after the butler had gone. 'Explain yourself.'

Ilam sighed. 'Anna Crossley, my foster sister, has been getting rather too fond of me recently. Eustacia saw it, but I didn't.'

'Who gave you permission to call my daughter by her Christian name?' Lady Hope demanded haughtily.

'I told him he might, Mama,' put in Eustacia. She had been watching Gabriel with considerable interest. He was showing none of the lovelorn symptoms which males usually exhibited on meeting her mother for the first time.

'You had no business to do so.'

'On the night of the ball, everything came to a head,' Ilam went on, ignoring this interruption. 'Anna became distraught and ran off. Several of us went to look for her.'

'I went to the gardens of Illingham Hall,' Eustacia put in. 'I thought that she might have gone there. When I arrived, I discovered that Lord Ashbourne had found her and was about to take her back to the ball. Then Gabriel arrived and . . . and misunderstood the situation. I tried to stand between them and Gabriel hit me by accident.'

Lady Hope looked very slightly mollified. 'Hmm. Perhaps you are not quite the complete oaf that I took you for; but a gentleman should never indulge in fisticuffs in front of a lady, no matter what the provocation. However, it seems to me that this girl you have mentioned has a lot to answer for; unless it was some action of yours that made her run off in the first place.'

'It was, my lady,' Ilam replied, flushing a little. 'She is only a child and not to blame. She had discovered in the most brutal way that I was in love with someone else.' He glanced down at Eustacia. On his face was the expression that she had searched for and failed to find when he had looked at her mother. Her heart began to beat rapidly. Slowly, she got to her feet and took a step so that she was standing beside him.

'Indeed,' exclaimed Lady Hope. 'And how did she make this discovery.'

Ilam opened his mouth to speak, but was

silenced by the quite unexpected sensation of a small but capable hand tucking itself into his.

'We were kissing, Mama,' said Eustacia.

'What?' demanded Lady Hope. This time her voice was definitely intended to wake those seated in the gods. 'You had the effrontery to kiss my daughter? Without permission?'

'I gave him permission, Mama,' corrected Eustacia, turning as red as Ilam. 'We were kissing each other.' There was a soft chuckle from Ashbourne's direction Before her ladyship could say another word, Ilam spoke. 'Lady Hope, this is not the moment that I would have chosen, but I love your daughter and most earnestly desire permission of yourself and her father to pay my addresses to her.'

Eustacia squeezed the hand that she was holding, and Ilam winced. She lifted it, and saw that the knuckles were bruised. 'Why, Gabriel, what have you done?' she asked.

'No doubt he has been brawling again,' said Lady Hope with dignity. 'Young man, your effrontery knows no bounds. I do not need to go over recent events I am sure, for you to understand that I have grave doubts about the suitability of a match between yourself and my daughter. Your ancestry, your violent temper, your impulsive nature, your ill manners and poor judgement all tell me that I would be unwise in the extreme to place my only daughter into your care. There would have to be some extraordinary evidence of your worthiness for me to consent to such a match. I am sure that her father will say the same.'

'But Mama, I love him,' Eustacia protested.

'In his defence, I feel bound to say that Ilam is not to blame for his ancestry,' put in Ashbourne, surprising no one more than his own son.

Before any more could be said, the door opened and Sir Wilfred stood on the threshold. 'I found Morrison, but someone had beaten me to it and already knocked him down,' he said in response to his wife's greeting. 'By George, I'd like to shake the fellow's hand.'

22

The marriage of Gabriel William Stafford Montgomery, Viscount Ilam and Eustacia Mary Louisa Hope took place three months later, on a glorious October day when the trees that surrounded St Peter's Church seemed determined to dress the day with added glory.

The whole week that preceded the wedding ceremony was one of the finest and warmest October weeks that anyone could remember.

The days leading up to the wedding were very busy indeed. There were last minute alterations to be made to Eustacia's gown, the details of the breakfast to be established and the house to be cleaned from top to bottom. Amidst all the excitement, Ilam and Eustacia managed to sneak away on more than one occasion.

'I don't think I've ever been happier to see anyone in my life than when your father appeared and said what he did,' Ilam told Eustacia as they walked along one of the avenues at the far end of the gardens that surrounded Woodfield Park.

'So was I,' agreed Eustacia. 'The one thing

that was guaranteed to sway Mama in your favour was if you had played a part in avenging the insult that Morrison inflicted upon me. I dare swear you acquitted yourself as well as Charlie would have done in your place.'

'You flatter me, my dear,' smiled Gabriel. She had told him about the mythical Charlie and his virtues very soon after his suit had been approved by her parents. Indeed, Lady Hope had become so reconciled to the match that she had ceased talking about Charlie, and had begun to speak of 'dear Ilam' instead.

Once Gabriel's offer had been accepted, Lady Hope had insisted that if she had a wedding to organize then she needed to go home as soon as possible. Sir Wilfred and Lady Hope had stayed at the vicarage for only one night before returning to their own house with Eustacia accompanying them. Since then Gabriel had taken every possible opportunity of riding over to see her.

'How could I do any other?' he asked. 'I told you, I wanted to knock his teeth down his throat.'

'Did you really knock him down? For me?'

'Twice,' he answered. Then when she looked at him questioningly he added defensively, 'He didn't stay down the first time.'

343

'Oh, Gabriel,' sighed Eustacia. The viscount pulled her firmly but gently behind a large tree, and then enfolded her in his arms.

'I don't know how it should be,' he said, 'but when you look at me like that I find I simply have to kiss you.' He suited his action to his words.

Eustacia looked up at him mischievously. 'I was wondering whether that might be the case,' she said demurely.

He had come from Illingham three days before the wedding, and was staying at the White Horse in the village. On previous occasions, he had been allocated a room in Woodfield Park, but this time, Lady Hope insisted that it would be bad luck for the groom to stay under the same roof as his bride.

Ashbourne also came to stay, but set up his temporary establishment in the Red Lion, situated in another village three miles away.

Eustacia tried to encourage her betrothed to stay in the same inn as his father, but the viscount refused. 'We are speaking to each other civilly,' he told her. 'You'll have to be content with that.'

'You must not think that I want to interfere,' she said to him, as she fiddled with the buttons on his waistcoat, 'but it makes me sad to think that you cannot be close to him as I am to my parents.'

He took a step away from her and turned so that he was not looking at her. 'He's never shown any interest in me. Why should I bother with him?'

Eustacia thought about what Dr Littlejohn had told her, about the hardness of Ashbourne's own father. 'Perhaps he did not know how,' she suggested, following him, placing a hand upon his back and stroking him gently. 'Gabriel, you have spoken about Anna, and made allowances for her being just a child. Ashbourne was only her age when he was married, and barely older than that when he became a father. Can you not make allowances for him, too?'

He turned, looked down at her thoughtfully, then said abruptly, 'Don't let's talk about him now. There are other things I would much rather do.' He pulled her into his arms for a long passionate kiss. Eventually he drew away from her and murmured in a voice that was not quite steady, 'Oh God, I wish it was our wedding day. I can't wait for you to be my wife, Stacia. I think you know why.'

She blushed. 'And I can't wait for you to be my husband — for the same reason.'

'Shall you mind marrying in that same church?' he asked, after another lingering kiss. 'If so we can always elope, although I

345

think your Mama might be a trifle disappointed.'

'No, it's quite all right; I don't mind at all,' she assured him. Nevertheless, there was a shadow lurking in her eyes that he resolved to do something about.

★　★　★

Two nights before the wedding, Sir Wilfred and Lady Hope held a grand ball in honour of their daughter and her husband-to-be. There were some living locally who recalled that this was not the first time that Miss Hope had prepared for a wedding, and when her second engagement had been announced, one or two had been inclined to indulge in a little laughter at her expense. The sight of Ilam's powerful frame and the sound of his title and that of his father soon caused the amusement to shrivel on their lips. Most friends and neighbours were glad to learn that Sir Wilfred and Lady Hope's only daughter would have another chance of happiness, and with a gentleman whose physique, fortune and status quite cast Morrison Morrison into the shade.

Needless to say, the Morrisons were not present, having very wisely decided to go abroad for the autumn, but the ballroom was full of plenty of other guests. Mr and Mrs Granby attended with Evangeline, who was dressed in a gown of a colour and cut that was far more suitable for a married woman than a single girl. Eustacia only managed a few words with her, but guessed that she had probably made a scene in order to get it. She seemed to have a number of gentlemen buzzing around her like bees around a particularly exotic flower.

Lord Ashbourne was not one of their number. Knowing his reputation for rakishness, Eustacia fully expected to see him making at least one attractive lady the object of his gallantry. Instead, he seemed to regard himself as being a kind of secondary host, chatting with the dowagers, exchanging snuff with Sir Wilfred, and enjoying a protracted conversation with Dr Littlejohn. He even conversed with his sister, who seemed, at the very least, to be prepared to be civilized with him.

At one point, whilst she was waiting for Gabriel to bring her a glass of lemonade, Eustacia glanced across at her future father-in-law. He was standing alone, looking, as always, as if he ought to form the model for an illustration in a book of fashion for gentlemen. It was not that he looked like a peacock. On the contrary, his style was more restrained than that of many other men present. His coat and breeches were of a shade that looked black in one light and blue in another, and his waistcoat was of palest peach with silver embroidery; but the cut of his garments was so exquisite that they looked at one and the same time more comfortable and better fitting than those of any other man present.

What kind of man was he really? From her mother's accounts, she had learned that he was an unprincipled rake, a judgement which was confirmed by Jessie Warburton. Lady Agatha said that he was a gambler, and Gabriel saw him as a neglectful parent. Yet with Anna, he had been kind, gentle and understanding. Who was the real Ashbourne?

As Eustacia observed him, she saw him idly watching the crowd. Then she actually caught the moment when his interest was suddenly captured by something — or someone — that was very important to him, and his expression almost became one of yearning. Following the line of his vision, she saw Gabriel coming towards her with her lemonade. Like his father, he was dressed in a restrained style; not so much from reasons of fashion, she suspected, but more because he didn't like dressing up. He still cut a very fine figure, and

Eustacia, filled suddenly with pride, forgot about everything else apart from the look in his eyes.

Another guest who graced the gathering that evening was Jessie Warburton, accompanying Lady Agatha. To Eustacia's great surprise, Henry Lusty was also with them.

'I encouraged him to come,' Lady Agatha told her goddaughter as they took a turn about the room.

'You encouraged him?' echoed Eustacia in surprise. She was recalling how Lady Agatha had chased the hapless young clergyman with an umbrella.

'I did it to annoy Ashbourne,' said her ladyship tranquilly 'He's so used to thinking of Jessie as only having eyes for him. It'll do him good to see that she's got another suitor.'

It occurred to Eustacia, as she watched Jessie, that Henry Lusty might not be the only suitor beating a path to Jessie's door. Miss Warburton had benefited from her stay with Lady Hope. Eustacia could see the marks of her mother's good taste written all over Jessie's elegant golden evening gown.

'Yes perhaps, Godmama, but it did not seem to me that you would ever be likely to be seen anywhere in Mr Lusty's company,' Eustacia ventured.

Lady Agatha laughed. 'Oh, that,' she

replied. 'That little scheme of mine is quite put behind me. Thanks to Ilam, I shall soon be installed in the Dower House at Ashbourne. I've already convinced Lusty that the whole business was more than half due to his overactive imagination.'

'You mean your plan to' — Eustacia dropped her voice — 'to bring down the Church of England?'

'Bring down the Church of England?' she responded in shocked tones. 'And I, a vicar's widow? Certainly not. Besides,' she went on mysteriously, 'I have other fish to fry.'

A short time later, Eustacia had the opportunity to exchange a few words with Jessie Warburton. 'Henry Lusty has asked me to marry him,' said Jessie. 'Part of me is inclined to accept.' Luckily, since Eustacia could not think of a response to this, Jessie went on, 'Eustacia, I cannot change the way that I feel, but I must have something of my own. If I carry on the way that I am, I shall have nothing but an empty heart and an empty home and a huge collection of futile dreams. Yet part of me is still holding back.'

'I wish you happy whatever your choice,' replied Eustacia. 'You deserve to be.' She thought for a moment. 'I have a book that has helped me a lot, and I would like to give it to you, if I may. It does at least acknowledge that women have rational minds that can be employed in all kinds of situations. I think you may find it useful, whatever your decision.'

'Thank you,' Jessie replied. The next time Eustacia saw her, she was dancing with Henry Lusty.

That evening, Eustacia had the pleasure of dancing with her future father-in-law. It was a pleasure, too, for he was an excellent dancer, and knew how to make a lady look — and feel — as light as a feather.

'My son has good taste,' he said when the movements of the dance permitted. 'You will make a charming viscountess.'

'Thank you,' she replied. 'All I want to do is to make him happy.'

'A laudable ambition.'

'If only you could make up your differences.'

At once, his face took on a shuttered look. 'I fear that is beyond even your skill,' he said, and then began to speak of something else. As the dance ended and they reverenced one another, he said, 'Confess it, my dear, if you had seen me first, you might have been tempted.'

Eustacia laughed. 'Oh no, my lord,' she replied audaciously, taking his hand as he led her off the floor. 'You're much too pretty for my taste.'

He burst out laughing. Ilam, who was doing Jessie Warburton the same courtesy, frowned a little. 'Pretty! I don't think I've ever been called that before,' Ashbourne said, as soon as he was able.

'What were you laughing about with my father earlier?' Ilam asked her suspiciously as they were going to supper.

Eustacia smiled. She had noted that he was beginning to speak of his father in that way, rather than referring to him as Ashbourne. She thought it a promising sign. 'I told him that he was too pretty for my taste,' she said. Gabriel stared at her uncomprehendingly. He glanced about him, then drew her through a door in the corridor into a small parlour.

'Stacia, are you sure — *really* sure — that you prefer me' — he paused — 'to him?'

'To your father? Of *course* I'm sure,' she told him. She laid a hand on his arm. 'You're the man I love; *you're* the man I'm marrying — remember?'

'Yes I know,' he replied. 'But what if you had met him first? What then?'

'It doesn't follow that I would have liked him better,' she answered. 'Remember my mother met him before she met my father; yet my father was the man she fell in love with and married.' She paused. 'I only wish I was a bit more like her. Men used to pretend to be interested in me; then later on I would discover that they only did it so that they could be with her. However much one loves one's mother it can become a little tiring.' She sighed.

Gabriel sat down and pulled her onto his knee. 'Listen to me,' he said. 'You're perfect; absolutely perfect, just as you are, and I love you; *not* your mother, but you.'

Looking into his face, she saw the same expression upon it that she had seen before he had first confessed his love before the whole company in the vicarage at Illingham. She reached up and touched his cheek. 'And I love you,' she answered. 'Not your father, but you.' He kissed her; she kissed him back; and once they had started, they found it quite impossible to stop.

A few minutes later, one of the female guests at the ball opened the door, quite by chance. She hurried off to find Lady Hope, telling her in shocked accents that the happy couple had better be summoned to supper quickly, as Lord Ilam seemed to be set on enjoying a meal of quite another kind!

★　★　★

Eustacia could not help feeling a little strange as she set off with her father in the carriage on her wedding day. It was not that she did not trust Gabriel; of course she did. He was not Morrison Morrison. It was just that she wished that she had never had that experience of going to the church and being jilted in that way. Somehow, those memories coloured what was happening now.

The previous night she had gone to bed in a happy haze, fully expecting to dream of Ilam. Instead, she had dreamed that she had gone to the church alone and on foot. It had been filled with people she knew, both here in her own village and at Illingham. As she had stood at the end of the aisle, which seemed to be much longer than that of St Peter's Church, she could see no sign of Ilam. She began to walk up the aisle, and as she did so, everyone started to point at her and laugh. Morrison Morrison, who was standing facing her dressed as a clergyman, was laughing the loudest of all.

She woke up wringing with perspiration, and sat up in bed at once, staring about her. It was still night-time, but she did not get to sleep again for a long time. When she did so, she enjoyed a dreamless rest, but she woke with a faint oppression of spirits. She soon pushed this mood to the back of her mind as her mother helped her to get ready, but as she got into the carriage, the dream came back.

Her father, seeing her thoughtful expression, asked her if she was all right and she answered in the affirmative. She just wished that it could have been a different church. Almost she wished that she had eloped as Ilam had jokingly suggested.

Walking into the porch would be the worst bit. Everything had been as it should be until she had walked into the porch and seen that Morrison was not there. If only she did not have to wait to see Gabriel until she had got inside the porch!

They walked through the lych gate and she could feel her legs start to tremble. Her father looked down at her concernedly and she returned his gaze with a wobbly smile. 'Look,' he said, pointing. She turned her head towards the church, and there was Gabriel standing in the porch. He looked so handsome in his blue coat and white breeches that she found that her knees were trembling for quite another reason.

In a complete departure from tradition, Sir Wilfred released his daughter's hand from his arm and laid it on that of her groom so that they could walk into church together.

'How did you know?' she asked him, as they reached the back of the church. He shrugged and grinned. 'Oh Gabriel,' she sighed, and those members of the congregation who turned at that point, witnessed another departure from tradition as the groom enfolded the bride in his arms *before* the service and soundly kissed her.

We do hope that you have enjoyed reading
this large print book.

Did you know that all of our titles
are available for purchase?

We publish a wide range of high quality
large print books including:
Romances, Mysteries, Classics
General Fiction
Non Fiction and Westerns

Special interest titles available in
large print are:
The Little Oxford Dictionary
Music Book
Song Book
Hymn Book
Service Book

Also available from us courtesy of
Oxford University Press:
Young Readers' Dictionary
(large print edition)
Young Readers' Thesaurus
(large print edition)

For further information or a free
brochure, please contact us at:
Ulverscroft Large Print Books Ltd.,
The Green, Bradgate Road, Anstey,
Leicester, LE7 7FU, England.
Tel: (00 44) 0116 236 4325
Fax: (00 44) 0116 234 0205

Other titles published by
The House of Ulverscroft:

CLERKENWELL CONSPIRACY

Ann Barker

When Captain Scorer died in action, his wife Eve was obliged to seek refuge with her cousin Julia. Treated as a poor relation and pursued by Julia's admirer, Eve is thankful when escape is offered through the bequest of a bookshop in Clerkenwell. She has no knowledge that Colonel Jason 'Blazes' Ballantyne, her husband's commanding officer, has been ordered by William Pitt to make enquiries concerning a codebook that has been left in the bookshop by French spies. When certain incidents and rumours convince Jason that Eve has a dubious reputation, it doesn't prevent attraction flaring between them . . .